The Novel of

HOBSON'S CHOICE

(formerly titled Hobson's)

by

HAROLD BRIGHOUSE
and CHARLES FORREST

Northern Classic Reprints

PRINTWISE PUBLICATIONS LTD
1992

© PRINTWISE PUBLICATIONS LIMITED
47 Bradshaw Road, Tottington,
Bury, Lancs BL8 3PW.

Warehouse and Orders
40-42 Willan Industrial Estate
West Ashton Street, Salford M5 2GR
061 745 9168   fax; 061 737 1755

ISBN No. 1 872226 36 1 limp bound
         1 872226 37 X hard back

Previously published under the title
HOBSON'S by Constable & Co., London.
First published in 1917.

Illustrations chosen, additional material and book edited by

Cliff Hayes

Cover illustration: Salford Railway Station, New Bailey Street.
Illustrations by H. E. Tidbury and taken from the book
MANCHESTER OLD AND NEW

Book retyped by SYLVIA HAYES
Printed and bound by Manchester Free Press, Paragon Mill, Jersey Street, Manchester M4 6FP. Tel: 061 236 8822

Introduction

I wasn't even looking for it. I was in Salford Local History Library quietly looking for a book called 'The Manchester Rebels' when one of the librarians, who look after you so well there, said: "Hobson's". "Pardon?", I replied. "If you're looking for a book of local interest to reprint, why not read Hobson's?", he said.

"Hobson's", I wonder if that's the same as Hobson's Choice, I thought? I wonder why it's not called Hobson's Choice? I took it and sat down just to see if it explained why; the play I knew was by the Eccles writer Harold Brighouse yet the book was credited to him and Charles Forrest. Oh well, I'll just read the first chapter and see what the book is like. Like everyone else, I remember the film and have seen the play, but a book?

I started to read, very lightly skimming the words just to get the feel, and the measure of the style. There I was, back in Old Salford, Charles Laughton setting the world to rights with the Moonraker's bar parlour worthies. The humour and wit of the words and the Manchester-Salford rivalry had smiles coming from the first page. John Mills sprang into my mind's eye as soon as the words Will Mossop appeared on the pages. Oh, what a pleasure and delight!

They threw me out at closing time, pointing out that the book was a rarity and not to be taken away, but I was back next day and, after threatening to haunt the place for the next two weeks, they agreed to let me take the book away for a weekend. It was like meeting an old friend, I knew what was coming up, what was happening next. Yet it didn't matter, the craft and skill of the words made it a pleasure to read on. I finished the book and wondered why no-one had told me about this book before, why this hilarious book had never become recommended reading? The answer proved very simple – not many people knew that there was a book available. They knew of the film, they knew of the play, but a book? "Never seen a copy" was the usual reply, and indeed copies of the book are very few and far between.

Well, if I can enjoy it why not you? If ever a book deserved to be re-printed - if only to bring some humour and laughter into today's bustle - this must come very high on the list. I've added some illustrations from the period, and it has been completely reset as the type of the original book was looking worn, but it is an honour to put before you such a gem of Northern life; to reintroduce the friendly, colourful characters that you know so well.

Harold Brighouse did write the play in 1916 and it was an immediate success, and it seems that Charles Forrest asked or was asked to re-write it as a book. Charles and Harold knew each other from a club they both belonged to called 'The Swan Club' which met most weekday lunch times in the Swan Inn off Market Street, Manchester, and which included some of the leading theatrical lights of the time. Charles Forrest was a playwright and author who had written books about his native East Anglia and was in Manchester, as many others were, to be involved with Miss Horniman's plays at the Gaiety Theatre.

Harold Brighouse wrote many other plays but none achieved the success of this one. The book Hobson's was published in 1917 and it doesn't seem to have been reprinted since, even when British Lion made the film in 1953, although in play form it has always been available.

Stand by for one of the funniest books ever written on Northern life. Get ready to be charmed and amused by some of the wittiest sayings ever put on paper, and savour the humour of gruff Lancashire life. For many, many years you've had no choice if you wanted to enjoy this story. NOW, you've got ...

HOBSON'S CHOICE

About Harold Brighouse

HAROLD Brighouse was born in Eccles in 1882. He attended Clarendon Road School, Eccles, and then won a scholarship to Manchester Grammar School. His father William was a teetotalling Liberal, a local J.P. and the director of a cotton spinners and manufacturers. It was his father's love of books that was passed to young Harold. William Brighouse was a 'proprietor' (a term for member) of the Portico Library in Manchester and his son continued the connection, and indeed Harold's sister who lived in Worsley was also a 'proprietor' and left £350 to the Library in her brother's memory.

Harold moved to London in 1902 where he worked as an assistant buyer for a firm of textile shippers. Whilst he was in London he became caught up in the revival of the repertory movement and by the time he returned to Lancashire he had the plays of George Bernard Shaw and others to inspire him.

He joined the RAF for the First World War, and by this time he had written and had produced two plays. But it was in 1916 that Hobson's Choice first saw the West End stage. He himself said that only by exceptional merit would a Northern play overcome the London Mayfair prejudice. But with Hobson's Choice he had such a play which ran and ran not only in London but on Broadway too.

Harold Brighouse was no one-hit wonder. Any amateur dramatic society knows of the wealth and quality of his one-act plays and those looking for a quality production that is different would do well to look up 'The Price of Coal,' 'What's Bred in the Bone' or 'The Happy Hangman'.

He was always an avid writer and reviewed books for the *Manchester Guardian*, and was a regular contributor to the 'Back Page' and the literary column for many years. When he felt he had to move back to London in his middle years to be nearer the theatres, he still came back North for rest and rejuvenation. Walking in the Peaks and the Lake District was said to be his way of unwinding.

This short introduction cannot do justice to the genius and the ability of Harold Brighouse. Those that knew him and wrote of him said he was "excellent company and a rewarding talker": a "Northern gentleman in touch with the people".

A list of his plays would fill a page and, although he didn't technically write the book Hobson's, he did subsequently try his hand and wrote two Lancashire novels. He even wrote a swash-buckling adventure called 'Captain Shapeley'. If you can get hold of a copy of his autobiography 'What I Have Had' is well worth a read.

Harold Brighouse died in July 1958, on the eve of his 76th birthday. He collapsed whilst walking down the Strand in London.

Fortunately or unfortunately Hobson's Choice will always be the one play that he will be remembered for.

So, lights, camera, action ... here we go with 'Hobson's Choice'.

Cliff Hayes

Reviews of Hobson's Choice from 1992 ...

"Brilliantly funny and atmospheric, and a good old Lancashire forerunner to Last of the Summer Wine."
Peter Riley, Salford Journal

"Evokes warm memories of a still-remembered Salford – a wonderful book." *Mike Sweeney, Piccadilly Radio*

"A welcome re-issue of a great Northern classic that manages to combine a vivid portrait of commercial life early this century and sexual politics still relevant in the 1990s." *Janet Reeder, Metro News*

... and from 1917

"Hobson's Choice is altogether admirable."
Mr. Arthur Machen in The Evening News

"The comedy is as brilliant between the book covers as it is on stage." *To-day*

"Full of a most delightful wit." *The Scotsman*

"Very clever work - rich in humour." *Glasgow Herald*

"It's human nature! ... We laughed and laughed again, ... and indeed the good people were deliciously absurd, but always the staple of their fun was their real humanity."
The Daily Telegraph

Acknowledgements

Thanks to Tim and Tony at Salford Local Studies Library for all their help. Tony Gibb once more provided the book from which the illustrations were taken. Thanks again to Manchester Free Press for their hard work.

Contents

Chapter		page
1	The Twin Cities; Introducing Henry Hobson; Upishness and Give & Take	9
2	The Mossops; Walking Out on Sunday; Will Mossop Buys a Hat	28
3	In The Bar Parlour; Nothin' For Nothin', and Little For Sixpence; No Matrimony Here	40
4	Love and Indigestion; Peel Park; Christian All Day Sunday	57
5	Your Will or Mine; Get It Over With, Lad	73
6	A Test For Will; Going To See Mrs. Hepworth	87
7	Settin' Up Shop; Both of This Parish; What A Day	103
8	Education's A Wonderful Thing; Alice Gets Promotion and Vickey gets Put-On; Smears, Blears & Erasions	117
9	The Butting Ram Incident; Vickey & Freddie are Caught; Clog Dancing on Sunday	134
10	Seth Finds a Lodger; Help Please, Maggie; Gettin' Used to Kissin'	150
11	Second-Hand Furniture; Pompous and Circumlocutory Precision; Liquor and Lawyers	166
12	Riding Elephants; The Wedding Supper; Consulting Mr. Shugwell	182

13 Father Comes Round; The End of Upishness;
   Come To Bed Willie Mossop 202

14 Column and a Half in The Salford Reporter;
   Mrs. Figgins gets invited back; Giving Advice to
   Henry; Resigning His Office 225

15 Time to Stand Up; The Green Rabbit or Tubby
   the Housemaid; A Tussle With The Doctor 242

16 Maggie's the Medicine Needed; The
   Phenomenal Will Mossop; Boldauciousness;
   William Henry Mossop 258

DEDICATION

To the two gentlemen who gave us this marvellous story – Harold Brighouse and Charles Forrest; also to Charles Laughton, John Mills and the rest of the cast who created the memorable film version.

CHAPTER ONE

The Twin Cities

The Irwell is a river in Lancashire. It rises in the hills of northeast Lancashire, where there are moors, and has a mile or two of cleanly life. Good, pure water is the first essential to a dye works, and the second is a drain to take away the slop. The Lancashire man, being born with a hard head, a desire to prosper, and no sense of beauty, found pure water on the moors and a natural drain in the river Irwell. That is why there is no dirtier river in England today than the Irwell.

The Irwell runs south from its source through Bacup and Stubbins, of the romantic name, to Bury and to Manchester, where it becomes the Ship Canal, is disciplined by locks, joins with the Mersey and empties itself, by one of the finest estuaries in the world, into the Irish Sea at Liverpool.

It is a symbol of Lancashire. It begins fair and ends fair, and underneath the dour ugliness of a ruthless industrialism the valley of the Irwell has its hints of beauty still. As their river is, so are the people, Let them be miners, warped in body with continued cramping in the coal mines, cotton-mill operatives, stunted by generations of labour in moist and heated air, farm labourers in the still comparatively large agricultural area, or tradesmen in the towns, with all there are, beneath the grime of smoke and the hard struggle to exist in overpopulated districts, those same almost furtive peeps of beauty, indigenous and ineradicable, which remain unconquered in the Irwell Valley.

Manners, in the politer sense, do not exist in Lancashire. Forms and ceremonies may be all very well for the leisured Londoner, but the Lancashire man is out for business. In London, a salesman talks about the weather and makes discreet approaches to the business of his call. He wastes his own and the buyer's time. They don't waste time in Lancashire - at least, not in that way. "Owt?" says the salesman. "Nowt," says the buyer. Then, if they are friends, they may discuss the cricket scores, and Yorkshire's chances against Lancashire; if not, the salesman goes and there's an end of it, until he calls again. He always calls again. He will call weekly for five years, the "Owt" and "Nowt" will be the sum total of his conversation with a buyer, but in the end he'll gain a customer. He knows it. The buyer knows it. It is one of the ways they have of testing men in Lancashire. You might call it a kind of long-distance tact. The salesman with a silk hat and sleek coat and personal charm is a failure in Lancashire. "It's dogged as does it."

Manchester is the metropolis of Lancashire though Liverpool people hate to think it. There is a saying "An Oldham lad, a Manchester man and a Liverpool gentleman," and Manchester men will tell you Liverpool is welcome to its end of the saw: they prefer to be men. The trouble is that they are apt to make a pose of it. Lancashire heartiness is true enough, "jannock" as they call it, but in any metropolis the rugged side of native characteristics is naturally rubbed away, and they resent the polishing in Manchester, make an affectation of candour, and trade a little on their county's reputation for uncouthness. Veneer on rotten wood is a deadly sin, but sound oak is none the worse for polishing.

Queerly enough, Salford, which economically is a part of Manchester, though geographically and indeed civically divided from it by the Irwell, is a stronghold of Lancashire character, pure and unrefined. The many-bridged river makes a barrier which is in some respects impassable. Interdependent as the places are, they do not mix. Pathetically, but with true Lancashire obstinacy, Salford attempts a hopeless rivalry, refusing offers of amalgamation, maintaining its own town council and its own mayor, its own gasworks and police, and equipping a large Technical School to compete with Manchester's. It is not business. Even the Salford man admits it, but business in Lancashire, the first home of co-operative trading, is still individualistic, and communities, as such, can commit every crime in the commercial calendar if, individually, their members prosper. In Manchester, at the present day, the finest city site is derelict, an eyesore and a byword. Some years ago the town Infirmary was there, but the building had become too small and a huge new place was but where there was room for it, leaving the most central site in all the city to become the King Charles' Head of Council debates, some wanting an open space, other a municipal Cotton Exchange, others the original

THE IRWELL AT ORDSALL.

scheme of an Art Gallery that shall be worthy of their city's wealth. Meantime, grass grows in Piccadilly, Manchester, and periodic visitors are left to wonder where the manchester man's reputation for business ability comes in - until they meet one. Then they find out that a Manchester man doing business for himself is a different kind of wildfowl from the same man thinking municipally.

However, this novel is about Salford, which is Manchester's Cinderella, and, of course, all Salford is not as black as its blackest parts. It has, indeed, large residential districts which are still pleasant, and held, in 1879, the chosen houses of merchant princes. Kersal, perched on a lofty cliff high above the Irwell, and Pendleton, which faces it above another of the winding river's bends, were lordly suburbs in their day; and even now, despite the coming of the electric tram to bring the jerry-builder with it and the motorcar to enable the merchant prince to fly from the invasion, there are mansions still amongst the smoke. True, when the older generation dies, the younger will probably sell the house and gardens to some speculative builder and make new houses in Cheshire, or by the sea at Southport, or Llandudno or amongst the Derbyshire or even the Westmoreland hills, but meantime a certain mellowed opulence clings about the Salford suburbs and fights a losing battle with a growing population's curt demand for room to live. But Salford is not beautiful, though, as elsewhere, the artists's eye may perceive a beauty in it, and a Whistler of the Irwell might find nocturnes there. The sun makes golden haze of smoke, the jet black river glides below, high warehouse walls leap up, their red brick mellowed and their stone soft velvet with its fur of soot. Brick is the builder's chief material in Salford,and however mean a brick-built town may be, a stone-built town is meaner still. There are stone-built places in Scotland, in Derbyshire, even amongst the hills of Lancashire which bring a shiver to the spine of the beholder. Brick does not do that: it has warmth, but stone is at once the noblest and the most ignoble building material.

Salford consists of long, interminable rows of small

brick houses, all exactly like one another, two large breweries, cottonmills, bleachworks, dyeworks, printworks, bleachworks, rubberworks, churches and chapels, and a Roman Catholic cathedral, railway stations, two cattle markets, a racecourse, some coal mines, the river Irwell and the principal docks of the Manchester Ship Canal, a large Irish population, grime, filth, and human beings extraordinarily endowed with the will to live. They must be, or they couldn't live in Salford, and not only do they live but they enjoy life; coarsely, perhaps, but, according to their lights, thoroughly. Work in the weaving-sheds is hard and hours are long. But play is hard as well. See them at Blackpool in August Bank Holiday week! Or rather, if your tastes are delicate, do not. They might offend you. Lancashire at play is no sight for the fastidious, but for the human observer of humanity the rarest spectacle extant.

In 1879 Salford was further from Manchester than it is today. You did not jump on the penny car and run into Manchester to one of the great shops if you required a shirt. When it became necessary to buy one, and not a day earlier, you visited the shop in Regent Road, or Chapel Street, and did your business like a decent neighbour with the tradesman round the corner. Even the big houses in the Crescent were not above shopping in Salford. The shops were unpretentious and dependable, and Salford people had an eye to quality and none at all for aesthetic decorations. They were conservative. If a man's mother bought his boots at Hobson's when he was a baby, he went to Hobson's when he was grown up. Hobson's was his boot shop for life: he would as soon think of changing the colour of his hair or his political opinions as change the boot shop where his mother bought his first pair of boots for him.

Introducing Henry Hobson

That is why it was good to be the proprietor of a boot shop in Chapel Street, Salford, in the year 1879. It was doubly good when you were yourself engineer of your fortunes, creator and organiser in your strenuous youth of the business which, now that you were mature, ran itself on oiled wheels. So thought Henry Horatio Hobson as he sat on the horsehair sofa with the antimacassars in the living-room of his shop, putting on his boots, and surveying in the intervals of that slow and painful process his industrious daughters in the shop. It was a painful process because Hobson was fat, very fat, and his vital parts suffered uncomfortable compression when he bent; and a slow process because a man must breathe to live, and Hobson did not intend to die whilst he retained any capacity at all for enjoying the fruits of his youthful toil. At his time of life ease was a man's due, and Mr Hobson always took his due, gloated over his due and enlarged it till you could scarcely see the due in the enlargement. His shop, he felt, was a perfect machine which ran almost spontaneously. Allow for the trifling assistance rendered by his three daughters and it did run spontaneously, bewitched to ceaseless activity by the skilled guiding touches of the masterly magician Hobson, administered in a few casual moments seized on his way to or from the Moonraker's Inn.

Mr Hobson was not a Falstaff, but he had Falstaffian qualities. His eye was genial, his sensuality frank, his popularity with men immense. It is one of the quainter customs to regard a man who does himself well as a jolly good fellow. Let a man be lavish with his money in a tavern, satisfying his thirst and his self-importance by buying drink for others, and he obtains a reputation for open-handed generosity. That the reputation is bought at the expense of the man's home is nothing to his boon companions.

Mr Hobson liked to make his fellow-men happy - but not his fellow-women. Women, to him, were an inferior race, created for the servile use of man. In the morning especially, he looked upon his daughters with a jaundiced eye. Morning was Hobson's worst time: until he had paid his first visit of the day to the Moonraker's Inn, life was a weariness indeed. That was why, as he sat up after putting on his second boot, wheezing, heavily, he stared in pained astonishment at the little scene which met his eye through the glass door leading to the shop.

Maggie, his eldest, was at the books. Victoria, called Vickey, his third, was up a ladder disturbing the Salford dust from the stock. That was as it should be. Women were made for mechanical duties like book-keeping and menial offices like dusting. But his second daughter, Alice, was revealed to her astonished parent in an attitude of familiar intercourse with an unknown youth who must have entered the shop during Mr Hobson's second campaign with his boot-laces. There was no mistaking their attitude, either. Hobson knew life, and, as he gathered his strength preparatory to rising in his wrath, the thought occurred to him that Maggie and Vickey by their exaggerated aloofness were clearly aiding and abetting the conspiracy against his peace of mind. Not that he objected to Alice's getting married. Rather the contrary, in fact. Hobson could run that shop with one hand tied behind his back, and the girls were mere encumbrances with appetites. Well, he might keep Maggie. Some one must tie the parcels up. But what annoyed him was the thought of secrecy. When Alice married he would have his finger in the pie, or know the reason why. He rose to his feet, but checked himself as he saw the young man part from Alice, raising his hat (and thereby earning the lasting contempt of Mr Hobson), moving towards the outer door and being accosted by Maggie before he reached it.

"What can we do for you today?" said Maggie.

Mr Hobson could not hear, but he could see, and he drew back behind the door. He knew that gleam in Maggie's eye. It meant business.

Albert Prosser hesitated, and was lost. The glittering eye of the Ancient Mariner was soulless glass compared with Maggie's.

"Well, I can't really say that I came in to buy anything, Miss Hobson," he stammered.

"No, folks don't buy things in the morning in Salford," said Maggie, and she gleamed at him.

"It's a working town."

"Yes," he tried bravely, "I have work to do. I must get back to the office."

"And we have work," she said, "and this is not an office. It's a shop, and we're not here to let people go out without buying."

Albert put his hand to his pocket and produced a penny.

"Well, I'll just have a pair of bootlaces, please."

Maggie had a small mat in her hand. Near Mr Prosser was a cane-bottomed chair. It was not the sort of chair for lolling in, but it was serviceable. Maggie was between him and the door, he was between her and the chair.

"What size do you take in boots?"

"Eights," he said, with pride. Eights is a smallish size in Salford. Then he realised his mistake. "Does that matter to the laces?" he asked, with the ghastly facetiousness of a death-bed jest.

"It matters to the boots," she said, and dropped the mat. A very slight push did the rest. Before a repartee occurred to him, Mr Prosser was sitting on the chair and Maggie was on her knees in front of him unlacing his boot. She surveyed it with contempt.

"It's about time you had a new pair," she said.

"These uppers are disgraceful for a professional man to wear. Vickey, number eight from the third rack, please."

Albert Prosser, qualified solicitor, became acutely conscious of a hole in his sock. Alice attempted a rescue. It was a forlorn hope and she knew it, but Alice loved Albert and she tried.

"Mr Prosser did not come in to buy boots, Maggie," she said.

"I wonder what does bring him in here so often," said Maggie, taking the box from Vickey. Vickey's sympathies were wholly with the victim of salesmanship, but inside the shop she followed Maggie's lead. She tried with some success to make up for it outside.

"I'm terrible hard on bootlaces, Miss Hobson," Albert explained.

"Do you get through a pair a day? You must be strong."

"I keep a little stock of them," he said. "It's as well to be prepared for accidents."

Maggie was busy lacing the new boot. "And now you'll have boots to go with the laces, Mr Prosser. How does that feel?"

"Very comfortable," he said, and spoke the truth. Just for the moment the gleam was not in use. By its aid, Maggie could have sold him a boot that pinched like a vice, but that was not her way. She wanted customers to come again.

"I'll put the other on," she said.

"Oh, no, Miss Hobson, I really don't want to buy them. They're very nice boots, but - "

"You can't go through the street in odd boots, Mr Prosser." Maggie laced the second boot. "I'll send the old pair home to you with the bill. We'd better sole and heel them first. That'll be a pound for the new pair and three-and-sixpence for mending."

"What!" he gasped.

"And you don't need to buy a pair of laces today," she continued, placidly lacing his boot.

"Because we give them in as discount. Braid laces, that is. Of course, if you want leather ones, you being so strong in the arm and breaking so many pairs, you can have them, only its tuppence more."

Mr Prosser rose. "No, no, thank you," he gasped. He saw the door and nothing else. His flight was ignominious. No circumstances can quite excuse a lover for ignoring his beloved, but Albert's neglect of Alice as he fled was almost pardonable. He had work to do at the office.

Maggie returned calmly to the account-book. She was accustomed to success. But Alice was angry. She had the protective instinct towards Albert, and she meant Maggie to know whose property he was. She got her blow in first.

"It's all very well for an old maid like you, Maggie, but if father won't have us go courting, where else can Albert meet me except here?"

"Courting comes first," protested Alice, and all Salford

would have agreed with her. An undue haste in marriage makes the neighbours talk. But Maggie scorned propriety.

"It needn't," she said, and picked up a lady's slipper with a high heel, a cotton plush upper and a fancy buckle. They were about the on l y things Hobson's sold which were not made on the premises. Hobson bought these from Leicester, scorning them, but selling them at a high profit for mill-girls to use on Saturday nights in the dancing halls of Regent Road. Maggie despised the flimsy slippers and their use. Saturday night, indeed, was her busiest time. "See that slipper with a fancy buckle on to make it sell?" she said. "Courting's like that, my lass. All glitter and no use to nobody." She dropped the bauble with a world of scorn.

Uppishness and Give and Take

Mr Hobson decided to emerge, but though Alice's affair made urgent call for action, he was not going to rush into eruption without first taking counsel in the bar-parlour of the Moonraker's. It cost him some effort to refrain, for on the previous evening he had attended a Masonic function, and was in consequence peculiarly short-tempered today. Nevertheless, he decided not to be precipitate. Once or twice lately his younger daughters had astonished him by an independence of spirit and an ease of repartee which he considered unfeminine. It had only been small matters, but his confidence was shaken, and he meant this time to make no mistakes. Clandestine amours were a serious affair, and his explosion, when it came, must be effective. Brandy and the company at the Moonraker's would sharpen his wits.

Slowly his face was cleared of half-incredulous astonishment and wore its wonted mask of genial good humour. He took his hat, a compromise in felt between a topper and a billycock, and stepped into the shop. He stopped in front of Maggie's desk and addressed her with the carefully casual air in which he always alluded to his outgoings to the inn.

"I'll be back in a quarter of an hour," he said.

Maggie did not trouble to look up. "There's liver for dinner," she said, "so don't be late."

Hobson consulted his watch. "It's an hour off dinner-time," he said.

"So that," she said, turning a page, "if you stay more than an hour in the Moonraker's, you'll be late."

Now, Hobson spent at least four hours a day at the Moonraker's. An Englishman's home is his castle, and his tavern is his club. His daughters knew it and he knew that they knew it, but, by general consent, the fact was never mentioned. It was officially understood that Mr Hobson went out on business. Maggie's candour outraged all convention. Decidedly, things were not going well with Henry Horatio Hobson today. First Alice's amour, next Maggie's ruthless rending of the veil, and, to crown all, Vickey - Vickey, his baby, Vickey, the beauty of the family - leaned over the counter and remarked, "If your dinner's spoiled it'll be your own fault."

He stared speechlessly. Hobson, the oracle of the Moonraker's parlour, orator, the wit, stared tongue-tied at his youngest daughter. Then he tried to put in practice a debating dodge which he found useful at the Moonraker's. When in doubt, swear. An oath comes trippingly. Delivered with a proper emphasis, it shouts the opposition down and gives the cornered arguer a moment's pause for thought. So Hobson swore.

"Don't swear in here, father," said Alice.

Hobson glared. Then he took his hat off deliberately and placed it on the counter. To postpone a visit to the Moonraker's was unprecedented, but here was a case for heroism.

"No," he said; "I'll sit down instead." You picture Mr Hobson straddling across a chair, that small cane-bottomed chair whereon young Prosser underwent his agony, with his back to the door and his inflamed face turned towards his audience of three. The stout form bulged beyond the little chair which bore his weight miraculously like another Atlas holding up the world. Mr Hobson prepared himself. He cleared his throat. He spat upon the floor. Deliberately, defiantly, daring Maggie with his eye as he did it, he spat, and thereby broke an ancient treaty and announced that this was war. A rumbling came from Mr Hobson's throat, faint premonition of the thunder-clap to come. Then words emerged.

"Listen to me, you three. I've come to conclusions about you. And I'll none have it. Do you hear that? Interfering with my goings out and comings in. The idea! I've a mind to take measures with the lot of you."

Maggie looked condescendingly from her books. She could humour the child in his tantrums. "I expect Mr Heeler is waiting for you in the Moonraker's, father."

There is no side-tracking a real orator. Once wind him up, and he must go till he runs down, and Mr Hobson had been strongly wound.

"Heeler can go on waiting. At present, I'm engaged in addressing a few remarks to the rebellious females of this house, and what I say will be listened to and heeded, so think on. I've seen this coming on ever since your mother died, and I'll tell you what it is: there's been a gradual increase of Uppishness in this house. Ay, Uppishness towards me." He paused to note effects. Curiously enough, there were no effects. Uppishness was deadly sin. He had accused them of it and they appeared unmoved. Mr Hobson felt depressed. He had that same embarrassed feeling which one gets on reaching the top of a staircase in the dark and raising one's foot to reach another stair which isn't there. He spoke more loudly.

"Providence has decreed that you should lack a mother's hand at the time of life when single girls grow bumptious, and must have somebody to rule. But I'll tell you this, my ladies, that you'll none rule me."

He glared at Vickey. Vickey smiled. She was exceedingly pretty when she smiled.

I'm sure I'm not bumptious, father," she said softly.

He pounced upon her. "Yes, you are. You're pretty, but you're bumptious, and I hate bumptiousness like I hate a lawyer."

That was not mere figure of speech. Mr Hobson did

CHAPEL STREET, SALFORD.

hate lawyers, and Albert Prosser was a lawyer, though Mr Hobson did not know it. Therefore the accidental shaft hit Alice hard.

She intervened. "If we take trouble to feed you, it's not bumptious to ask you not to be late for your food."

"Give and take, father," came from Vickey.

"I give and you take," said Hobson; "and it's going to end."

Maggie looked up again. "How much a week do you give us?" she asked.

"That's neither here nor there," he said. "It's immaterial." (In sober truth it was.) "It's not the point. At moment, I'm on Uppishness, and I warn you your conduct towards your parent's got to change. But that's not all. That's private conduct, and now I pass to broader aspects and I speak of public conduct. I've looked upon my household as they go about the streets, and I've been fair disgusted. The name and fame of Hobson has been outraged by members of Hobson's family, and Uppishness has done it."

"I simply don't know what you're talking about," said Vickey, feeling herself addressed.

"Vickey," her father said, "you're pretty, but you can lie like a gas-meter. Who had new dresses on last week?"

Alice blushed. Vickey tossed her head. Maggie watched: she rarely had new dresses, and, in fact the value of the dress she might have had was equally divided between Alice and Vickey. Maggie had no use for fine feathers. Her eye was her fortune.

"We shall dress as we like, father," said Vickey, "and you can save your breath."

"I'm none stopping in from my business appointment for the purpose of saving my breathe. I'm here to speak my mind."

"You know you like to see us looking nice." Vickey was vaguely coy.

"I do," he said. "I like to see my daughters nice. That's why I pay my friend Joe Tudsbury the draper, ten pounds a year a head to dress you proper. A well-dressed daughter is pleasing to the eye, and likewise good for trade. But I'll tell you, my ladies, if some women could see themselves as men see them they would get a nasty shock; and I'll have words with Tudsbury, and all, for letting you dress up like guys. I saw you two out of the Moonraker's parlour on Thursday night, and my friend Sam Minns - "

"A publican!" interrupted Alice.

"Aye, a publican. As honest a man as God Almighty ever set behind a bar. My friend Sam Minns asked me who in thunder those bombastical pieces were. And well he might, too. You were making exhibitions of yourselves in Chapel Street with a hump added to nature behind you."

Vickey gasped a scandalised protest. "Father," she began, but might as well have tried to dam Niagara with a champagne cork.

"The hump was wagging, and you'd the kind of waists that's natural in wasps and abominable in women, and you set your feet on the pavement as if you'd got chilblains, which is a libel on any boots that come from Hobson's shop, and you held your heads like a giraffe's with a bad stiff neck, and you were gone at the knees, and I say it's immodest."

"Don't you know it's the fashion to war bustles?" asked Alice.

"You should open your eyes a bit to what other women wear," said Vickey.

"If what I saw on you is any guide, I should do nowt of sort," said Hobson. "I'm a decent-minded man." He stood. No chair could bear his peroration. "I'm Hobson. I'm British middle class, and proud of it. I stand for common sense and sincerity. You're affected, which is bad sense and insincerity. You've overstepped nice dressing and you've tried grand dressing, which is the occupation of fools and such as have no brains. You forget the majesty of trade and the unparalleled virtues of the British Constitution" - drunk or sober, Mr Hobson could pronounce that phrase - "which are all based on the sobriety of the middle classes, combined with the diligence of the working classes. You're losing balance, and you're putting the things which don't matter in front of the things which do, and if you mean to be a factor in the world of Lancashire or a factor in the house of Hobson, you'll become sane."

"Do you want us to dress like mill-girls?" asked Vickey, undaunted.

"No," he roared, "nor like French madams, neither. It's" - he paused - "it's un-English, I say."

Now, if you want a little healthful exercise in Salford, a useful plan is to go up to the first man you meet and call him a bastard. It will be necessary for you to get off the mark rapidly and thereafter to run for your life. But there is another and an even surer way. Call him, instead, a foreigner, or better still, a bloody foreigner. It is the last insult. No one who is not a first-class adept in the art of self-defence would dare to risk it on a man, but a father addressing his children is a privileged person. Hobson called their conduct un-English, and thought to see them reeling at the blow. Maggie was still book-keeping, Vickey simply smiled, and Alice merely seemed to be stating a fact when she said, "We shall continue to dress fashionably, father."

Hobson began to feel like a man wrestling with a

feather bed, but he pulled himself together. He remembered Albert Prosser.

"Then I've a choice for you two," he said. "Vickey, you I'm talking to, and Alice. You'll become sane if you'd go on living here. You'll control this Uppishness that's growing on you. And if you don't you can get out of this and exercise your gifts on some one else than me. You don't know when you're well off. But you'll learn it when I've done with you. I'll choose a pair of husbands for you, my girls. That's what I'll do."

"Can't we choose husbands for ourselves?" asked Alice.

"You!" he roared. "I've been telling you for the last five minutes that you're not even fit to choose your dresses for yourselves. You'd choose husbands as you'd choose your clothes. Flash and nasty, made for show and not for wear. If a woman dresses like a fool she'll marry like a fool; aye, marry a lazy lounger with a collar sawing his ears, and a reek of oil on his hair, and a pair of hands that never did a day's work in their life" - which was not wholly unrecognisable as a caricature of Mr Albert Prosser. Alice recognised it, rather to Mr Hobson's annoyance. He wanted the assistance of the Moonraker's before he tackled that matter seriously, and regretted that he had allowed himself a premature allusion.

But Maggie made a diversion. She put her pen down and came round the counter to Mr. Hobson.

"You're talking a lot to Vickey and Alice, father. Where do I come in?"

He stared, puzzled. She hadn't worn a fashionable dress. "You?" he asked.

"If you're dealing husbands round, don't I get one?"

"You with a husband!" he laughed. "That's a good one." And it was. Hobson was quite sincere. Maggie's celibacy was as much a fixed idea as the inviolacy of the British Constitution.

But Maggie was serious.

"Why not?" she said, a little dryly.

He spoke with rough good-humour. "Why not? I thought you'd sense enough to know. But if you want it said, you're past the marrying age. Eh, you're a proper old maid, Maggie, if ever there was one."

Maggie was drier still. "I'm thirty," she said.

"Aye," Hobson agreed, with pleasant contempt.

"Thirty and shelved. Well, all the women can't get husbands. But you others, now, I've told you. I'll have less Uppishness from you, or else I'll shove you off my hands on to some other man. You can just choose which way you'll have it.

He took his hat and opened the door.

"One o'clock dinner," Maggie reminded him.

He turned. "See here, Maggie, I set the hours at this house. It's one o'clock dinner because I say it is, and not because you do. Do you know that?"

Maggie nodded. "Yes, father," she said. She never let power run to waste. Strength frittered away on unimportant things turns into weakness.

"So long as that's clear, I'll go," he said, and stepped into the street.

"Dinner's half-past one," said Maggie Hobson.

"He'll not be back before."

Chapter Two

The Mossops'

The household consisted of Hobson and his three daughters. The late Mrs. Hobson had succumbed some years ago to the strain of controlling Hobson's convivial expansiveness. Maggie was younger then, and Mrs. Hobson looked after Hobson, and Hobson looked after his business. Now he looked after himself. Maggie ran both shop and house and her sisters did as she told them, in both departments. There was no servant. A Salford man with three daughters would have regarded a domestic servant as criminal extravagance. Twice a year, in the spring and late autumn, a charwoman made her appearance for a week and the house was "turned out" from attic to cellar. It interfered with Mr Hobson's comfort, but he never grumbled. The spring and autumn cleans are as inevitable as the Sunday School processions and Whit Sunday. In Lancashire, women are nothing if they are not "house-proud," and cleanliness in Salford is a god to be worshipped not by prayer and fasting, but by energy and elbow-grease. The Hobson girls were vigorous young women, and it was well for them they were. Salford weeds out its weaklings young.

Four workmen made and mended boots in Hobson's shop. They laboured in the cellar underneath the shop. The law was so far observed that a card printed with the requirements of the Factory Act hung somewhere on the wall, but dirt had long since made its print illegible, and Inspectors hunted larger game than Hobson's. The cellar had no natural light and no ventilation. Its walls had once been white-washed. It stank of leather, gas and human beings. And in it worked the craftsman, Willie Mossop, the foreman, Tubby Wadlow, and two other hands whose personality was varying. Men came and went, but Wadlow and Mossop remained unchanged.

Will Mossop was big for a cobbler; a large, ungainly, lumpish, whey-faced lad with cunning hands which made the finest boots in Lancashire. He didn't know it. He only knew he loved his work and received the sum of eighteen shillings a week for doing it. Nor did Hobson nor Hobson's customers know it either. Hobson knew he had a good, cheap workman, who never complained and made no misfits. Customers knew Hobson's for a reliable shop where they charged a reasonable figure and sold a boot that didn't pinch. No one but Maggie knew that Willie Mossop's boots were things of beauty, great craftsmanship, the perfect adaption of means to end. People from the better parts of Salford, from around St. Philip's Church and from the Crescent, came to Hobson's for their made-to-order boots, and Maggie knew the reason why. It was one part neighbourliness and three parts Willie Mossop's genius. But Willie did not know. How should he know?

In the year 1820, a naked baby was found by the porter at the gate of Salford Workhouse. The night was cold, but the baby's constitution was heroic. He survived. They called him Ben Mossop because Benjamin is in the Bible, and Mossop was the maiden name of the clerk's grandmother. At the age of seven, Ben Mossop left the workhouse to begin life in the Agecroft coal-pits. The Lancashire miner of today is a rough, good-hearted, brutal, wife-beating, pigeon-fancying, whippet-racing, hard-drinking, generous mixture of the cruder virtues and the cruder vices. He is the best trench-fighter in Flanders because he can dig a mine and is inured to hardship. And some of his women-folk are glad that he is there. After a recruiting rush from Pendlebury, early in the war, half the women wrote with chalk upom their doorsteps, "Peace at last." The other half were weeping. There were no young men left in Pendlebury. And in 1827, when Ben Mossop first went down the pit, miners were savages. If a child-slave dodged the lump of coal they threw at him, they launched a pick-axe. If he evaded that, they collared him and used their belts. Ben Mossop still survived. There were unbelievable things done in coalpits where brutalised men in distant galleries were absolutely safe from observation. Ben Mossop thought the ravenous rats were friendler than men.

He grew in years, in hardihood, in knowledge of evil. His rough vitality attracted women. Where nearly all his mates had grown deformed through stooping, or suffered in an accident, or been twisted to amuse a tyrant, Ben stood straight and strong, a noted fighter, great at drinking ale.

A woman looked into Ben Mossop's eyes, beneath their air of callous recklessness, and saw a gentle soul. She married him; their son, Will Mossop, came, and, at first, they both knew happiness. Her softness healed his bruises, and the man Ben Mossop might have been flickered to life till ale and habit grew too strong again. Ben Mossop, sober, was a man, with a taste for canaries and a skill in breeding them; drunk, he was a beast, the terror of his son. Cock-fighting, ratting and bullying his son were Mossop's pastimes when the drink took hold of him. As he had suffered when a child, so should his son suffer. It was proper and natural for children to be beaten. It was what children were for.

It stunted Will. He had his hands, those wonderful hands which seemed miraculously able to do anything. He had his mother, whom he was powerless to protect, and, for the rest, his mind was a blank slate on which who would, could write. When a child's life depends upon his agility in dodging a clog shied at his head by a drunken father, mental development is apt to be arrested.

Ben died in a drinking-bout, and his widow soon lay by his side in the huge cemetery in Weaste. Will was then twenty and earned eighteen shillings a week at Hobson's. He was now thirty-one, was still receiving eighteen shillings a week and would continue to receive eighteen shillings a week in perfect content in return for creating masterpieces of leather craftsmanship if he were allowed. But he was not allowed.

Tubby Wadlow looked up. When a man of Mr Hobson's weight crosses a floor, those in the room below are made aware of it.

"That's the master going out," said Tubby.

"Aye," said Will, and kept his eyes upon his work with the same concentraction which Maggie Hobson bestowed upon her books.

"I'll go up, then, and see Miss Maggie," Tubby said.

Timothy Wadlow was called Tubby because he had a paunch, and a workman with a paunch was remarkable in Salford. He was Hobson's foreman. He had received twenty-five shillings a week since Mrs Hobson died. Until that time Hobson had been his own foreman and Tubby had received a pound a week to reward him for twenty years' service. The cause of his promotion was architectural. The cellar-workshop was entered only by a ladder descending from a trap-door in the floor of the shop. To descend a perpendicular ladder without inconvenience required more nerve than Mr Hobson now had in the early morning, and more steadiness than his legs had later in the day. So Tubby was made foreman and soon fell into the habit of taking his orders for the day from Maggie, after the burgess had gone out.

Tubby climbed the ladder with ease of custom, took the precaution of knocking on the trap from below, and raised it. As the shop became visible to him, he started with surprise and almost fell..Maggie was attending to a customer.

Walking Out on a Sunday

Customers, as Maggie had unkindly hinted to Albert Prosser, were rare events in the morning. Hobson's did more trade on Saturday night than in the whole of the rest of the week. Afternoons were always slack and morning practically blank. They work for their livings in Salford, and shopkeepers must work their hardest when others are at play. It is a notable fact that Mr Hobson did not visit the Moonraker's on a Saturday night.

But Mrs Hepworth was no ordinary customer. She

lived at Hope Hall, and her carriage brought her to Hobson's. It was only the second time that she had come, and even Maggie felt a little anxious. Mrs Hepworth was somebody.

She was sitting on the little chair, poking a new boot into Maggie's face.

"Who made these boots?" she asked.

Maggie knew, but a firm must be impersonal.

STATUE OF SIR ROBERT PEEL IN PEEL PARK.

"They are our make, madam. Executed on the premises."

"Then who executed these?"

Tubby made a noise. It might have indicated a desire to speak. The mistress of Hope Hall looked at him.

"Did you?" she said fiercely.

"What's wrong with them?" asked Tubby.

"Can I get a plain answer to a plain question?"

Tubby's eyes met Maggie's, and she gave assent.

"They're Willie Mossop's making, if you want to know," he said.

"I came to know. Send Willie here."

Mrs Hepworth was accustomed to obedience. Tubby obeyed, and went below. Defensive silence reigned above. Both women, in their different spheres, were of a type. Will Mossop showed above the trap.

"Are you Mossop?"

"Yes, mum."

"Come here." He came. She pointed to her boot. "Did you make that?"

Willie bent down and peered, short-sightedly.

"Yes," he announced, "I made these boots last week."

"Take that," she said, and Willie dodged to escape a blow which didn't come. The expected had happened too often in Willie's past for him to take a risk. "Take it," she said, and held a visiting-card before his eyes. He took.

"You see what's on it?"

"Writing," he said, struggling to read it. "Only it's such funny print."

"It's the usual italics of a visiting-card, my lad. Now listen to me. I heard about this shop from Mrs Bolton in the Crescent, and what I heard brought me here for these boots. I'm particular about what I put on my feet. Mossop, I've tried every shop in Manchester and Salford, and these are the best-made pair of boots I've ever had. You'll make my boots in future. You hear that?" she added, turning to Maggie. Maggie nodded. She was thinking too fast to speak. "You'll keep that card, Mossop, and don't you dare leave here to go to another shop without letting me know where you are."

Maggie emerged from thought. "Can I take your order for another pair, Mrs Hepworth."

"Not yet, young woman. But I shall send my daughters here. And, mind you, that man's to make the boots."

"He shall," said Maggie opening the door for Mrs Hepworth. She bowed her out. Maggie did not bow often, though Mrs Hepworth could not be expected to know that. But Maggie had her reasons.

Willie was spelling out the card. She came to him.

"Willie," she said, "me and you'ull go a walk on Sunday afternoon. I'll see you after school."

Will Mossop dropped the card and fumbled for it on the floor. If Mr Hobson had asked him to come and have a drink, he would have been less surprised. Fully to understand his surprise one should know something about Sunday Schools in Salford. They are popular institutions. They are popular with parents because elderly digestions require a period of perfect peace in order to deal with Sunday's dinner, and children are safely and respectably out of the way at Sunday School. They are equally popular, if not with children who have enough school during the week, at any rate with young adults. Opposing sexes find in Sunday Schools a sanctioned meeting-place. In bulk, the intercourse is quite promiscuous. Mary takes her after-school stroll with John one Sunday and with Dick the next. But if the same maid pair with the same man for three successive Sundays, tongues begin to wag. He "goes with" her, and to "go with" a girl bears the same relationship to an engagement as an engagement does to a marriage. It is slightly more tentative, a preliminary trial-trip, unauthorised but regular, a starting-place to which one may return to make a new beginning with another partnership. It is begun by some such invitation as that which Maggie now extended to Will Mossop. Maggie instructed a class of infants in the rudiments of Christianity, and a well-instructed, highly disciplined class it was. Will Mossop attended a young men's class at the same school.

"I'll meet you at the door," she continued.

"Eh, Miss Maggie," he protested. A meeting at the very door meant starting off together in the glare of publicity. The shyer sort were wont to start off singly, sometimes in opposite directions, making a circuit and meeting at a corner by appointment some ten minutes later. This was brazen.

"That's settled, then," she said, and walked into the house.

The shop was alien atmosphere to Will. He bolted for the ladder. He could think straight in the reeking cellar.

Will Buys a Hat

The fact is, Will Mossop was "tokened" to Ada Figgins. That was the thought which prevented him from bursting with pride at the prospect of him Will Mossop, eighteen shillings a week bootmaker, walking out on Sunday afternoon with Maggie Hobson, his employer's daughter. Morever, such an invitation as Maggie's though more usually extended from a man to a woman, was one of the recognised approaches to the kind of intercourse which led to matrimony.

Nothing is more certain than that Will Mossop did not desire to marry Maggie. He did not want to walk with her. Or did he? How much of his reluctance was fear of Hobson, should Hobson hear of it, how much was loyalty to Ada, and how much abject craven terror of Ada's mother, his landlady?

He did not disklike Maggie, neither did he particularly like her. He admired her cool efficiency. Maggie was never flurried, whereas his life except for those suave hours when he was shaping leather in the vitiated air of Hobson's cellar was one eternal flurry. Like a rabbit, he felt safe only in his burrow. But he had the habit of obedience, and particularly did he obey Maggie Hobson. She had an eye..He was was aware tahat he would obey her now, but his very soul trembled at the consequences. He hated Maggie. Why should she interfere with him? He felt quite sure he hated her..He would like to be seen walking on Sunday with his employer's daughter..But suppose the wrong people saw him? Indeed, there were no right people at all. People who did not know them would be blind to the stupendous compliment she paid him in walking with him. People who knew them would inevitably talk to Hobson or to Ada, to Vickey or Mrs Figgins. He could see nothing in it but catastrophe.

"Tubby," said Will Mossop during a lull in the sounds of cobbling, "do you know much about women?"

"No," said Tubby; "I'm a man of sense."

"Aye," said Will, and worked in silence.

"Out with it, lad," said Tubby.

"Nay, ut's nowt."

"And you're a liar, Will. You're in trouble and I can give a guess at where it comes from, too. It's that ginger-headed wench you lodge with that's the cause."

As a matter of fact Ada Figgins had hair of the sunniest copper imaginable, only they hadn't heard of Rossetti in Salford in 1879, and copper-coloured hair was a misfortune to its owner..But it was Ada Figgins' glory, and Willie Mossop knew it, or he felt it. The man who fashioned leather as he did, had the instincts of an artist. He admired her hair. It was the only admirable thing she had. The rest of her was clemmed anaemia. That was because her diet consisted principally of strong tea and mixed pickles.

The word "clem" is good old English. Ben Johnson uses it in *The Poetaster*, and a note translates it as "to stock the guts together." But to clem in Lancashire means to starve. It was an overworked word during the Cotton Famine at the time of the American Civil War. Ada Figgins was clemmed. a feeble-spirited, poor-bodied daughter of a dauntless mother. Will was engaged to her. Mrs Figgins purposed it, and what she purposed usually came to pass with Will. His one contribution to the arrangement was a faint desire to see Ada with her hair down. In no other way, physical or mental, did he desire her.

"I'm tokened to Ada Figgin," he confessed.

"You're the largest size in witless fools in Salford," Tubby told him.."After all I've told you of the ways of women, to go and let a starveling rat the likes of her get hold of you! I warned you. I told you to come and lodge with me and keep away from booby-traps. But you'd none flit and now you'll pay for it."

"I didn't see how I could move," said Will.

"No, It'ud take three furniture vans three days to shift your belongings, wouldn't it? You're a young man of great possessions, and the greatest of them's just damned lunacy. When's the wedding?"

"It's not got that far yet," said Will. "I only spoke last night."

St. Philip's clock struck twelve. "That's dinner-time," said Tubby. One of the transitory "hands" was brewing tea at the fire in jugs. Tubby and Will approached the fire, the other men withdrew from it. Thus was the caste system honoured in Hobson's workroom. Long-service men sat by the fire, the nomads had a corner in the cold, and would no more attempt to trespass on the older inhabitants' preserves than an up-to-date trades unionist would work more rapidly than the regulation rate.

Tubby ate the bread and meat, washed down with steaming tea, unqualified with milk, directly from his jug. Will substituted cheese for meat.

"Tell me about it," Tubby said.

"I dunno as there's much to tell," said Will. "It happened-like."

"It would," said Tubby; "and her mother made it happen."

"Aye, well, she did talk to me, did Mrs. Figgins. She's been saved, you see, and thinks a lot about her latter end, and what was going to happen to Ada after she'd gone to glory. Spoke a lot about that one time and another. And Ada knitted me a pair of socks. Warm 'uns, and all. I've got them on."

"It used to be an apple," Tubby said. Will missed the allusion.

"Ada 'ull be lonesome-like when her mother dies, and that's a fact. And I looked at it like this. I'm very near one of the family now with lodging there so long. I mean - it's not like marrying a stranger. I could'nt, Tubby. Not at any price.

Strange women are a thing I can't abide. But I'm used to Ada, and the shock 'ull not be so bad. I always like the chill taken off the water when I wash myself Saturday nights."

"You're not in love with her." Tubby was blunt. The bathing simile annoyed him slightly. Tubby did not take baths.

"I don't know, Tubby. I don't know whether I am or not. I've never been in love before, so how can I tell whether I am or not this time? I know I've promised to wed her. And I've struggled, Tubby, I've struggled hard."

""You're a fly in the web of the spider."

"I'll hear no disrespect to Ada, Tubby,"

"Then I can shut my mouth. I thought you asked for my advice."

"Aye, but it's not about Ada, though. I'm tokened to her, and what's done is done. It's about Miss Maggie."

"Miss Maggie," said Tubby startled.

"Aye," said Will. "She's after me, and all."

Tubby decided that Will had lost what wits he ever had.

"Art mad?" he asked.

"I wish I were," said Will. "I might be safe in asylum." And he told Tubby of Maggie's surprising command.

Tubby apologised. "It's the women that's gone mad. Not Thee. Two women after thee - three, counting Ada's mother - and thee the biggest, silliest fool in Salford."

"I am," said Will complacently. "But facts don't seem to matter to a woman."

"Let's take a look at you," said Tubby. "Maybe there's something in you that I've missed. I've only worked aside you fifteen year and I can't know much about you yet. You've a lump of a body, and a face like a piece of dough. You've got great feet and calves like the leg of a chair. You don't walk, you shamble, and your mind's a void. You make boots like an angel, but that's nowt to a woman. I'm judging your externals., Will, and the verdict is you're guilty, and there's not a single word to say in favour of you. I'm trying to be kind, but I must be just. I can understand Ada Figgins.

She's a measly, red-haired atom, and anything in trousers is a gift to her. But Maggie Hobson's off her head, or else you're dreaming it."

"It's not a dream," said Will. "She said it and she meant it."

"That's Maggie's way," said Tubby. "She does mean what she says."

"What am I to do?" asked Will.

"Do! You God-forsaken idiot! Do! Thank Heaven for the blindness of women, and buy a new hat against you go your walk with Miss Hobson on Sunday. And leave the rest to her. She knows what she wants."

Will Mossop bought a hat.

Chapter Three

In the Bar Parlour

Mr Hobson emerged from his shop into the mirk of Chapel Street. After the disturbing events at home, its drab familiarity was soothing, to his troubled soul. Outsiders might have said hard words of Chapel Street, but Mr Hobson loved its dirt, its unpretentious shops, its two-horse trams to Manchester, and its frank unloveliness. Money was made in Chapel Street, and that was all that mattered.

    He loved the fly-blown, soot-stained windows and the bulging walls, irreparable roofs whose slates might fall at any time, the absent-minded pavement of the side-walk and the sudden yawning cellar-entrances protected by the flimsiest of railings. These were things that made a man look lively when he went to his inn, and made his livelier return adventurous. It is certain that the now departed soul of Mr. Hobson looks in pity on the modern weaklings who invoke the aid of tip-accumulating hotel porters and nurserymaid taxi drivers. In his day a man took his chances and Mr Hobson loved things as they were. Interference and reform were the fetishes of Radicals, and, for him, the stark-grey sky was luxury enough, and clattering clogs made a music to his ear.

    The street was comfortable to his soul, and the short walk in the sunshine to his body. It restored him to nod patronisingly to Sam Welch, who kept the tripe shop and was lounging at his door, to be saluted by a policeman and to shake the hand of a Conservative Town Councillor. Nevertheless, Mr. Hobson was depressed. His absolute authority had not been flouted, but it had been challenged, and Mr. Hobson saw trouble ahead with his daughters Vickey and Alice. Maggie was different. She had some sense.

Sam Minns noticed the depression. He knew Mr. Hobson's moods and silently poured out brandy. In equal silence Mr. Hobson drank it up.

"More," he said, and took his usual chair in the bar-parlour of the Moonraker's - Sam Minns obliged.

"Morning, Hobson," said Jim Heeler, the grocer. "Up late to-day?"

"I've been detained," said Hobson, and he drank again.

"Good health," said Mr. Joseph Tudsbury.

Hobson's eye was not as Maggie's was, but it could cow Mr. Joseph Tudsbury. "I'd be in better health if it were not for you," he said. "Do you think I make an annual contract job with you for letting my daughters dress like trollops? Ten pounds a head makes thirty pounds, and half of that is profit. You'll be fifteen pounds a year out of pocket for doing this, my lad."

"I've dressed them in the fashion," protested Tudsbury.

"Then to hell with the fashion!" said Hobson.

"Salford's a decent town."

"Hobson," said Heeler, "this is not the language of friends, and I hope we're all friends here."

Sam Minns poured alcohol upon the troubled waters, and Hobson drank again. "You've lost time to make up today, Mr. Hobson," he cooed sympathetically. The patient responded to treatment.

"All right, Joe," he said. "I own I'm short today, and cause to be, and all. Jim, you've got daughters."

"Aye," said Jim, in a toneless voice that committed him to nothing.

"And they're about the years of mine," said Hobson. "Do yours worry you?"

"I can't say that they do." said Jim. "They mostly do as I tell them, and the missus does the leathering if they don't."

"A strap's a handy thing," said Mr Minns. "I always wear one."

"I never found a strap much use with women myself," said Tudsbury. "I've a system of fines with the shop assistants."

"You've got no daughters," said Jim Heeler, "or you'd know they need the strap. There's nothing like daughters for getting above themselves. You can sack a shop assistant, but you can't sack a daughter."

"You can marry her off," said Minns, who had accomplished the feat three times by putting the goods on exhibition in the bar.

"I've thought of that," said Hobson. "But I'm none for rushing at it. I wish their mother was alive." His audience stared. It was an opposite wish which Mr. Hobson used to utter when the lady was alive. "I do. I know what you're thinking, but I do. A wife's a handy thing, and you don't know it proper till she's taken from you. I felt grateful for the quiet when my Mary fell on rest, but I can see now I made a mistake. I used to think I was hard put to it to fend her off when she wanted summat out of me, but the dominion of one woman is paradise to the dominion of three."

"You're a bit upset today, Henry, that's plain," said Jim.

""I'm a talkative man by nature, Jim," said Hobson. "You know that."

"Talkative? My lad, that's not the word. A nagging woman's talkative. But you - why, damn it, Henry you're an orator! I doubt John Bright himself is better gifted at the gab than you."

"Nay," said Hobson modesty. "Good wine needs no bush, and you needn't flatter me. I know I'm gifted."

"Aye," said Minns. "You're the best debater this barparlour ever hears, and it's the regret of my life that you don't come in on Saturday nights."

"They'd not appreciate Hobson on a Saturday," said Tudsbury.

"Eh?" said Hobson.

"Too fuddled," Tudsbury explained quickly. Mr Hobson was mollified. He spoke for sober ears.

"Oh," he said. "Well, that's the fact. In the estimation of my fellow-men I give forth words of wisdom. In the eyes of my daughters, I'm a windbag."

The bar was horrified. Jim Heeler even rose in his seat.

"Nay," he said. "Never!"

"I am," said Hobson. "They scorn my wisdom, Jim. They give back-answers. They've grown uppish."

"They do," said Jim. "I know. It comes of living an indoor life. They get the idea that they're important in the world because they're boss in the kitchen!"

"A woman's foolishness begins where man's leaves off," said Mr. Hobson.

"They want a firm hand, Henry," said Sam Minns.

"I've done my best," said Hobson. "I've lifted up my voice and roared at them."

"Beware of roaring at women, Henry. Roaring is mainly hollow sound. I favour silent strength, myself" said Mr Heeler,

"Aye; as you said, your missus does the leathering," said Mr Tudsbury, glad to make a point at anybody's expense so long as it was not the offended Hobson's.

"Strength of character is what tells with women," persisted Jim Heeler.

"Do you mean to tell me my character's not strong?" said Mr Hobson

"No, but I tell you you're on the wrong track, Henry. You quit roaring at 'em and get'em wed."

""I can see that's what it's coming," said Mr Hobson. "But I'm an amateur at making matches. It comes natural to a mother, but a man's a bit at sea. It's not often I'm in doubt," he added hastily.

"Men's common enough," said Heeler. "Are you looking for angels in breaches?"

"I've got a son myself," said Sam, "and he's a bachelor at present."

"I'd like my daughters to wed temperance young men, Sam," said Mr Hobson.

"Good Lord!"said Mr Minns. "You keep your ambitions within reasonable limits, Henry," advised Jim. "You've three unmarried daughters sitting on your chest. You can't pick and choose with a wholesale line like that."

"Two, Jim two at most. Alice and Vickey. They're only window-dressing in the shop, but Maggie's a bit of use sometimes, when there's an extra busy time, you know. She can be handy at little things, can Maggie, if she's watched proper. And you know, Jim, when it comes to marrying, our Maggie's what you might call on the ripe side."

"Ripe?" said Mr Minns. "I've known them do it at twice her age." "Still," said Tudsbury, "leaving Maggie out, you've still got two."

"One will do for a start, though. It's thing I've noticed about lasses. Get one wedding in a family, and it runs through the lot like measles."

"Well, we're getting down to business now," said Mr Heeler. "We know what you want. You want one young and you want him temperance. The last item makes him a bit of a fancy article, but when you're overloaded with stock that looks like sticking by you, it's worth sacrificing something considerable to set it moving. Question is, how high are you prepared to go?

"How high?" said Mr Hobson, puzzled. "Oh, I'll get my hand down for the wedding do all right."

The bar permitted itself a smile. Smiles at Hobson's expense were rare luxuries, but that sapient gentleman was showing innocence indeed. Achilles had a heel.

"Er - " began Mr Tudsbury, but thought better of it. His footing was slippery today. Jim took the plunge. "A warm man like you 'ull have to do more than pay for a wedding do, Hobson. What's the price of an outfit, Tudsbury?" Tudsbury became the shop-man for the moment. "A lady's trousseau for a daughter of any one like Mr Hobson with a shop in Chapel Street can be supplied for forty pounds," he said. "Special price, that it. It's sixty to a customer."

Hobson's mouth was open, but he did not speak. Apparently he did not intend to. So Jim resumed.

"Aye, that's about it."

"Cost me a hundred each for mine," said Minns.

"No wonder," said Tudsbury tartly. "You let them shop in Manchester,

""And then, there's settlements," said Jim.

"Settlements!" roared Mr Hobson.

"Of course," said Him. "You have to bait your hook to catch a fish, Henry."

"Then I'll none go fishing at all," said Mr Hobson.

""Hang it, Henry, is it likely a man will drop from the skies and take a daughter off your hands, scot-free? There's nothing for nothing in this world, my lad, and very little for sixpence. You've got to pay for peace and quiet like other things."

""Aye. Well, I've changed my mind. They can stay single and chance it."

"Fact, is Henry, I have a likely man in mind."

"Oh, aye," said Mr Hobson. "And what's your commission on the settlement?"

"Come, come," said Sam. "That's not quite worthy of you Hobson. Jim's doing his best, and a man who wants a

THE OLD BULL'S HEAD, GREENGATE, SALFORD.

temperance son-in-law is hard enough to please without you making bad to worse."

"I take it back," said Hobson. "I'm sorry, Jim, but none of your settlements for me."

"You save their keep, you know," said Tudsbury.

"They work for that. Not hard, I'll grant you, but they're none of them big eaters."

"And their wages," said Sam Minns. The other three looked pityingly at Minns.

"Wages?" said Mr Hobson. "Do you think I pay wages to my own daughters? I'm not a fool." And feeling that he could at this point retire with credit, Mr Hobson rose and left abruptly.

"Hobson's upset to-day," said Mr Tudsbury.

"Upset?" said Minns, "And so he deserves to be. A man of his sense wanting a temperance son-in-law. The thing's unnatural."

""Well," said Mr Heeler, "he's a widow-man, and there's no denying it, a man does miss his wife. You can get used to anything. There's a man I know who lives at Widnes where the bone factories are - "

"And the smells," said Tudsbury.

""Aye; well, one day he thought he'd go to Blackpool because he'd never seen the sea. He gets out of train, and he goes along promenade and he sees the sea, and he gives a sniff at the Blackpool air. 'They call this the finest air in England, do they?' he says. 'Not for Tommy Blackstock. It's unhealthy. I'm off to Widnes.' And he was, and all. He took the next train home to the stink he knew. And I reckon it's the same with wives," said Mr Heeler.

Nothin' for Nothin, And Little for Sixpence.

Mr Hobson left the inn dissatisfied. To say that he was dissatisfied is, in fact, to give an inadequate impression of the turmoil of his mind. It had been borne in upon him that there was a subject on which he was palpably unable to lay down the law in the Moonraker's bar-parlour; one, on the contrary, as to which he could himself compelled to sit at others' feet. The attitude was unfamiliar, and Mr Hobson hated the unusual. He was an oracle, and oracles should be oracular.

On men, and on affairs, on life, and even women in a certain way, he was a first authority. Bid him discourse on these and he would pour out words, not honeyed, but (like cherries) brandied in a ceaseless stream of practised eloquence, and shrewd words too. But in the problem of his daughters, their hinted threat of domestic rebellion and his proposed cure by marriage, he had stooped to ask advice, and as deliberately now reject it. Walking down the street he faced his dilemma boldly.

Taking a Salford man's short cut to the heart of things, he pondered the demand for settlements and saw that it was just. True, the late Mrs Hobson brought him no wealth, but her father had none to give, while he was Hobson of Chapel Street. What was the lowest sum of money which Hobson of Chapel Street could creditably bestow upon a marriageable daughter? He decided on five hundred pounds. Two daughters at five hundred pounds apiece. Which was absurd. Therefore he had made a mistake, and marriage was not the way out.

After all, Alice and Vickey were of some little use. Alice was comely, and her white arms were undoubtedly attractive against the brown paint of the counter. Besides, she could cook. And Vickey, though a shockingly yielding saleswoman, had a pretty face which counteracted her incompetence when selling to young men. But if he kept them, it must be on his own terms, and his suspicions were alert. That morning's episode might mean nothing, or a great deal. Albert Prosser was unexplained and Hobson wanted him explained, but asking Alice would not do. That was the worst of women. You never knew where you were with them, and wherever you were, you were certain to be wrong.

What it all came to was that he must ask Maggie. In point of fact, Hobson had for years been "asking Maggie," but he didn't know it. This time he did it consciously. He proposed to enlist her aid, flatter her a little, tell her how old and sensible she was, and how a mature woman of her years should stand for a mother towards her younger sisters. He hoped diplomatically to divest himself of all responsibility. It was about time Maggie did something for her living, and he meant to put things on a new basis from that day. Maggie should be responsible to him for the good conduct of her younger sisters.

By the time he reached the shop, Mr Hobson was decidedly happier. It only remained to announce his decision to Maggie.

Maggie looked up at him embarrassed. Such a phenomenon could hardly pass un-noticed.

Hobson notice. "What on earth are you doing with the costs book Maggie?" he asked.

"I'm looking up the cost of things." she said. "What for?"

"Just curiosity. I reckon a little shop could be opened on a capital of a hundred pounds.

"I managed on less than that," he said. "But things were cheaper then."

"Aye," said Maggie, and she closed the book and looked at him. Hobson conceived it wise to change the subject.

"Dinner ready?" he asked.

"Not yet, You're early to-day."

"It's after one." "Dinner's for half-past."

"I said one."

"Yes, father. One for half-past. If you'll wash your hands it'll be ready as soon as you are."

"I won't wash my hands. I don't hold with such finicking ways, and well you know it."

"Then you've to waste ten minutes."

"My time's money," he said, "and I don't waste either." And Hobson meant it, too. A liar is a man who speaks what he knows to be untrue. He drew the chair to the counter and sat facing her. "Maggie," he said, "I'm getting an old man now. I'm bestowed with care, and the heavy burden of responsibility. I carry the whole weight of this business on my shoulders, and I have my office at the church" - Hobson was vicar's warden at St. Philips's, and found it good for trade - "and I've made a lot of sacrifices. I'd be in Town Council at this moment if I hadn't put my privet duties in front of the public need. I've been approached more than once, but I gave up the idea for you, and I know it disappointed Minns. But I'm a family man, and I saw family first. And if I stick to you, I look for some return. I've had the care and trouble of bringing up three daughters, and if they don't know all there is to know about boots and clogs, it's not my fault, but theirs. And I ask you, Maggie, if I don't deserve reward?"

"What's wrong?" she asked.

"Alice is wrong, and Vickey is wrong, and their clothes are wrong, and their minds are light, and they're lacking in respect to me. It's like this, Maggie. I'll run the shop, but I look to you to take their mother's place with them. They're uppish, and you've got to see it's stopped. I spoke of marriage, but I've made inquiries and I find it will not do."

"Why not?"

"Because it won't. That's why. I find that folks are greedy, and I'll none satisfy their greed. There's awkward things called settlements, and I'll none settle. I've got no brass to throw away, and so those girls 'ull bide; but they'll bide humble, and I look to you to see they do it. You're old enough to take a bit of worry off my shoulders now. You're a sensible woman, Maggie, and you've got to set about those girls and put 'em in their place. It's not a man's job, and they're motherless. It's yours."

"You told them to get married."

""Aren't I explaining that I've changed my mind?"

""That won't change theirs," she said, and paused; then added grimly, "or mine."

"Dinner", said Alice, opening the house door.

Hobson was looking into Maggie's eye, thinking doggedly. He had never thought so hard in all his life before.

"We don't waste time," said Maggie. "There's liver for dinner, and you're fond of it."

"Alice," said Hobson, with controlled savagery, "you take your head into kitchen and cook that liver hard. I've a fancy to chew leather today. "Aye," he turned on Maggie as the head of Alice disappeared obediently and gladly. "I like leather. And you're leather, my lass, tough, ancient leather. But I can chew thee, and I will chew thee."

Maggie laughed. She had been at the costs book and she knew she could start a shop on a hundred pounds, and though Hobson paid no wages to his daughters, she had a shrewd idea where she could raise the capital in case of need. It was a pleasant laugh, but Hobson recognised the ring of steel in it.

"So you'll none change your mind? "he sneered.

"I ask you, my lass, have you a mind - owt above the lumber-room most women have?"

"Most women have a matrimonial mind," she said, and went into the house.

Hobson sat down to gasp more easily, but gasping leads nowhere, and he was hungry. He decided to follow Maggie in.

No Matrimony Here

Maggie Hobson had been behind the counter for as many years as she could be seen above the counter, and a shop counter is one of the most wonderful inventions of man. Man made the counter, but the counter has also made man. It has made him a better-mannered creature, more tolerant of the ignorance of his own sex and the cunning of the other. It has fostered social reform, for nobody would have found his neighbour's grievances half so interesting if the shop counter had not been invented.

Maggie had tolerance enough, but a young lady who has handled and seen the weakness of mortal feet for more than six thousand days is naturally a trifle disillusioned and fully determined for her own part to wear the shoes of her own selection, and to stand up in them very confidently and charmingly. And if the shoes of her sisters pinch them, she is equally confidently and charmingly resolved, out of professional and family pride, to do her best to furnish the ease they desire. And Maggie did not share her father's deep-rooted objection to change.

Each of Mr Hobson's daughters was aware that change was coming to the Hobson household, and each had clear-cut views as to how the change would affect herself. But Hobson himself, lulled by security, was still quite unaware of change. There had been little upsets before; this was another, that was all - a storm in a tea-cup, a toy rebellion needing only the application of a strong man's thumb to kill it as dead as a squelched window-fly. And a man must have a sense of proportion. Daughters were details, and food was on the table. Mr Hobson was silent for seventeen and a half minutes by the parlour clock. He dried his plate with a thick piece of bread, marvelling how excellent God had made the gravy from pigs. Pig ran to beauty in its juice. He set down his knife and fork. He smiled. A little shuffling of plates, and Mr Hobson went on to apple dumpling. He smiled easily now: the more his middle tightened, the more his top-piece relaxed and smiled. He considered cheese. He accepted largely of cheese, on the real principle of eating to satisfy appetite, and on the abstract principle that the more cheese, ripe Cheshire cheese, one ate, the less the digestion suffered. And when Mr Hobson turned the quart ale-mug upside down on his plate, angels visited him the angels of paternity, of goodness and faith, of gentleness, kindliness and laughter. Further, Heaven's most blessed messenger came close, the Harbinger of Sleep.

"I don't know, my girls," said he a little drowsily from his arm-chair, "but I had something on my mind to say to you. I believe I had warnings to give. But I feel lenient mentally because I feel strict physically. Only I state in brief what I have stated to Maggie already. While I live, my daughters shall be spinsters. No matrimony here."

Mr Hobson nearly closed eyes beatifically, but they were open enough to observe the effect of his declaration.

Vickey gasped, shamelessly her father thought. Vickey,

too? Well, she was easy to deal with. Alice pursed up her mouth defiantly. This was slightly more serious, for Alice was strong-minded, and he had received ocular demonstration of Mr Prosser's intentions. Still, Alice could be managed, and Mr Hobson mentally took the gold ring off her hand for ever.

But he awoke very rapidly when Maggie spoke. Yet all that Maggie said was, on the surface, altogether unexceptionable.

"Just as you like, father."

Need any man's heart flutter and tremble at subservient words like these? Are they not messages of comfort and assurance to a much-tired, settlement-evading father? What need to sniff treason in a gentle affirmative of this kind?

But Hobson was the father of Maggie. Therefore he maltreated his dinner, disregarded his digestive necessities. He sat upright.

"When I hear you state in a cold, agreeable tone that the matter is 'just as you like, father,' I'm aware the matter is just as you like, Maggie, I distrust you, my lass. You are hatching devilment, my lass.

Maggie and Alice swung the tablecloth corner and corner. They did not look at each other. Fear was in the face of Alice, but the drollest shade of fun about the mouth of Maggie.

"I'm making plans," she said. "And a husband's included in them."

Mr Hobson put carefulness aside. Digestion could go hang for once. He rose to the perpendicular.

"When?" he demanded.

Alice hung on the reply as well, this was new to her.

Maggie put her fingers on the table and counted one, two, three. Four Sundays from this week-end. Any time after that when we get a fine day, I shall be wed."

"I'll tell you something, Maggie, as is maybe news to you. If you're counting on a settlement from me, you're on wrong horse, my lass!"

"I'm not," she said. "I want no settlement. You can add

amount of mine to Alice's and Vickey's father."

"I'll add nothing to nothing," he said, "and that makes nothing. So your lad wants no settlement? No, and I'd think not, neither. But he'll pay me one. I've taught you a trade, Maggie. You're a skilled apprentice, and he'll pay me for you."

"No," said Maggie, with lips firmly but daintily prim.

"He'll pay, I tell you, or he'll none get you away from me. What's his name?"

"His name?" she said. "I'll tell you when I've got him."

"What!" roared her father. "Art counting chickens before they're hatched?" He fell back in his chair the happiest man in Salford. "Eh, Maggie, but you nearly frightened me. Not got the lad yet, eh? No, lass, and never will. I called you a proper old maid, and I judged right, and all. I never knew an old maid yet as hadn't a husband coming on in a month. Aye, you can tell a horse by looking in its mouth, same as cab-drivers do, and a hardened old maid is known by her boasts of fascinated young men. Eh, but I'm glad to see you show the signs and symptoms of it, lass. I nearly broke my inside when you first broke the news. Aye, but I'd no call to fret myself." Mr Hobson grew genial, his breath came more easily, he rolled complacently. "The lad that tackles you is a bold lad, I'd admit; but I say he may be bold, but it's undeniable from the fact of his tackling you that he has a slate loose. And the lad that has a slate loose is none a match for me. I'd wager I'd persuade thy lad out of matrimony faster than you could persuade him into it. But I don't mind your having these fancies, lass. Fancies are valuable for keeping females quiet and content. So you go back to shop, Maggie, and tell Tubby he can go back to cellar again. I'm glad you've spoken your mind. It's a great relief to know your mind is taken up with ideas. I thought at first it was taken up with a real man. But it is not so. And again I say, go into the shop, Maggie, and prosper.

The orator took breath, very well pleased with his speech, and himself, and Maggie and Alice. For, of course, the whole includes the part, and when Maggie was crushed all the family was crushed.

The sisters exchanged looks. Not Vickey; she had vanished into the kitchen to enjoy the washing-up rather than suffer paternal examination. But Maggie and Alice looked at each other, and the dialogue of their looks was this -

"Father has spoken, but I have not replied." Both sisters said this.

"I shall reply when I have done what I am going to do," said Maggie's look.

"If you'll stop and prop me, I'll have it out with him now," said Alice's eye.

"It's best. I'm with you," Maggie said.

Alice began. "Father, she said nervously.

"I'm - I'm going to marry Albert Prosser," burst out Alice.

"Who allowed you to ask Albert Prosser?" asked Mr Hobson.

"Albert Prosser asked me, and I said 'Yes,'" retorted Alice.

"That was nice of Albert Prosser and very nice of you. I don't want to know Albert Prosser. He may be mayor of Salford or a dustman. Still I say, it's nice of both of you." Mr Hobson had found his genically satiric mood. It was a mood which worried Alice, and well Mr Hobson knew it.

"I'm glad you think so," Alice lied bravely.

"It's rum what some folks think I think," said Mr Hobson.

Maggie judged it time to shock her father out of this humorous mood. Confidentially she assured Mr Hobson that in her opinion he thought very little.

Mr Hobson saw red. If there is a maxim more devoutly believed in the County of Palatine than another, it is that "What Lancashire thinks to-day, England thinks tomorrow," and here was his own flesh and blood telling him his thoughts were of no account. Mr Hobson rose. This feminine alliance demanded extinction, and Mr Hobson was ready to supply demand.

"She's better off than you, choosehow, Maggie," he

said. "She's got a lad with a name, but" - the batteries were turned on Alice - "I saw him this morning, and if Albert Prosser is the name of that long-shanked, jumped-up, tuppenny-ha'penny clerk I watched making sheep's eyes at you in the shop - "

"You needn't be common about it," Alice defended her choice.

"Common! Me!" Hobson shouted. "That's your word, Alice, a word you've grown too fond of. What is 'common'? Is truth common? Then I am common, but if you think a refined fourpenny-bit like your Albert Prosser is in the same street with a common sovereign like me, you're making the mistake of your life. Good for church collection is fourpenny-bit Prosser, but good in market-place is common sovereign me. But I'm none repeating myself. Repetition is weakness, and I'm not weak. I have the measure of Mr Albert Prosser, and that's a pound a week as a copying clerk, with a shine on his breeches you could see your face in, and darned elbows. That's Albert Prosser as he is."

"He's the smartest man in Salford," said Alice.

"He'll need to be before he catches me asleep," said Hobson. "He'll be smart if he gets a settlement from me, and he'll none marry you without."

That was perfectly true. A solicitor, who has much to do with other people's settlements, naturally expects a settlement of his own, and Alice was aware of it.

"My lass," he went on, with great kindness, "I can see you grateful hereafter. I'm saving you affliction. But I'll none be kept longer from my natural repose. Get into shop."

Alice looked at Maggie, who was silently deciding that her own affair came first, Alice could wait. They went into the shop, and Mr Hobson composed himself for sleep, and slept as lightly and serenely as a cherub resting on a summer cloud. One passing thought he had, but put it from him - Vickey. Vickey had gasped curiously at dinner. But Vickey! Pooh! a child. He put suspicion from him, and he slept, carefree, at peace with all the world.

"I've made an end to that job," was his final thought as consciousness departed.

CHAPTER FOUR

Love and Indigestion

It is a strange thing, Love. They have made many beautiful songs about it, chiefly because they do not know what else to do with it. In the Latin primers, which are invented for use in schools where fees are paid, and paid quarterly, the streaky-haired young animal and the spindle-shanked young puss can conjugate you at the top of their voices, "*amo, amas, amat*"; but to say "I love " at the top of the voice does not imply that the streaky-haired young animal and the spindle-shanked young puss actually know the meaning of what they say. And when they conjugate the verb together in later years as the sleek-haired young fellow and the elegant-figured young lady, the ignorance persists. No sensible person can set forth the laws of love. But every sensible person can set forth the laws of the conduct of love. Mr. Hobson was a sensible person, nobody ever lived who was more sensible than Mr. Hobson. He did not say anything about love; he did not know what it was; he had never seen it; he disbelieved in the theory of love; he heard people talk about love, but for his own part he ranked it as an affliction, a transitory but re-current pain similar to indigestion. It was not so bad as indigestion. Indigestion, despite the advertisements in the newspapers, was incurable. It might be curable if one ate within reason. But to eat within reason was to rob eating of its joy, and thus to eat reasonably was to eat unreasonably. Mr. Hobson could do without love, but he could not do without eating. He adjudicated the love affairs of his daughters on the same basis. His final and irrevocable verdict had been, as we know, neither love nor matrimony. If love existed it had to be cured, as indigestion could be cured, by doing without the food of love.

It was not likely that this arbitrary and unjust decision would have stood without appeal had not the circumstances of love been yet more prejudicial to the hopes of love. Vickey hedged with her father when her father was curious. Mr. Hobson would have cut her off from grace for ever had she confessed that she "walked out" with Frederick Beenstock. Vickey was truly a Church of England maiden, but she had very little religious fanaticism. It did not matter much to her that her Freddie was "Chapel," it mattered immensely to her that he was nice when he kissed her. She was that sort of young lady who was made for nice kisses. But her beloved was, from Mr. Hobson's point of view, the most obnoxious choice she could have made. His father, Nathaniel Beenstock, was more than a Nonconformist - he was a pillar of Nonconformity. He carried that large and influential centre of Congregationalism, Hope Chapel, Salford on his shoulders, so to speak. He wore piety and a frock-coat in the mornings along the aisles of the chapel; he only obscured his piety and his frock-coat at the entry of the minister, when he graciously allowed the minister to shine for a brief hour. He wore childish piety and a manufactured paternal smile in the afternoons at Sunday School. But his wearing apparel was allowed for by his purse. He opened his purse for the chapel more often than any other member. The chapel was his idol. And to further the ideals proclaimed in the rostrum of his idol Mr. Beenstock secured a seat on the Town Council. Mr. Hobson, as a staunch and worthy representative of the Conservative and Church party, had been invited to fight Mr. Beenstock. But Mr. Hobson refused, owing to family reasons. He was grateful he had a family. His family saved his face, his purse, and his reputation. Nonconformity was strong in Salford, Mr. Beenstock was the strongest figure in the strongest sect, and his defeat unpurchasable by beer. Mr. Hobson privately and wisely decided it was better far to be the autocrat of the Moonraker's Inn than Junior Councillor in Bexley Square. Of course he did not privately admit he would be beaten by Mr. Beenstock; he knew it privately all the same, and loved Mr. Beenstock very, very little. And if he loved the father very, very little, naturally he detested the son very, very heartily.

Whilst Alice could avow herself to Maggie and Vickey, and steal brief interviews with Albert Prosser in the shop, or even, when worked up, declare her intention to her father, and be squashed on general principles only, poor Vickey had to hide her affair even from her sisters. Her sisters might sympathise, but they might also sympathise in an unguarded moment. One suspicious word let fall in Mr. Hobson's presence, and never again would Vickey know nice kisses and dream nice parlours with Frederick Beenstock on Sunday afternoon.

Sunday afternoon was Vickey's invariable opportunity. She cut her Sunday School, Freddie cut his, and while Hobson slept and Maggie taught, they took their hour. How good it was, and how it lasted through the week! It was a concealed love, but concealment concentrated the love, repression fed it, threats inflamed it, paternal vetoes made it unbearably sweet. It is an excellent thing to have a cantankerous parent. But there was considerable embarrassment in three out of four people who met at Peel Park gates this particular Sunday afternoon. Maggie and Will were going in and Freddie Beenstock and Vickey were coming out. Freddy raised his hat nervously; mentally he was picturing his father. Freddie ought to have been at Sunday School, and his father was not a pleasant picture when he was agitated over Sunday School attendance. Will Mossop dropped Maggie's Bible. he was carrying it with a high sense of formality. He experienced immediate relief when he dropped it, not because he disliked serving Maggie, but because ladies' property always worried him. He felt too conspicuous carrying that book. Vickey Hobson's secret was out, but she kept her head enough to get her blow in first.

"Hello, our Maggie," she cried. "Are you going with Willie Mossop?"

That, of course, was Vickey's jest, one of those pleasant quips that do much to level the superiority shown in the senior offshoots of a family. She really wondered why Maggie was walking with Will, and expected some light joke by way of explanation. But Maggie's face was firm.

"I am." Vickey knew the tone. Maggie spoke in that tone when she decided question in the shop. "Mr. Beenstock, I believe?" Maggie was smiling indulgently at Freddie.

"Yes, Miss Hobson," said that blushing youth.

Maggie nodded pleasantly, the kind of nod with which a matron welcomes an eligible. "Ill be seeing you at tea, Vickey," she added, and passed on. Will Mossop did not speak. He was beyond words. Not only had Maggie abducted him under the collective eye of the disgorging Sunday School, but she had announced in so many words to Vickey that she "went with" him. His pulses leapt, but mighty fear was on Will Mossop. He walked with Maggie Hobson, but Ada Figgins sat unseen upon his back.

Vickey turned round and watched them go through the high gateway which was erected to commemorate the day when Queen Victoria came to Salford. (It was also the day of Vickey's birth, and the Constitutionalist had called his daughter after his queen.)

"Well!" said Vickey Hobson.

"What's the matter?" asked her swain.

"If you need telling that, you're slow at thinking," she replied. "Haven't you and I got enough difficulty in front of us without Maggie's putting more? Do you see yourself calling *that* your brother-in-law, because I don't. Maggie can just think shame to herself to be seen on a Sunday afternoon with a boot-hand in Peel Park."

"She saw us, though," said Freddie.

"There's that about it, certainly, but she'll not boast about it, neither, seeing the company we found her in. If our fat's in the fire, her fat is there, and all, and we'll frizzle together."

"I was thinking of owning up to my father about us, Vickey, anyhow."

"Well, don't. Not yet, until I've heard what Maggie's got to say."

"All right," said Freddie; "only she'll not rule me."

"Nor me," said Vickey. Mr. Beenstock held his peace. He knew who ruled the roost at Hobson's. He was an outsider, and outsiders see most of the game. Then Cupid reasserted sway and took their talk in charge.

Peel Park

Hobson was perfectly right. At thirty, in the year 1879, a woman was "on the shelf." She had failed to take her chance, and it was only left to her to stand aside and let the youngsters win. Maggie had other views. If circumstances arose to make a change desirable at thirty, or at forty either, Maggie was quite prepared to make that change. Celibacy for its own sake did not appeal to her, Will Mossop did. At first, she only saw his hands. In her neat tabulating mind, Will Mossop's hands had long been indexed in a special way. The man behind the hands was raw, so raw that Maggie felt him safe from any rival onslaughts of her sex. She left out Ada Figgins, for she did not know of her. She felt that she could bide her time.

Hobson's homily brought matters to a head. His cool assumption, that she, Maggie Hobson, was as other women were, content, because she was thirty, to dedicate her life to him, a vestal virgin worshipping before the altar of filial piety, made Maggie clench her teeth. If husbands were to be dealt round she meant to have her share, the first and biggest share. She had the remarkable vision of Will Mossop as the biggest share. Hobson could change his mind, but Maggie knew hers! She wasn't the changing sort.

And so, dismissing Vickey from her mind, Maggie walked with Will through the gateway of Peel Park, past the statues and the Museum, down the many steps to the Park below. She walked with pride, her little figure stiffly held, her back inflexible, a buxom, black-haired little person with the largest will in Lancashire. Maggie was made for wear. Young men looked round when Vickey passed, they rarely turned to take a second glance at Maggie. Young men lack sense.

Today a few turned round, not to look at Maggie but at Will with Maggie. He shambled by her side. If comparisons

62 *Hobson's Choice*

VICTORIA GATES, PEEL PARK.

occurred to them, they thought, perhaps, of that then familiar spectacle in the streets, a small foreigner with a dancing bear. Will's clumsiness was ursine, but if it be true that the first essentials of good dressing are a man's boots and hat, he had redeeming points. He wore the hat which Tubby Wadlow made him buy, and, of course, his boots were very good indeed, because he made them. Each workman at Hobson's was allowed to make himself two pairs a year in his own time but with Hobson's materials. One need not blame Hobson for that. It was merely one of those small sentimental concessions by which astute employers the world over reconcile workmen to inadequate wages by throwing in a perquisite which costs them very little. And Hobson did not believe in letting the cobbler go ill-shod.

If you go through Peel Park and take the path along the Irwell, you arrive at something which resembles country. There struggling farmers strive against the smoke and make a milk-round pay. There, too, the Salford lovers come. Along the road from Agecroft Bridge you may observe, at short intervals, against the fence, patches where all the grass is worn away by men's and maiden's feet. The benches in the Park are left for age to rest its weary bones upon. Young love must have the fields at hand, and as there are no benches, and the walk is long enough, must take its stand and lean against the fence. In each worn patch, a pair of lover stood. They rarely spoke. Proximity was Paradise enough.

Maggie found a patch unpeopled and shepherded Will into it.

"Show me your hands," she said. Will Mossop fumbled with her Bible. She took it from him and tucked it underneath her arm. He held out his hands.

"They're a bit rough," he said.

"Yes, they're rough, but they're clever, Will. They can shape the leather like no other man's that ever came into the shop. Who taught you, Will?"

"Aw, Miss Maggie, I learnt my trade at Hobson's."

"Hobson's never taught you to make boots the way you do." She held his hands and Willie's shuffling feet expressed his agony. He liked it, and Ada Figgins in the body was far away, but Willie had a conscience. "You're a natural born genius at making boots. It's a pity you're a natural fool at all else," she added, and dropped his hands.

"I'm not much good at owt but leather, and that's a fact. I feel at home with leather in my hands, and strange-like when I've nowt to occupy my mind."

"When are you going to leave Hobson's?" she asked.

Will had a shock, much the same sort of shock which a man might feel if asked suddenly, "When are you going to murder your mother?"

"Leave Hobson's?" he gasped. "I - I thought I gave satisfaction."

"Don't you want to get on?" she said. "You know what Mrs Hepworth said to you. You know the wage you get, and you know the wage a boot-maker like you could get in one of the big shops in Manchester."

"Nay, I'd be feared of my life to go into one of them fine places."

"What keeps you where you are? Is it the people?"

"I'm just used to being there," he said.

"I'll tell you something, Will. Maybe it's news to you. There's two things keeps that business on its legs. One's the good boots you make that sell themselves, the other's the bad boots other people make and I sell. We're a pair, Will Mossop."

"You're a wonder in the shop, Miss Maggie."

"And you're a marvel in the workshop, Will," said the other half of the Mutual Admiration Society.

"Well?"

"Well what?" said Will.

"It seems to me to point one way."

"What way is that?"

"You're leaving me to do the work, my lad," she said. Will shuffled uneasily.

"I'd like to go home," he said. "It's getting tea-time."

"You'll go when I've done with you," she said, a little grimly. "I've watched you for a long time now, and

everything I've seen, I've liked. I think you'll do for me."
"What way, Miss Maggie?"
"Will Mossop, you're my man. Six months I've counted on you, and it's got to come out some time."
"But I never - "
"I know you never," she said. "Or it 'ud not be left to me to do the job like this."
"I'm a bit 'mazed, Miss Maggie." Will mopped his brow. "What dost want me for?"
"To invest in. You're a business proposition in the shape of a man. My brain and your hand 'ull make a working partnership."
Will was relieved. So this was all it meant! Astonishing enough in all conscience, but at least this was not matrimony. "Partnership," he said. "Oh, that's a different thing. I'm - I'm not very quick at understanding, Miss Maggie, and I'll make a clean breast of it. I thought you were asking me to wed you."
"I am," said Maggie Hobson.
"Well, by gum!" said Willie Mossop. "And you the master's daughter!"
"Maybe that's why. Maybe I've had enough of him, and you're as different from him as any man I know. I know I've spoken boldly, Will, but it's the only way with you; and I tell you this, my lad, it's a poor sort of woman who'll stay lazy when she sees her best chance slipping from her. A Salford life's too near the bone to lose things through the fear of speaking out."
"I'm your best chance," Will echoed.
"You're that," she said.
"Well, by gum! I never thought of this."
That wasn't strictly true, as his new hat proved. But Will was playing for time. There was Ada.
"Think of it, now," said Maggie.
"I am doing, only it's job I'm slow at, and the blow's a bit too sudden yet. You know, I've a great respect for you, Miss Maggie. You're a shapely body, and you're a masterpiece at selling in the shop, but sithee, lass, I'm bound to tell the

truth, now, aren't I? And I can't honestly say that I'm in love with you at all."

Maggie faced it. "Wait till you're asked," she said. "Just now, I want you hand in mine and your word for it that you'll go through life with me for the best we can get out of it."

Will overlooked her hand. "We'll not get much without there's love between us, lass," he said.

"I've got the love all right," said she.

"You're desperate set on this," he said. "It's a puzzle to me all ways there are. "What 'ud your father say?"

"He'll have a lot to say and he can say it. It'll make no difference to me."

"We're bound to think of the master. Much better not upset him. It's not worth while."

"I'm judge of that," she said. "You're going to wed me, Will."

He shook his head. "Oh, nay, I'm not. Really and truly I can't do that, Miss Maggie. I can see you're going to be upset, and I don't like disturbing your arrangements, but I'll take it kindly if you'll put this notion from you: I'd be obliged, Miss Maggie, and - "

"When I make arrangements, my lad, they're not made for upsetting. The only thing that troubles me is why I didn't tell you yesterday. Then we could have been called in church today. It wastes a week my leaving it till Sunday."

"Oh, well, its got to come out sooner or later," said Will. "I might consider it, Miss Maggie, only what makes this so desperate awkward is that I'm tokened.

"You're what?" she said.

"I'm tokened to Ada Figgins, Maggie. I'm tied up."

"Then you'll get loose and quick. Who's Ada Figgins? Old Mrs Figgins's daughter?"

"Maggie, you'll not go there!"

"Won't I?" said Maggie Hobson. "Where is it?"

"It's where I lodge," he said, "in Ordsall Lane."

"Come on," said Maggie. Willie came. But his dull obedience was a milk-and-water virtue contrasted with the swift energy of his commander.

Christian All Day Sunday

The daughters of Mr. Hobson walked out with their ineligibles on Sunday afternoon with a sense of perfect freedom and absolute security from the menacing eye of their parent. The reason was a commonplace one, but, like all commonplace reasons, founded on a rock - the one invariable event of their Sabbath life. Mr. Hobson slept.

The sleep of Mr. Hobson was not an ordinary sleep. Sunday afternoon slumber is a British institution, but Hobson's sleep was also individual. The whole of the previous week, its satisfactions and dissatisfactions, contributed to the Sabbath slumber, but the experiences of the Sabbath morning contributed more. Mr. Hobson, after Saturday night's exertions in the shop, awoke late and rose heavy-headed on Sunday. He breakfasted dully, and only the prospect of exhibiting Hobson as Hobson in St. Philip's prodded him out of dullness. He neither winked nor blinked during the sermon although he might at times lose the thread of the discourse. But that was because he was thinking hard in his own mind. He admitted that the recital of the Litany was his vulnerable hour - and that temptation may be forgiven him.

On the return journey, Hobson was alacrity itself. His conscience was clear and proud, as a churchwarden's ought to be, his stomach was clamorous and his appetising dinner as commanding as a bugle call. Everybody sat down to Sunday's dinner with great content, the girls because it was the only dinner they could eat with security from shop calls, and Mr. Hobson because virtue was added to appetite. None can feed in beauty unless the soul is consciously clean. The perfect feeder is the virtuous feeder.

Mr. Hobson has been sketched at dinner time before. It is not necessary to enlarge again on his physical enlargement. Only his spiritual enlargement, his mental content and his radiating smile must be recalled. He dismissed his daughters to their washing-up and dressing-up with benign generosity; he watched them indulgently as the trio issued forth to

Sunday School. The unwritten law concerning tea was too securely a fundamental conception of his daughters to require reiteration. They undertook Sunday tea by turns, one of them forsaking religion and other pleasures early to return to get tea ready.

"Eh!" said Mr. Hobson, in his majestic solitude. "This is better than yapping at females on matrimony."

He snuggled his shoulders more effectively into the back of the arm-chair, and shifted his seat into that slanting position which requires no effort for the body to hold itself up, and no effort to save itself from slipping off.

"Ease," quoth Mr. Hobson a little later on and a little more somnolently. "Ease, I like it. It is good for me. I am a Christian in my body on Sunday afternoons."

He folded his hands on his stomach. He gazed at his hands, but without interest. Mr. Hobson's mind was vacant for twelve minutes. He did not sleep, he created a vacuum within himself. he did not want to sleep. Foolish as it may sound, one misses the beauty of it if one sleeps. Hobson was half submerged; a spark of reflective intelligence struck up above his slumberous whole like the mast of a sunken ship. He seemed to himself to be talking through his eyes. Therefore he made no audible sounds, but carried on a tremendous conversation with himself in a conspiracy of silence.

"Eh, but in the mood of tranquil understanding, I grow a wonder to myself, an indisputable marvel. I have realised myself. I have reached my harbours in sound condition, and the three harbours are firstly Heaven, which I have attained inasmuch as the churchwarden's office I hold is like the conductor's office on a tramcar. I'll get as far as any passenger in the holy conveyance. Heaven is the first harbour, home is the second, and hotels are the third. Heaven, home, hotels, Henry Horatio Hobson, a gratifying combination. In my youth I dreamed I had to choose between the Prime Minister's job, owing to my natural gift of oratory, and the mayorality of Salford, owing to geography and my business faculties. But I say heights are none worth the climbing. I fill a unique hole instead.

He slept profoundly, fully submerged at last, but horrid dreams assaulted him. He awoke nervously, in terrible fear, with a cold sweat on his body. The parlour was empty, not even a tortoise-shell cat washed its face on the hearth, but, for the moment, Mr. Hobson was convinced that his wife was sitting opposite on the other side of the fireplace, addressing him with all her old perversity. It was dream

CHORLTON ROAD CONGREGATIONAL CHAPEL.

carried into consciousness. The lady had been dead many years - safely dead, to Mr. Hobson's mind. He had loved his Mary dutifully, but she had never rightly understood the perversity of her own opinions and the faultless rectitude of his opinions. She was in Weaste Cemetery, and, so long as her daughters were not troublous, he did not greatly wish her back.

"I don't like nightmares," he said fretfully.

"Mary had remarkable qualities, or I'd never have married her. But they were the remarkable qualities that make the Empire what it is and the home what it ought not to be. Home is a Paradise, but only when wives and daughters have been properly subordinated to their useful but inferior positions. That is the paternal and masculine ideal, but disappointment is the fate of man. I never heard yet of a properly subordinated female, and the lad that boasts of a subordinated family is the same lad that would sit down on a hedgehog and say he liked the prickles. Aye, women have an ungodly capacity for frustrating the ideals of men. And sometimes I nearly fear my daughters may yet frustrate my ideal; my ideal of economy, of peaceful daughterly service. It is a handsome ideal, and I may be allowed to fear their contrary designs. But they cannot frustrate me. I have that quality of wisdom that sits on females. I am Hobson, I have measures for all sizes and fits. I take my Sabbath sleep in security.

Having turned the conversation from the disagreeable subject of his wife to the agreeable and flattering subject of mastering his daughters, Mr. Hobson settled anew. Again lethargy, warm and kind, holy delicious, settled upon him.

"Eh," he murmured. "It's worth while to come awake to realise the nature of sleep. I don't envy emperors or cotton kings. My mother wasn't envious either. I get it from her, my generous disposition. Eh, she was pious, too, but she had a command of plain language. I have heard her round up a coalman in plain words that made coloured or bad language tedious and insignificant. We're a notable family, we Hobsons. I'm all for the middle class myself.

It occurred to Mr. Hobson that the appreciation of his own class was too secular for Sunday. For, whatever one may think of his discourse, it was Mr. Hobson's idea of a holy overhauling, a pious and penitential self-examination. The arm-chair was the seat of his humility in which the churchwarden rightly attempted to purify his life of fault and failure. Sunday was holy, afternoons and morning, and if Mr. Hobson seems to have avoided abject self-confession and the hard stool of the penitent it is solely due to the fact that he was sternly anti-Roman. He frowned on self-flagellation. But his thoughts took higher aim: he discovered devoutness and purity of religion in himself.

"I am fat," he allowed, "but fat is accounted to me for righteousness. Religion goes with width. Lean people are often religious humbugs, and chapel humbugs into the bargain. There are fat chapel folk, a very few. But my argument is not defeated. No argument on reasonable topics can be based on Nonconformists. A man like Beenstock makes my inside ill. Beenstock has weight about him, but I'd as soon meet a mountain of rotten beefsteak as Beenstock. And a mountain of puffy, stinking, deteriorated green-juiced beefsteak is the exact similitude of Beenstock. And," decided Mr. Hobson judicially "if I can honestly and religiously so describe Beenstock on the Sabbath, I cannot very easily imagine my description of Beenstock on a weekday. I have heard that Beenstock exhausts the adjectives of his fellow-councillors, and if Salford language is exhausted over Beenstock, the language of the universe is deficient to supply owt that says more, and in that case Beenstock is inexpressible."

It is right that pious exercises should finish with a restoration of confidence in the devotee. Mr. Hobson felt amazingly better at the conclusion of his soliloquy, and was only mildly irritable when the clink of tea-spoons on tea-saucers roused him into full wakefulness.

"Where's family?" he demanded of Alice, suspiciously but not rudely.

"Outside," said Alice, very patiently. She had returned

from a devastating experience with Albert Prosser. Albert, in fact, had avoided her. The Sunday School that afternoon had been treated not only to the spectacle of Maggie's capture of Will, but of Albert's sullen evasion of Alice.

"School is going on for a long time today," said Mr. Hobson, more to pass the time than with any detective intent.

"School was over at half-past three." Alice mentioned the fact for Mr. Hobson to make what he liked of it.

"It's four minutes to five now, my lass."

"They don't feel like coming in before five on Sunday."

"Why not? Home's home, I hope."

"After the heavy dinner they must walk it off." Alice was more patient than ever.

"Oh," grunted Mr. Hobson. A father gets very unsatisfactory answers to his questions. And Alice reflected that very unnecessary questions were asked in families, and if the questions are awkward ones, so much the worse for the inquisitor. With the conduct of Albert Prosser to worry about, Alice meant to evade her father till his mind grew tired of ferreting out rats that would not bolt.

Chapter Five

Your Will, or Mine!

Mrs. Figgins belonged to the gin-worshipping tribe of tartars. She rented two and a half rooms in a dingy house in Ordsall Lane, Salford; but her address is no true or complete indication of her nationality. Englishmen ought all to be like Mr. Hobson, and all true Englishwomen like his mother of pious and respected memory. Mrs. Figgins had the instincts of the hungry animal; and lived mainly by instinct. She scrubbed floors under the compulsion of primitive necessity; saw no necessity of any kind to wash her own floors; robbed Will Mossop systematically of most of his savings as a strong-minded landlady should; stole such articles belonging to her employers as could be stolen by any intelligent thief; and betwixt the successful application of gin and instinct managed to live very happily, according to her own ideas of happiness. It was a pity her own ideas of happiness did not correspond with her daughter's or Will Mossop's. She pushed Ada out to work in the weaving-sheds when Ada would have greatly preferred to get through life on the minimum of exertion. Ada had a fundamental fancy for her own bed. And Mrs. Figgins had also successfully pushed Ada on to Will Mossop, who, whilst meekly accepting the gift, would much rather have done without any matrimonial beds whatever. But Mrs. Figgins was the sort of lady who is neither convinced by argument nor open to argument. She knew what she wanted and took it.

And Maggie Hobson, who also happened to be a lady who knew what she wanted and took it, knew some of the characteristics, redeeming and otherwise, of Mrs. Figgins.

Will Mossop had once bashfully entreated Maggie to employ his landlady for the spring cleaning. And partly to recompense the painful boldness of Will, Mrs. Figgins had been employed. The whole business had been schemed by Mrs. Figgins, and she had spent some familiar language upon her lodger before she got him up to the asking point. Mrs. Figgins went nowhere without a previous introduction; it added honesty, morality, cleanliness and wholesome respectability if one secured an introduction. Mrs. Figgins felt no real need of these qualities, but strange as it may appear, she had hopes of pickings, insignificant acquisitions, at Hobson's and she needed the time granted to the trustworthy, in which to make a discriminating selection. It says much for the genius of Mrs. Figgins that she finished the spring cleaning at Hobson's considerably richer in unlawful than lawful rewards, and without a breath of suspicion upon her clearly mirrored character. Mr. Hobson himself allowed she was a decent woman (the decent woman had considerable talent for faithful flattery), and Maggie had been well enough satisfied with her work to help her connection by a friendly word to cleanly purchasers in the shop. In short, the jobs that Mrs. Figgins thought worth while, were mainly due to the Hobson introductions.

The influence of a landlady on young men is only comparable to the influence of a wife on her husband. A great many young men fly into the arms of matrimony to escape the dominion of their landlady. And we honestly believe they do escape many evils. A young man has no longer any need to perish of cold rather than die under the contempt and callous temper exhibited by his landlady when he suggests the fire might be a little more heat and a little less heating bricks. In the freer state of marriage he can growl at his wife; and examine the coal merchant's bill for himself. Further, he has liberty to growl at his coal merchant if the bill be exorbitant. And many other such liberties there be for married men.

Will Mossop was a more wretched figure than ever as he followed his lady-love intent upon raising trouble with

Your Will, Or Mine! 75

Mrs. Figgins. He knew exactly how relieved Mrs. Figgins had been when she had got him tokened to Ada, and he could therefore estimate exactly how displeased Mrs. Figgins would be when she heard he was also tokened to Maggie. He pleaded with Maggie as they went along. Maggie was not at all sympathetic; she did not seem to appreciate the fact that he had to go on living with Mrs. Figgins after Mrs. Figgins had been annoyed. Maggie's lips grew more tightly closed than ever as he pleaded, until at last Will, fearing the outbreak of Maggie might well be worse than the outbreak of Mrs. Figgins, pleaded no longer, and slunk along by her side in the humility of a broken dog.

They turned the last corner, and Will began to run. He meant to get there first. Mrs. Figgins was brewing tea when Will burst in.

"Miss Hobson's coming," he gasped.

"She'll be wanting some cleaning done, I reckon," said Mrs. Figgins, hastily unfastening her apron and jerking it into the oven, which happened to be the handiest hiding-place. And "cleaning" was, perhaps, exactly what Maggie did want done.

Ada was lounging slackly in the rocking-chair. She had the lounging temperament, but her hand went briskly up to fumble with her hair. She still wore curling-papers at tea-time on Sunday afternoon!

Curling-papers were permissible in the morning, and might of course be worn all day during the week in the weaving-shed. But a Salford girl who wore them after one o'clock on Saturday or after breakfast-time on Sunday was a self-confessed drab. It wasn't done.

Anaemic Ada did it, though. She had this much excuse, that she was not going out with Will till night and wished her hair to look its frizzled best. She as ashamed of her hair's colour, but, at least, she could distort it with the best.

Maggie gave her no chance. Maggie could run as well as Will, and she came in as Ada made a frenzied onslaught on the papers in her hair. Ada stood up, revealed to Maggie for the torpid slut she was.

"Why, Miss Hobson, this is a surprise," said Mrs. Figgins. "Will you 'ave a cup of tea? I were just brewing it."

Maggie ignored Mrs. Figgins. She was watching Ada. "So this is her," she said, and looked at Will.

"Aye, that's Ada," he said.

"I thought as much," said Maggie Hobson, speaking volumes.

"They're tokened, 'im and 'er," said Mrs. Figgins, maternally. "We're all very 'appy about it."

"Will's got a happy look," said Maggie. "Young woman, do you know you're treading on my foot?"

Ada was vaguely looking to see how far Maggie's boot extended. She stepped back to be sure.

"Me, Miss 'Obson?" she said.

"What's this with you and him?"

"Oh, Miss 'Obson, it is good of you to take notice like that."

"I'm noticing a lot," said Magggie. "I'm noticing this room has not seen soap-and-water for many a day, and the curtain's black with dirt. There isn't a plate on the table that's not cracked, and you haven't washed your face today, nor your neck for a week."

"Ada's not strong and I've been busy cleaning other folks' houses," said Mrs. Figgins in defence. In spite of Maggie's frank criticism, she was not to be regarded as a woman, but as an influential employer.

"Oh? Do you get a lot of cleaning to do at this time of year?" asked Maggie.

"No, but - "

"No, It's a pig-sty, Will, and time you said 'good-bye' to it."

"You leave my Will alone," said Ada, warming to a fight.

"He may be yours and he may be mine. That's why I'm here. We've got to see."

"There's no seeing about it," said Mrs. Figgins.

"They're tokened ."

"We'll come to that," said Maggie. "Look at him, Ada.

Take a fair look, lass. There's not much there for two women to fall out over, is there?"

Will's best was pretty bad. Just now, he hardly looked his best.

"Maybe he isn't much to look at," Ada said.

"But you should hear him play."

"Play?" said Maggie. This was news. "Are you a musician, Will?"

"He plays the jews' harp beautiful," said Ada.

"Well," said Maggie with whimsical joy, "Will has now come to the waters of Babylon. He is hanging up the harp and weeping, if he likes to weep for you."

"I don't see you have any call to interfere with our pleasures. Me and Will can love one another without your help." Ada made the declaration very proudly.

"Can Will make love, Ada? I'd call it a pretty poor performance if the experience I have had with him is anything to go by."

Ada opened her mouth. "You? You've been going with him this afternoon," she said jealously.

"Will belong to me, and you have made him come out with you, as if he'd given me the go-by. I call it a shame. I do; and - and presumshalls." Ada felt an extraordinary word would state her grievance very much better than a common one.

"I hasn't given you the go-by," cried Will, eager to justify himself in the eye of Mrs. Figgins. For those eyes were beginning to light up with the wicked light that generally preceded the exhibition of Mrs. Figgins, her primitive self. "But she'll have me, Ada, if you don't be careful."

"She'll not." Mrs. Figgins was very decided about it. Maggie was growing less of an employer, much more of a fellow-woman. And Mrs. Figgins had a very short way with fellow-women who disagreed with her. "They're tokened," she declared, inviting contradiction of the statement. It is the gage of battle amongst the gin-worshing tartars; the statement throws down the glove, the contradiction picks it up; the encounter follows rapidly, very rapidly in most cases. The female tartar knows the value of the first hair-clutch.

"They're tokened?" Maggie made no direct contradiction. "They're handcuffed."

The illuminative comparison did not disturb Mrs. Figgins. She invited contradiction again, this time on a generality.

"Right is right," she said, "all the world over, and what's ours isn't yours."

"No! That it isn't," cried Ada offensively.

She got a glare from her mother. Mrs. Figgins could conduct her duels without assistance; she was a veteran duellist of considerable reputation.

"What's truth of all the world over isn't true of you. Might is right in your case, and decent thought for Will Mossop doesn't come into your plans."

"I am marrying him to my daughter." Mrs. Figgins was enjoying self-restraint before self-indulgence.

"That's why I said it." Maggie took Ada into her glance.

"Insulting my daughter; insulting me." Mrs. Figgins started to work up her temper. It did not require a lot of working.

"I don't wrap up the truth any more than Ada hides her curl-papers at four o'clock on Sunday."

"I am a woman of the people," said Mrs. Figgins, and grasped the broom-handle. She advanced on Maggie; a terrifying apparition, prophetic of black eyes, broken noses, scratched faces and disordered and well-mauled hair. But Maggie stood her ground. She laid hold of the long black poker in a business-like manner. Mrs. Figgins came on like a company of Scots Greys in a bayonet charge; she drove at Maggie with pulverising intentions. Maggie stepped aside, grasped the broom as it stopped short against the wall, and rapped Mrs. Figgins's knuckles smartly with the poker. Mrs. Figgins expostulated and dropped the broom-handle, but before she could close with Maggie for her special cat-play the poker was threatening the remnants of her facial beauty in a very importunate manner. Mrs. Figgins stood still and gazed at the silent fire-iron. She realised she was up against an expert in the theory of self-defence, one who recognised that female combats were to be conducted on ruthless principles if victory was to be secured. She had relied upon the legendary fastidiousness of the middle classes and relied in vain. Maggie happened to want Will, and if Mrs. Figgins stood in her way, so much the worse for Mrs. Figgins. Maggie could cope with her.

"Lumme," gasped Mrs. Figgins, aggrieved as well as surprised.

"You have got three texts on your walls," said Maggie, with great self-possession.

"And the peace of God in my heart," lamented Mrs. Figgins; defeat made her extremely pious. She had not suffered physical defeat as yet, but she had been humbled by the ready tactics of her opponent. She had lost confidence and therefore talked earnestly and plaintively of Providence.

"I know," said Maggie, while still the poker menaced. "And you have also got your cupboard open. And the gin-bottle, I can see may have vinegar in it, but the clock on the mantelpiece behind me is the one we missed from our kitchen three years ago. We had the whitewashing people in when you were there that time, so we laid the theft to one of them. But you have whitewashed the whitewashers, Mrs. Figgins. And if you'd like to go to your bedroom you may go."

Mrs. Figgins had no objections to the police court as a police court, or to prison as a prison. But unfortunately a police court soiled one's respectability, and a prison blackened one's character. It was unjust, but a charwoman was not allowed to go to prison if she liked. So Mrs. Figgins decided that her bedroom was preferable to prison.

Maggie felt decidedly easier. She had vanquished the tartar without losing hair, teeth, or eyes, without a scratch on her face and without a rent in her garments.

"Now, Ada Figgins."

"Yes, Miss 'Obson." Ada exhibited respect for the victor, but it was sullen respect.

"I can tuck Will Mossop under my arm. He won't object to wedding me, and you haven't any objections that count for much."

"Oh, yes, I've! I call it a shame, a dreadful shame of yer to come pinching 'im when he were tokened, you hussy!" hissed Ada recklessly.

"Don't lose your temper, Ada, when you hair is in curl-papers," advised Maggie.

"I shall, I shall, then!" shrieked Ada.

"Listen to me, my lass." Ada subsided in spite of herself; she recognised that the thief of love was greater than the inspirer of love. "I said neither you nor Will had objections that counted for much. That's true, and you needn't look as though you were going to lose your head over it. It won't pay. But I have got objections, Ada Figgins. I don't want Will Mossop against my conscience."

"Much conscience you got." Ada was rude.

"I have this much. I am playing fair; which is more than your mother has done with Will. Will!" - she turned on the gawky spectator - "how were you tokened to Ada?"

Will was scared. He mumbled. Ada was eyeing him also. The gaze of four female eyes was unendurable agony.

"Out with it, my lad." exhorted his lady.

"I was cornered," burst forth from his lips. He broke from the optical spell, rushed out of the room and downstairs into the street, praising Heaven he was not worse damaged. Maggie let him go.

"What is your idea of Will Mossop's life in the days to come?" she asked of Ada, very business-like indeed.

"Eh! He'll be married to me," said Ada complacently.

"That may suit you, but it'll none suit Will."

"Oo said it wouldn't?" demanded Ada fierily.

"I say it, my lass. The fact is, you're ready to be tied up to the lad and live on him, and do nothing for him that does nothing for yourself at the same time. Pah! You don't even keep your rooms clean now you're engaged. What'll they be like when you've had six months of married life? You have got no plans neither for yourself nor for Will."

"Folks like us doesn't have plans," retorted Ada.

"We draw our brass and spends it. That's all the plans we need; and if you have come up here to lecture like a

Church Visitor you can take yourself off home. I'm not afraid of you, even if my mother is. I haven't stolen your dirty clocks. I haven't washed in your house. I have got my man and I'm keeping him. If we live in a pig-sty it's nowt to you." Ada was very truculent; she had the high squeaky voice that often accompanies high-coloured hair; she imitated the maternal position of offence, arms akimbo.

But Maggie had no time for repetitions.

"It is nowt to me how you'll live. But you'll live as a spinster for all of Will Mossop you'll get. I didn't know how things stood till I came in here. You had got in first with Will, before me, who want him just as much as you. Why, I don't know, but I do. Listen, my lass; if you had shaped you'd have kept him. But you don't shape. You've got no ideas of his future, and the idea of your own future seems to be you'll lie on the bed you made last week. And I won't see Will Mossop tied up to anybody of that nature. The lad is a sight too fine beneath his clumsy awkward flesh for you to spoil."

"I'm glad I'm wedding one as has your good word."

"It's time you came to sense, Ada Figgins."

The childish obstinary of the slut annoyed Maggie; also it made Maggie look very young, almost enthusiastically and passionately a woman in love. Like solid parents, slatternly females have their uses, they heighten other people's enjoyment. Maggie had entered the appartments of the Figgins family with a purely business idea of Will Mossop. She had meant to secure his release by common sense consciousness, but the vehemence of Mrs. Figgins and the dull and ignorant hostility of Ada fanned common-sense into something more spiritual, fervid and real. Maggie laid bare her innermost faith.

"I haven't lived my life with my eyes shut. And what I have seen of men from behind a shop-counter has made me respect good men. They're rare, but God can turn out some surprising stuff, quality stuff, when He has a demand for it. And Will Mossop us a good man, as meek and sweet as I am strong and hard. And more than that, Ada Figgins; more than jews' harps - he can touch and fashion leather into beauty. When I see a man like that, that can make beautiful things, like God a-making of green things in the spring-time, I love that man. And when I am as near to him as I am to Will Mossop, and free, I marry that man. And what he hasn't got in sense, business brains, and knowledge of the world enough to keep his talent clean, I supply him with. You cannot, and you know it. And you'd let him be an eighteen-shilling shoe-hand, until your habits dragged him down to a ten shilling shoe-hand. I can see the tale of your years with Will before it's written. And it shall neither be written nor happen to be written. You have had your chance with him, you have given him nothing, neither a clean lass in yourself, nor a clean home for both of you, nor courage nor self-respect for himself.

"You're hard enough on me," protested Ada tearfully. She had not much stamina for a whirl-wind.

"I'm being kind to the man I love," answered Maggie passionately.

"Oh! You fancy yourself. Nobody is good enough for Will but yourself. And you're a sight too good for him if he only knew it." Ada was jealous still.

"I am good for him, my lass. He is good for me, too good for me; same as every babe that's born is too good for its mother. And what am I going to do or him, to make it right I should take him from you? You want to know that? Why, lass" - Maggie was tender-voiced at the thought of it, at the vision of her future - "why, I am going to work for him."

Ada stared. It was an astonishing declaration, but Maggie was also a little fascinating in moments like these, even to a rival.

"Work! It's the most beautiful thing in all the world, when God has set you in the right place. And Will and me are in the right place. I can run a boot shop. I have run Hobson's for fifteen years, Ada Figgins. And Will has worked in our cellar, where he must not work any longer. The lad is a great craftsman, and I want him to come out of our cellar to take his stand where he ought to be, amongst the men Salford is proud of. You know whether you can help him to that. You know whether I can help him to that. Will loves neither of us.

He doesn't know anything about love. He's affectionate, but he will only love the woman who nourishes him. And that means he has got to be taught - taught pride in his work, see fruits of his work, hear the words of men on the fruits of his work. You'll never get love out of a blighted life, Ada Figgins, nor anything but little love out of a little-natured man. I'm giving him his chance to come through and be something finer than the shambling figure he is now. But you have first claim upon him; you say you love him. And if you love him, you know, or ought to know, what is best for him. If you give him to me to make him, he shall never regret it," Maggie finished.

"Though I may," said Ada almost inaudibly.

"The price you pay for loving him; the price I pay is work, Ada, unending work."

But Ada knew, without any more words. Dimly, out of the murky haze of mind she had lived in until now, there rose the soul of Ada; such generosity and greatness, such light and purity, as come once in a lifetime when the small-souled people grow to great estate.

Ada renounced.

"Take 'im, Miss 'Obson." She fled to Mrs. Figgins in the bedroom.

But no one in Salford will ever drop their aitches more forgivably than Ada Figgins.

Get it over with, Lad.

It is the vocation of the great to discover the great. And Maggie Hobson had discovered something great, an action that moved her well-nigh to tears. However sordid the entanglement of Will Mossop might have been, the fact remained that Ada and Will had been tokened, the sense of possession had entered into Ada, the weakling spinster of the sheds had fed her vanity, she had been possessed by a male in the sight of the neighbours; and beneath her vanity, inch-thick complacency, her slovenly, lazy habit of mind, there had blossomed the flower of love; a small flower and insignificant, one that would have very soon wilted and withered away under the terrible blighting increase of self-satisfaction, selfishness, laziness and indulgence. Ada had given up possession, she had invited the rage of her mother, the tempest of maternal fury, and, worse still, the comic humour of her neighbours and fellow-weavers. Maggie knew the greatness of the sacrifice, and desired to give Ada her dues in silence, the thanks and the reverence her nobility merited.

As Maggie stood on the pavement communing with herself, Will Mossop reappeared, as a frightened rabbit returns to its burrow when the night closes and the sportsmen and their dogs have gone. Will had nowhere else to go, or he would not have faced the wrath of Mrs. Figgins. And he was less desirous than ever of entering the house, when he saw Maggie between him and his goal. He was justly afraid that Maggie would attach him again. He shambled up, one eye on Maggie, the other on the space available between Maggie and the door. The eye of Maggie prevailed.

"I thought you'd gone home," blurted out Will.

"You'd have been very glad if I had?" inquired Maggie lightly.

Will was miserable; such a woman there never was for divining a man's thoughts. Then Maggie smiled on him and all was changed. Will liked the quality of her smile; it beguiled him, made him innocent, fearless and confiding. It assured him some one was tender towards him, and it was a great relief to find some one who could condescend to real likeable tenderness towards him. Maggie noted the manifest result of her smile.

"So you're going back there again?" she said.

"I shall have an awful time of it," admitted Will.

"Well," considered Magge,"I think you won't go back."

""I live there," said Will simply; "I have lived there as long as - "

"As long as is good for you. I can trust Ada, but I wouldn't trust her mother with a mopping-rag, let alone you. No; we'll go along and see Tubby Wadlow."

"Tubby," said Will hopefully.

"You're used to Tubby? Well, lad, it's maybe best you aren't frightened any more today. I shouldn't like being frightened by Mrs. Figgins myself. We'll put Tubby in charge of you, and if you're terrified of Mrs. Figgins in your sleep, Tubby can hold your hand."

Will smiled gratefully. He like the tender chaff, and he liked the news of his change of lodgings still more. He walked on beside Maggie with a sprightly step, and his head in a bewildered whirl.

"Eh! it's like an 'appy dream."

Maggie smiled as well, very contentedly.

"You do manage things, lass - Miss Maggie, I mean."

"No, you don't," dared Maggie, "You really mean'lass'."

"Nay," said Will, frightened by the bold ease of the girl; "Miss Maggie's right, eh, and, and - "

"Safer?" The cheerful provoking lips of Maggie derided him.

"Aye," said Will, involuntarily. "Nay, proper, "he corrected himself.

"We're nearly to Tubby's. We shan't have a proper chance there, but we have a safe chance now. You can kiss me if you like," laughed the metamorphosed saleswoman audaciously.

"Nay!"

"Thou's naying a lot this walk, my lad," responded Maggie, with loverly sharpness of tone. "Come! Here's my lips." She stopped in the middle of the pavement and offered them. "Get it over,lad!" she admonished him.

"Holy Names!" Will turned and fled again, muttering, "Kissing a lass, not if I know it. It's not my line. I cannot. I darsen't. But what a mouth for kissing, too."

Maggie came on behind, full of laughter. She was disappointed, but she had yearning for the pluck to fulfil her delicious invitation. Will would come to it all right when he got used to the idea. At present he was not. Still, it was all very well done, the topic of kissing had been introduced, and the next time he would not run away - at any rate not quite so fast. His education was beginning.

She overtook her kiss-shy lover at Tubby's door, and together they entered.

"Good afternon, Tubby," said Maggie cheerfully to her foreman, as he got up very hastily from a stool in front of the fire.

"How do, Miss Maggie. Come for tea wi' us bachelors?" he indicated the quiet but kindly figure of Mr. Jerry Bamber seated at the fireside.

Mr. Bamber inclined his head; the motion was perfect courtesy. Mr. Bamber did not need to rise to be polite to a lady. Courtesy was implicit in Mr. Bamber's whole. He had been a prize-fighter in his youth, and a remarkable aray of belts and cups adorned the walls of the room. Mr. Bamber was proud of his fighting record, in an unpretentious manner. Fighting had made him wise, silent, reliable and generous.

"No," said Maggie. "Will is come for his tea."

"We must have the couple." interposed Mr. Bamber, with happy significance in his tone.

"Not this time, Jerry."

"It is the custom, Miss Maggie," quoth Tubby, as shining of face as Old Sol himself. "I like turtle-doves. I'm a bachelor myself, but it would be a great treat if thou stayed tea with Jerry and me. We don't know much about billing and cooing, Miss Maggie."

"Tubby!" Will was scandalised at the liberty of speech in old bachelors.

Maggie laughed. "I have a job for you both."

Tubby and Jerry signified their willingness.

"Tubby must go round to Mrs. Figgins's for Will's things, and Jerry must go to look after Mrs. Figgins while he get them."

He looked blankly at Maggie, suspecting mischief, and he did not like mischief and Mrs. Figgins in the same breath.

"Oh!" - Maggie was quite cheerful - "Will has paid last week; but she'll want money for notice. And you can bring Will's things back with you, before she pops them. Then he can lodge with you."

Tubby was quiet, digesting all that these commands signified in terms of fiction.

"Jerry!"

"Aye, Miss Hobson," responded the light-weight.

"Can you make Will into a fighter?"

Will looked appealingly at Maggie, but she did not interfer whilst Jerry came across and sized up the candidate for the Noble Art.

"I might do something with him," announced Jerry.

"It's more than I expected," said Will humbly. Maggie laughed agreement.

"Not that I'll make much of him," said the candid Jerry; "but if you want him to be able to use his hands, I can manage that much."

"In a month?" queried Maggie.

"He won't be expert." Jerry was kind to ladies. Inwardly he chuckled mildly. "A man does not know his hand from a pudding in the first month."

"Well! till he is expert enough to stand up to Mrs. Figgins, I expect you and Tubby to do his fighting for him."

The bachelors laughed highly at this. Miss Maggie was a welcome visitor, a tonic joy this Sunday afternoon, and they promised to look after Will more zealously than they could well fulfil. Will smiled feebly but contentedly. He was at rest with none but men about him. Maggie left, with a promise to arrange finally with Tubby in the shop tomorrow morning. Then the bachelors sat down to tea and the extraction of woeful tales of women from Will Mossop.

CHAPTER SIX

A Test for Will

No one will ever persuade a Salford man that the week begins on Sunday. Sunday is the last day of week, and Monday the first of the next. Calendars are liars. They call every Monday "Black Monday" in Salford, and in certain trades it is found so useless to open at the usual hour that workmen are allowed till after breakfast-time to recover from their Sabbath dissipations. (In Lancashire the working-day begins at six a.m.)

Mr. Hobson was not Mondayish by reason of Sabbath alcohol, but for lack of it. His duties at St. Philip's, and the policy which lay behind them, prevented him from doing more than just calling at the Moonraker's on his way home from evening service. Monday was black indeed, and not till Mr. Hobson had absorbed his afternoon restorations did he recover from the distressing results of religion. "Nowty" is a Lancashire word which may be translated as "cantankerous," but cantankerous is a part of the whole. The whole was Mr. Henry Horatio Hobson on any Monday morning.

Alice and Vickey were in the shop. They, too, were "Mondayish," but there was reasonable cause for that. They shared a bedroom, and had spent most of the night discussing the outrageous conduct of their sister. Vickey, in this emergency, had told Alice of Freddy Beenstock, and the complicated situation meant a sleepless night, and finally resolved itself into an offensive and defensive alliance of the younger sisters against Maggie.

At this moment Maggie was dressing to go out. It was

THE ROYAL HOSPITAL, SALFORD.

the system at Hobson's to send bills once. If, after a reasonable interval, money did not arrive, a bill was not sent twice. Maggie was sent instead. It saved clerical labour and bad debts. Maggie passed through the sitting-room where Hobson sat accumulating resolution to put on his boots.

"I'm going after Montgomerys' debt," she said.

"It's going to sixteen pounds."

"And don't come back without it, now," he said.

"They're a rotten lot. Might be Londoners the way they live. Put it all on their backs and starve their bellies. All the goods in the shop window and nothing in the larder. Live in a big house in the Crescent, and get it cheap because there's a pork butcher rents what used to be the stable at the back. They're shoddy and I'm broadcloth, and I'll none have debts of that size owing from the likes of them."

"No," said Maggie; "but you gave them credit. I was out last time they came to buy, and you were in."

"What I did has nowt to do with you. Your job's to get that debt."

"I'll try," said Maggie, and she went through to the shop. The mutineers were watching and they were ready to attack.

"Look here, Maggie," said Alice, "we want word with you."

"I'm busy now," she said.

"You're not too busy to listen to what we're going to say, and you're going to listen, too. We've been put on by you for long enough, and I'll tell you this, you'll not mess up our futures if you think it, so look out."

"What's the matter with your future, Alice?"

"My future's Albert Prosser, and you know it."

"And mine is Freddy Beenstock," came from Vickey.

"I judged as much from what I saw yesterday, Vickey," said Maggie. "You had the look."

"And what I looked, I feel. I suppose I can be in love if I like?" said Vickey.

"It's like this, Maggie. We come first," said Alice.

"Do you?" said Maggie. "I'd a notion I was firstborn."

"And we're first wed," said Alice Hobson.

"And you can just make up your mind to that. If you want to make an idiot of yourself with Willie Mossop, you can do it after we've got wed and not before. You've got no right to spoil our chances."

"I'll not do that," said Maggie.

"You will," said Alice. "Do you fancy Albert Prosser's going to wed me with Will Mossop in the family?"

"If Albert's any sense he'll be proud to do it."

"He'll never marry me at all," and Alice nearly wept.

"You'll marry Albert Prosser when he's able, Alice, and that'll be when he starts spending less on laundry bills and hair cream.

Mr. Hobson heard the sound of altercation and he rose in wrath. One boot was on, the other foot was slippered, but he came. "What's this?" he said. A silence reigned.

"I'll be getting on to Montgomery's if they've nothing to say," said Maggie.

"We've a lot to say," said Vickey.

"You always have," said Hobson. "You pair of chattering magpies! There's Maggie's got more sense in her little finger than the pair of you put together." Things were looking bad for the prosecution, but the prisoner had a sense of justice, if the judge had not.

"Don't lose your temper with them, father," said Maggie. "You'll maybe need it all when Vickey speaks."

"It would be Vickey," Hobson said. "She thinks she can do owt because she can look at herself in the glass without a fright. What's Vickey been up to now?"

"I've done nothing," said Vickey. "It's about Will Mossop, father."

"Will?"

"Yes," said Alice. "What's your opinion of Will?"

"He's a decent lad," said Hobson cautiously.

"I've nowt against him - that I know of."

"Would you like him in the family?" asked Alice.

"Whose family?"

"Yours"

Maggie spoke quietly. "I'm going to marry Will," she said. "That's what all the fuss is about."

Perhaps it was as well that Sunday was Mr. Hobson's abstemious day. He went purple, and he sat down hard.

"Mossop! You! Marry!" he gasped.

"You see, father, when you thought me past the marrying age, you were making a mistake. I'm not. That's all."

"You are. You all are."

"Father!" said Vickey in protest.

"And if you're not, it makes no matter. I'll have no husbands here. I've changed my mind. I've learnt things since I spoke of husbands. There's a lot too much expected of a father nowadays."

"I'm expecting nothing," said Maggie.

"You!" he said. He came back to the main point, from which Vickey had side-tracked him. He began to see that Maggie was in earnest. What had she said? Marry Willie Mossop?

He looked at Vickey and at Alice. "Get away, you girls," he said. This was an affair for principals. "Go right upstairs. I'll none have gazers through yon door."

It is sadly disappointing for the engineers of conflict to be denied the sight of the battlefield, but Alice and Vickey decided that it was politic to go. No seconds were required.

Polite fighters may have their ritual, the approach salute, and guard, but in Salford a fight is a fight, and clogs and belts can play their part as well as fists. Maggie and Hobson had had their differences before today. They knew each other's strength and waived preliminaries.

"Mean it?" asked he.

"Oh, aye," she said. The case was stated.

"It's come to a falling out between us, then," he said.

"It needn't, though. That's as you like. I'm ready to go on - on terms."

"Terms!" he scoffed.

"You'll take your choice," she said.

"Aye, lass. I'll take my choice, and happen my choice

won't be thine. If you're wedding Willie Mossop, you and me part company. I'll none hear of it. Why, lass, his father was a workhouse brat. A come-by-chance."

"It's news to me we're snobs in Salford," she said. "I'm wedding Willie Mossop for sufficient reasons of my own. I've my life in front of me, and I'm settling what I'll do with it."

"Listen to reason, lass. Why, I'd be the laughing-stock of the place if I allowed it. I won't have it, Maggie, I tell you. It's hardly decent at your time of life."

Maggie tightened her lip. "I'm thirty," she said. "and I'm marrying Willie Mossop. And now I'll tell you my terms."

"Terms," he laughed. "You're in a nice position to state terms, my lass."

"Not so bad," she said. "You will pay my man Will Mossop the same wages as before; and as for me, I've given you the better part of twenty years of work without wages. I'll work eight hours a day in future, and you will pay me fifteen shillings by the week."

"Do you think I'm made of brass?" he asked.

"You'll soon be made of less than you are, if you let Willie go. And if Willie goes, I go. That's what you've got to face."

"I can face it, Maggie; shop-hands are cheap."

"Cheap ones are cheap. The sort you'd have to watch all day - and you'd feel happy helping them to tie up parcels and sell laces while Tudsbury and Heeler and Minns are supping their ale without you at the Moonraker's. I'm value to you, and I know it if you don't. So's Willie Mossop; and I'll tell you this" - her voice was mellow gold, and her face shone with the power and the strength and the knowledge from within - "I'll tell you this much, father, you can boast it at the Moonraker's that your daughter Maggie's made the strangest, finest match a woman's made this fifty years. And you can put your hand in your pocket and do what I propose."

Hobson had his point of view. It was not Maggie's. "I'll tell you what I propose," he said. He raised the trap and bellowed down it. "Willie" he cried, "come up."

THE ROMAN CATHOLIC
CATHEDRAL OF ST. JOHN'S,
SALFORD.

"One moment, Will," said Maggie.

"Do what I tell you," Hobson roared.

"All right," said Maggie. "Do, but put your coat and hat on first. Then come." She turned to Hobson. "Father," she said, "you'd better think a bit. You can have us with you or against. If it comes to a parting, I've my own idea about which of us will be hurt."

"There's other ways of killing pigs than shooting them," said Hobson, unbuckling his belt. "I cannot leather you, my lass. You're female and exempt. But I can leather him, and, by the Lord I'll do it, too. Come up, Will Mossop."

Willie came up, blinking, as the daylight hurt his feeble eyes after the murk of the cellar. He wore his hat and coat, but it was his old hat. Sunday hats are for Sunday wear.

"I've heard some news of you, my lad," said Hobson. "You've taken up with my Maggie."

"Nay, and I've not," said Willie. "She's done the taking up."

"That's like enough, Willie, but it's your misfortune either way. Love's led you astray, and I feel bound to put you right."

"Magie, what's this?" said Will.

"I'm watching you, my lad." And Maggie was. She stood aside, deliberately, watching, and if ever Maggie Hobson was nervous in her life, it was now. Externals did not matter. Broken skin would mend, but Maggie knew this was a test. Will Mossop at assay. Was he good metal or had Maggie counted wrongly? This time he would get no help from her.

"Mind you, Willie, Hobson was saying, "I'm none for sacking you. It's her that said 'Put on your coat,' not me. I've no objections to your staying here. I don't bear malice, but you've got an ailment and I've got the cure. Love's overcome you, and you've lacked the strength to cast it out. I'll lend you strength, my lad. I'll be your benefactor and I'll beat the love from your body in the kindest way. And if the first dose doesn't do it, Will, you'll get another dose for every day you come to work with love still sitting in you. I'll exorcise that love, my lad. It's a nasty devil, and it's got to come out."

"You'll not beat love in me. You're making a great mistake, Mr, Hobson." Maggie trembled. Will was stammering, watching the strap, and his fingers moved convulsively. Was Will a coward then?

"It's your mistake," said Hobson. "And you'll put aside this weakness for my Maggie if you've a liking for a sound skin. You'll waste a gradely lot of brass at chemist's if I am at you for a week with this." The strap swung ominously.

Willie looked at it. "I'm none wanting thy Maggie," he said. "It's her that's after me." Then something happened. Will Mossop stood erect. He looked at Mr. Hobson with a challenge in his eye. "But I'll tell you this," he said. "If you touch me with that belt, I'll take her, and I'll take her quick, aye, and I'll stick to her like glue."

Then Maggie knew. She was ashamed. She'd doubted him, but this was the stuff she always knew was there, her stuff, her great discovery, the stuff that she would mould to what she would.

A boot-hand did not challenge Henry Hobson in vain. Willie had asked for it. "There's nobbut one answer to that kind of talk," he said, and swung the belt. Will caught it in his hands.

"And I have nobbut one answer back," he said, and went to Maggie. The other end of the belt being in Hobson hands, Hobson went too. He pulled the belt, but went where Willie listed. "Maggie," said Will, "I've got to answer this. I've never kissed you yet, my lass. I shirked last night, but, by gum, lass, I'll none shirk now."

He dropped the belt. The result for Mr. Hobson was natural but unfortunate. He fell, but Will and Maggie did not seem to care. It is doubtful if they knew.

"I'll take you, and I'll hold you," Willie said, "and if Mr. Hobson raises up that strap again, I'll do more, I'll walk straight out of shop with thee and us two 'ull set up for usselves."

"Come on," said Maggie Hobson. "That's good enough for me."

The door closed noisily in Mr. Hobson's face.

"Going to see Mrs. Hepworth"

The casual observer would have seen Maggie in Chapel Street as an insignificant little woman with her arm firmly tucked under that of a lumpish, bewildered-looking lad. But Maggie walked on air, and every inch of her vibrated to an unsung song of love, and triumph and creation. It was as if an unborn fate was leaping in her, but her baby towered by her side and his name was Mossop, and his future just as much in Maggie's hands as any sucking child's might be. She glowed with pride in him, her choice, her child, her man to make and mould. Hobson the shop, her virgin past, like an unsubstantial pageant faded, left not a rack behind. Maggie Hobson was a thing gone by, and Maggie and Will began. Creative ecstasy was all.

Not so with Will. Will had not shed so easily the shackles of the past, and as Maggie, seeing visions, strode along, Will disengaged his arm from hers and stood, one troubled eye on her, the other on the shop. A dog called one way by a master whom he fears and called another by a mistress whom he loves presents the same pathetic sight of helpless indecision.

Maggie came back from dreamland. "What's wrong?" she said.

"I've got to go back," said Will.

"What for?"

"I must apologise to Mr. Hobson," said Will Mossop. "I don't know what came over me to treat the master as I did."

She took her arm firmly, postponing private dreams, and urged him to the road. "Be quick," she said, "we've got to catch that tram." They caught the tram. It was a dingy two-horse vehicle. Maggie was no great patroness of trams. Shanks' mare was good enough for her, and on her debt-collecting expeditions she was wont to walk, but she had things to do today and the tram did two of them for her. It got Will Mossop away from the shop and it took him to Hope Hall in the Eccles Old Road. It was not a long journey, and the electric cars which solve the larger traffic problems of today accomplish it in fifteen minutes, but in '79 the Woolpack Inn marked the division-line between the thick-set population and the larger pleasaunces beyond.

Long after then, indeed, it was the boast of the Eccles Old Road that no fewer than five members of Parliament had houses in it. The Heywoods, the Agnews, the Henrys, Armitages and the Howarths were the greater names, but

Hope Hall was a place apart. It had - what their abodes had not - a grey antiquity, not quite historic, though Lord Clive of India had once stayed there, but richly aged and set upon a hill in fine and mellow dignity. Yet not so dignified as once it was, for now the great house was divided into two, and in one half of it lived Mrs. Hepworth.

Will Mossop was going to see Mrs. Hepworth of Hope Hall! He did not know it. All he knew was that his conscience was hurting him, but that the unaccustomed movement of the tram, its palatial interior, and the fearful pride he felt in sitting side by side with Maggie Hobson (whom he, Will Mossop, had kissed) were rapidly soothing its stabs.

CATCHING THE TRAM.

Nevertheless, he had a guilty feeling. It was Monday morning and he ought to be at work.

Maggie said nothing, and the presence of two other passengers was more than enough to prevent Will's attempting to initiate a conversation. The conductor would have been enough. Besides, Maggie's eye discouraged it. Maggie was making plans.

"Weaste Lane," announced the conductor. Maggie rose, and Will followed her out of the tram. The gates and lodge of the Hall were at the top of Hope Hill, just where Weaste Lane begins. Maggie crossed to the Lodge.

"Maggie!" said Will, in scandalised protest.

Her jaw was set. She did not speak. Even the dauntless spirit of Maggie Hobson quailed a little at the enterprise before her. The gates were uninviting, but she opened them. "Be sharp," she said, and pushed him through. The gate clanged back behind them, bringing the drowsy lodge-man to the door.

"Hey, there!" he called, but called in vain. Maggie and Will were walking up the drive, and the lodge-keeper, a one-legged pensioner, was in no mind to try pursuit. Let those lazy fellows at the house do something for their livelihood.

"Maggie," said Will again.

"You hold your hush," she said. "Give me that card that Mrs. Hepworth gave you."

Willie produced the card, a little grimed, and Maggie put it in her bag.

They reached the Hall, and Maggie's lips were tightly closed. Hope Hall was not a Chatsworth but its entrance had impressiveness. "It's only so much stone," she muttered, and she rang the bell. After a decent interval, a footman came.

"Is Mrs. Hepworth in?" she asked.

He diagnosed the case. "If it's the tradesman's entrance you want, it's round the corner to the left," he said.

"It's not," said Maggie. "Is she in?"

He exercised discretion. "No," he replied.

"She's not at home."

"Then I'll come in and wait," said Maggie Hobson, and

was in. Will followed sheepishly. The footman stared. Young women of the lower classes were accustomed to fear his eye.

"You can't" he said, quite fifteen seconds after the event.

"Young man," she said, "that's Mrs. Hepworth's card, and I've come here on business. You take that card to her and you tell her Miss Hobson of the boot shop's waiting to see her." And Maggie looked at him. If doubt was in her heart there was no doubt in her eye. It had the calm assurance of, say, Lady Henry, the M.P.'s wife, calling in the afternoon on her friend Mrs. Hepworth. Yet she came in the morning and announced herself as Miss Hobson!

The footman decided to chance it. At the worst, he could excuse himself by exhibiting her own card to Mrs. Hepworth.

"But I gave my card to a man," said Mrs. Hepworth.

"There is a young man with her, madam," said the footman.

"I'll see them," she decided. "Show them in."

Maggie and Will were taken to the gracious Georgian room where Mrs. Hepworth sat at a walnut writing-desk, which had been new when Queen Anne sat upon the throne. It was a panelled room, and struck both Will and Maggie as bare and unfurnished.

"Good morning," said Mrs. Hepworth. "You're the man who made my boots."

"Yes, mum," said Will.

"Can I do something for you?"

"It's like this, Mrs. Hepworth," Maggie said.

"You said he wasn't to make a change without letting you know. Well, he's making a change. He's marrying me."

"I referred to a change in his employment," and Mrs. Hepworth smiled at the poor girl's simplicity.

"He's changing that, and all," said Maggie.

"That's what we've come about."

Mrs. Hepworth drew a piece of paper to her.

""Then if you will give me his new address, that will be all I want.

"It isn't all I want," said Maggie. "And there's no address to give as yet, and won't be if I fail with you."

"Sit down," said Mrs. Hepworth. "What is it you want?"

"I want a hundred pounds," said Maggie Hobson. "And I want your word amongst your friends that Will's the best bootmaker in the land. We're starting on our own, and a hundred pounds will set us up."

"Indeed!" gasped Mrs. Hepworth.

"Aye," said Maggie. "Will and me's a pair. I've got the head and Willie's got the hands, and all we need's a bit of capital to start us off. The rest 'ull come."

Mrs. Hepworth was amused. "You'll not miss anything for want of asking for it," she said.

"No," said Maggie. "I've a tongue in my head, and words were made for use. I've the gift of selling boots and he's the gift of making them, and it's a pity if we cannot come to terms with you. I'll pay you your money back with twenty per cent, in a year from now."

"And if I spoke the word security?" said Mrs. Hepworth, playfully.

"You're the security," said Maggie. "And the more you tell your friends to come to us, the more secure you'll be. There's brass in boots if they're made right and handled right. And the good-class trade's the paying end of it, and all."

"That sounds as if I'd been paying too much for mine," said Mrs. Hepworth.

"Nay, you've not," said Maggie. "Hobson's aren't robbers and Mossop's won't be neither. They'll give good lasting work and charge a decent profit for it because the boots they sell 'ull not wear out in three months."

"I don't know much about you," Mrs. Hepworth suggested.

"I'm not the running sort, if that's your meaning." Maggie said. "But a hundred pounds is the least I'll take. I've worked it out, and it can't be done for less. If you haven't got the money by you, you can guarantee me at your bank instead. It's all the same to me.

"I'll see." said Mrs. Hepworth. Maggie had interested

her, and Mrs. Hepworth liked to play the Lady Bountiful, but the number of small benevolences to be accomplished with a hundred pounds is almost infinite. This was a large hole to be made at once in the charity account - for, of course, it was as charity that Mrs. Hepworth thought of this.

"Nay, that won't do," said Maggie. "I must know. It's now or never, Mrs. Hepworth."

Labour is wont to call on Capital with cap in hand and in that mood of chastened humbleness which a proper perspective gives. Maggie's way was different: she stated her demand, and held a pistol to Capital's head. And Maggie's eye was gleaming.

A faint irritation began to harass Mrs. Hepworth. She was used to master and felt herself being mastered, but she decided to be amused instead at Maggie's audacity. It pleased her to think that, in Maggie's circumstances, she would have acted as Maggie did. And, after all, a hundred pounds was not so very much. She could afford to lose that sum, and it would be diverting to see how her investment would turn out. She decided to invest a hundrerd pounds in Maggie Hobson's audacity, in much the same spirit as that in which her son would put the same amount on a horse.

"You're in a hurry, then," she said.

"I've got a lot to do today," said Maggie. "I've a shop to find, and a bit of furniture to pick up cheap, and the banns to see about, the leather and tools to buy."

"Can't he do anything?" asked Mrs. Hepworth, indicating the silent Will.

"Yes," said Maggie. "He can make boots, and if there's any of your daughters in, it'll save his time and theirs if you'll let him be measuring their feet while you and me arrange about the money."

"No," said Mrs. Hepworth; "I'd rather bring them to your shop when you're ready."

"You said you'd send them to Hobson's, but they haven't been there yet.

"No," said Mrs. Hepworth. "And you should be glad of that. But I'll see they come to your shop."

"Certain?" said Maggie.

"Very certain," said Mrs. Hepworth. "I'm financing yours." And Maggie's heart gave one great leap, but all she did was just to nod. "And when they come," continued her financier, "I'll come myself to look around. When shall you be ready? In a week?"

"When can I have the money?"

"This morning. You can cash a cheque."

"Then the shop 'ull be open tomorrow," said Maggie. "And any time after six in the morning we'll be glad to see you there. I'll leave the address at your door tonight."

Mrs. Hepworth handed Maggie a cheque and looked at the bell. She decided not to ring it. She would see Maggie and Will to the door herself. Maggie was wondering what she ought to say. Her object gained, Maggie was lost. A restful mind made no more appeal to her than idle hands.

"I'm much obliged for this," she said. "I'm sure I - "

"Then make the most of it," said Mrs. Hepworth, interrupting, and she held her hand out. Maggie shook it, and for the second time, Will Mossop raised his hat. They hurried down the drive at the hot pace which Maggie set. The day had just begun and she had work to do.

Mrs. Hepworth stood on the doorstep, watching them. She had the knack of reading character in people's backs, and Maggie's back attracted her. Willie's did not. She turned, and her face revealed an easy mind. "I'll get my money back all right," thought Mrs. Hepworth.

CHAPTER SEVEN

Settin' Up Shop

"Well, by gum," said Willie Mossop, whose only notion of a hundred pounds was a pile of glittering sovereigns. "Tha means to say yon bit of paper means all that?"

"It does," said Maggie, walking with him out of the bank where she had opened an account with Mrs. Hepworth's cheque in Willie's name. Will's signature was laboured but it could be read, and he had signed where he was told. They knew Maggie at the bank and there had been no difficulties. Will Mossop had a current account credited with eighty pounds, and Maggie stuffed four five pound notes into her bag.

"And now," she said, "we want a shop, and I reckon a cellar's good enough. We'll not be there for long, but it's to be on a good street or Mrs. Hepworth's friends 'ull lose themselves in looking for it. Oldfield Road's about the mark."

The two main thoroughfares of Salford are Regent Road and Chapel Street, roughly parallel to each other, and Oldfield Road connects them, thus cutting through the most densely populated district. It was not quite a main street, but rents were proportionately lower, and as the Eccles Old Road customers would come, in any case, by carriage, Maggie argued that they could as easily be driven to Oldfield Road as to Chapel Street. And she trusted Mrs. Hepworth to see that they came. As for the clog-trade, it would be at her doorstep.

They walked down Oldfield Road, but Oldfield Road seemed popular with shopkeepers. That was a good sign, but Maggie wanted a cellar and there were none to let. They went over the ground again. At the corner of Liverpool

Street, Maggie stopped short. A depressed little man in shirt-sleeves and a black sateen apron emerged from a cellar entrance, locked the door behind him and went into the shop above. It was a draper's. Maggie followed him in, and Will followed Maggie.

"I want a yard of blue ribbon," she said. The man produced a box. "Do you make much use of your cellar? she asked.

"I keep a bit of stock down there," he said.

"It's a dry cellar."

"Pretty big?" she asked. "I'll take that shade."

He cut the ribbon. "A lot too big for the use I make of it," he said. "It's got two rooms and water laid on, and all."

"Why don't you let it, then?"

"It's handy at times," he said. "I'm short of room up here."

"How handy is it?" she said. "And would a rent for it be handier, because I'll pay you one."

"Depends what rent?" he said.

"Depends what room," she said. "Let's see the place."

He took the key from a nail behind the counter and they went down. A dim light filtered through the unwashed windows. It was a large cellar, divided by a wooden partition into two rooms. The floor was flagged, but it was as he had said, quite dry. The walls had been whitewashed recently, and, to Maggie's pleased surprise, there was a counter, used at present to support a stock of sheets.

"I want some bed lined," Maggie said. "I'll buy it here if we come to terms about the rent."

"What do you want the place for?"

"A boot shop and a living-room," she said.

"What's the rent?"

"Ten shillings a week," he said.

"Five shillings, "Maggie offered. "And it's something for nothing to you. That bit of stock can go upstairs."

"I might take seven-and-sixpence," he said.

Maggie took two pounds from her bag. "There's eight weeks' rent in advance," she said. "Is it a bargain?"

He took the money. "I'll close with you," he said. "The times are hard. There are too many Welshmen in the drapery business for an honest man to do much good."

"Times are likely to be hard," said Maggie, who was without national prejudice. "It's not the Welshmen's fault you've kept a place like this eating its head off. Well, get that stock of yours out of my way. I'm busy."

"I'll see to it tomorrow," he said.

"Will, take your coat off," Maggie said. "I'm going out, and if this place isn't clear by the time I'm back, you'll meet with trouble. When you've done that you can get the windows clean. Mr. Pratt will lend you a bucket.

"There's gas laid on and a separate meter," said Mr. Pratt. "If you clean the windows, you'll have children watching you."

"They'll watch us being busy then," she said.

"And that's all good for trade. Now, get a move on, Will."

In half an hour the cellar was cleared of Mr. Pratt's property, and Will Mossop was engaged in cleaning the windows when Maggie returned with some slices of what is known as "pig's cheek," and a loaf of bread, a small boy laden with crockery and utensils, a gas-inspector who was to check the meter at the point where Pratt's tenancy left off and hers began, and a sign-writer who was to paint the legend "William Mossop. Practical Boot and Clog Maker" on the door and windows. A coal merchant had an order for a bag of coal, and in an office up the road an astonished job-printer was quietly kicking himself for have undertaken to deliver handbills, headed letter-paper and invoice forms by five o'clock that afternoon. But he had no intention of breaking his promises.

"You can knock off now," said Maggie to Will.

"We've not done so badly, and it's dinner-time."

They picnicked at the counter, sitting on it, whilst the gas-inspector made his examination and the sign-writer did his job. Will Mossop watched the sign-writer. He was experiencing that noble thrill which comes when for the first time one sees one's name in print. Maggie watched the gas-inspector. He checked the meter and she checked him. She knew what gas-inspectors were.

Will wolfed his food and got down from the counter. He wanted to be near that sign-writer.

"You'd better make a meal of it," said Maggie, who was doing it herself. "We've got our hands full if we're to open in the morning, and the next time's a long way off. You've got a handcart to push this afternoon."

Willie accepted another sandwich, but he ate it in the street. From inside the lettering was of course reversed, but in the street he was able to gloat over the sign as the world was to read it. "William Mossop!" his name, his, Will Mossop's, who but yesterday - ! Excitement and dry bread had combined to choke him, and he ran down the stone steps to the water-tap.

"I'm ready now," she said. "Come on. I want all those windows covering," she added, to the sign-writer. "I'm not the one to spoil a ship for a ha'porth of tar. I reckon it's an afternoon's job."

"And more." said the man.

"Well, what's not done by night comes, won't get done at all," she said. "This shop's to open in the morning."

The gentleman who made his living by hiring out handcarts at ninepence an hour was in the habit of demanding a deposit from hirers who were strangers to him. But he refrained from asking Maggie.

Will pushed the cart by the gutter and Maggie walked on the pavement. She turned up Regent Road.

"Where are you going to?" asked Will.

"Manchester," said Maggie. "It's a pity, but we've got to buy some stock to make a show. Clogs and cheap fancy slippers and a few good ready-mades. It's the first and last time we'll trouble the warehouses if I get my way."

At the wholesale house in Manchester, Maggie Hobson saw the principal. It was probably the first time in his career that he had been personally interviewed about a ten-pound order, and certainly he had never allowed a special discount off such an amount. But Maggie Hobson asked for it, and what Maggie asked for she got. A merchant tackled by a determined lady, who knows his price-list quotations better than he does himself, is at a disadvantage.

"And now," she said to Will, as her purchases were loaded on the cart, "I want a bed."

"A bed," he echoed stupidly.

"I'm none sleeping on the floor," she said.

They sell flat-irons at the Flat-Iron Market, Salford, because they sell everything, but the market owes its name to the shape of the piece of land behind Trinity Church on which it is held. There, in one corner of the crowded area, is all the fun of the fair - coconut shies, merry-go-rounds, and strolling players who perform strange plays in canvas booths; *Maria Martin* and *George Barnwell* linger still in the repertoire of the vagabond actors who fill in a week between the dates of country fairs and "wakes" on the Flat-Iron Market at Salford.

Maggie ignored its lighter side. Concealing Will and the handcart well up a side street, lest any stall-holders should imagine she was really there to buy, she strolled with a nicely calculated air of casual sight-seeing amongst the miscellaneous rubbish exposed for sale. Household goods in every stage of decadence were tumbled on the ground. The naked earth itself is stall enough for the sellers of the Flat-Iron, and they squat amongst their dingy wares like Oriental merchants in some dim bazaar, as listless and as seemingly content whether they make a sale or not. Yet their half-closed eyes were sharp enough, and he would be a great Autolycus who could pick up a trifle from a Flat-Iron stall and make away with it.

You will see nothing new for sale here. Indeed, the trouble was to find anything which was merely old. The market was an exhibition of frailty and decrepitude. It was a depot for the off-scourings of the second-hand shops and auction rooms. What was unsaleable in them was sent for sale here, and, astoundingly, was sold.

Maggie found what she wanted, an iron bedstead,

bright red with rust, but strong and shapely still. She passed it by and bought a pan for fourpence.

"How much for the bed?" she asked.

"Fifteen shillings," said the saleswoman carelessly.

"I'll give you half-a-crown," said Maggie.

"Five shillings, and it's yours," said the woman.

"And I'd rather you cleaned it up than me." They praise their goods like that at the Flat-Iron.

"I'll take it," Maggie said.

"There's a mattress. Do you want that too?"

"Not much," said Maggie, shuddering. She went for Will and the bed was loaded on the cart.

"And now," said Maggie, "we can spread ourselves a bit. I want a new mattress and you want tools and leather, and I'll stint myself on neither. We want good sleep and we want good work.

It was a well-loaded handcart which returned to 39a Oldfield Road. A mattress (from Mrs. Burgess in Chapel Street, which was the best shop in Salford or Manchester either, as Maggie and the Eccles Old Road knew very well), an outfit of tools, which Will had chosen with slow deliberation and a knowledgeable eye, a stock of leather, a cobblers' bench, the bedstead, the fancy stock from the warehouse, and assorted groceries made a heavier pile than the little cart was built to bear, or Willie's back to push. But they arrived, and by the time Willie had the cart unloaded and returned to its proprietor, tea was ready on the counter.

"We're getting through with it," said Maggie cheerfully. "And I don't know that I'd begin to work tonight if I were you. We'll make it a holiday and have a walk tonight. It'll be a bit of exercise for us."

A man who has pushed a handcart with an increasing weight over seven good miles of Manchester and Salford streets hardly required exercise, but Will said "Yes."

"We've that handbill to deliver to Mrs. Hepworth's, so as she'll know where we are, and we may as well go round to Vicar's tonight to see him about the banns. With any luck, we'll be too busy later in the week. And happen I shall think of somebody I might get an order off for you to make a start on in the morning. I don't believe in working for stock."

Both of this Parish

"You'd better get your tools and leather looking shipshape whilst I wash the pots and go upstairs to buy bed-linen from Mr. Pratt," said Maggie, as they finished tea. "I like to see a place look workman-like. And if you've finished before I have, there's that bedstead to clean. I got some oil. Of course, that'll be the bedroom in yonder, and I'm wondering if we can run to a curtain across here to make that corner our living-room. Still, there's lots of time for that. We've not got to go thinking of luxuries yet." Hadn't they? But Willie Mossop had. Give a craftsman tools of his own choosing, materials of his own selection, and a space in which to arrange them to his convenience, and he asks for nothing more as luxury. To Will, tanned hides were what colours are to an artist, and no artist visiting his colour-man had ever chosen with more loving care than Will Mossop lavished on the choosing of the hides which now surrounded him. Their reek was incense to his nostrils, their ruddy browns rejoiced his eye. The day had been a dream, a wild rushed nightmare of bewilderment, but here was calm reality at last, and as he planned the corner behind the steps, and drove in nails whereon to hang his tools, and fingered hides with cunning hands which felt and knew that they were good, Will Mossop's soul knew peace.

He took his time, and Maggie, watching, gave him rope. She understood. As he to her, so they to him: the raw materials of each. So it was she who cleaned the bed while Will evolved a workshop out of chaos. But when he gave a sigh of satisfaction and stood up straight to stretch his back, she pounced on him like cat on mouse.

"Finished?" she asked.

"It'll about do," he said.

"Then get your hat and come along. And see now, put these in your pocket." She handed him a number of handbills.

112 *Hobson's Choice*

CHURCH OF THE SACRED TRINITY, SALFORD.

"I've put a lot in envelopes addressed to people I know and we can leave them as we go to Mrs. Hepworth's, but you'd better have some extra ones in case I think of any more likely customers. I'll call on them myself tomorrow, but we'll just leave these tonight to break the ice."

It is about two and a half miles from Oldfield Road to Hope Hall, and the Crescent was on their way. Bill-distributing is weary work, but as they turned out of Mrs. Hepworth's drive for the second time that day, no tram was in sight.

"It won't be long," said Will, who had discovered that he liked trams.

"My lad," said Maggie, "you'd better watch yourself. Extravagance is a thing that grows on folk, but it'll none grow much on us. Trams that aren't there when I want them, go without my money. We're fourpence better off for this, and the walk will do us good."

And it did Maggie good. It was a brisk and glowing Maggie who confronted Mr. Blundell with the terse announcement, "We're getting wed," but Will Mossop, used to the confinement of Hobson's cellar, his daily dose of exercise limited almost entirely to the distance between his place for work and his place for sleep, was a foot-sore, limping pitiable wreck.

Nevertheless, Mr. Blundell was not surprised. Even before Maggie spoke, he understood their situation. Mr. Blundell was used to interviewing young women with radiant faces and young men whose expressions varied from that consonant with an early Christian martyr's to that of an innocent man about to be hanged for a murder he did not commit. Nor was it in the least unusual for the young woman to transact the business of their call. The man was there because he had to be, but he let the woman do the talking.

"Indeed, Miss Hobson," said the Vicar, who of course knew Maggie very well as his warden's daughter and a Sunday School teacher to boot.

"And who is the happy man?"

"That will tell you his name," said Maggie improving the occasion and producing a handbill.

"Of course," said he. "I recollect you now. You come to the Young Men's Class."

"Aw," said Will.

The Vicar made a note. "Both of this parish?"

"Yes," said Maggie. "Both."

"Your age?!" he asked.

"I'm thirty-one," said Will.

"And - er - I must ask for yours, Miss Hobson, too."

"Thirty," she said, "and seeing we've a busy time ahead of us, I'll make arrangements now with you for the wedding, if it's all the same to you."

"Three Sundays for the banns and whenever you like after that," he said.

"Yes. Monday after the third Sunday," she said, at a quarter to twelve. If you'll book that now, I'll take it as settled, and we shan't need to bother you again till then."

The Vicar made another note. "And there's another thing," she said. "I don't know if you've read that handbill through, but we're setting up a boot shop, and it 'ud look particular well if we had your name down for the first order in our books."

"You're leaving your father?" he asked.

"There's reasons for that," she said.

"I go to him for my boots, Miss Hobson," said the Vicar in a voice which would have silenced any ordinary parishioner.

Maggie was not ordinary.

"I know," she said."And Will Mossop's the man who made them for you there. If your boots gave satisfaction, you'll have to come to us."

"I've certainly been satisfied," he said.

"Then I'll take your order now to save you the trouble of coming round to our shop. There's no need to take your measure, because I've a head that carries things like that and I know it by heart. One pair of boots as usual for Mr. Blundell, Will. You can start on them in the morning, and they'll be delivered by Thursday, sir," she added, turning again to the Vicar. "And thank you very much for your order. A good beginning's half the battle, and you're the best beginning in Salford."

Mr. Blundell meant to refuse. He didn't want a pair of boots, but Maggie's selling eye, tempered with genuine gratitude, was one too much for him.

"Well," he said weakly, and rose.

"Good-night," said Maggie. "And the wedding's for three weeks today at a quarter to twelve. I'd rather you than a curate, too."

"I shall hope to take it myself," he said.

"Good-night."

What a Day

"You were a bit short with the Vicar, Maggie," Will said, as they descended the Vicarage steps.

"What's the odds?" she said. "We're taking him some business, so it's only fair of him to give us some. Where are we? Oh, you're on your way to Tubby Wadlow's here, and I don't know that you need come back to the shop with me now. So we'll say 'Good-night.'"

"Good-night, Maggie," said Will awkwardly.

"You great soft thing," said Maggie tenderly, and kissed him hard. "I'll be expecting you come six in the morning."

"I'll not be late," he said; "but I reckon I'll be stiff."

"Oh, fiddlesticks!" said Maggie Hobson, and she turned down Chapel Street.

Mr. Hobson's state of mind that day was comparable with that of a man who has survived an earthquake, and, stunned by the initial shock, is only afterwards able to piece together his recollection of events. He had communicated to Alice and Vickey a freely censored version of the morning's episode, according to which Maggie and Will had been kicked out and forbidden to enter his door again. Truth is conformity to fact. The fact was that Maggie and Will had gone and had, apparently, no intention to return. The only possible explanation was that he had kicked them out. Therefore he spoke the truth.

Nor were Alice and Vickey to be much better informed by Maggie, who now went briskly through the shop and went upstairs.

"Well!" they said together, and ignoring duty's call, both followed her.

Maggie was packing clothes into a handbag.

"Who's in the shop?" she asked.

"Nobody," said Alice.

"If your stock gets stolen, Alice, it's nowt to do with me, but I'd advise one of you to go downstairs and keep an eye on things."

"You go, Vickey," said Alice.

"Go yourself," said Vickey. "You're in charge."

"Are you? said Maggie. "Did you get Montgomery's debt?"

"No," said Alice. "Aren't you going to tell us anything, Maggie?"

"I've got my hands full with myself just now," said Maggie. "For the next three weeks I'm too full up to think of you, but I may be able to do something for you later on."

"Father's in an awful way," said Vickey.

"Is he?" said Maggie, picking up her bag. "I reckon he'll be worse before he's better, too. Good-night." And Maggie paid her girlhood's bedroom the tribute of a searching look. But it was not to take a sentimental leave of it. It was to see whether she had forgotten anything, and she decided she had not. She took her bag and went.

In Salford, a holiday was usually one day, and it is spent by crowding into a hot excursion train travelling at least three hours, leaving the train, playing "rounders" in a field, eating, and racing at the last possible moment for the train and then three hours' journey home.

That explains why Maggie Hobson's thought, as she locked the cellar door in Oldfield Road after finishing the "pig's cheek" by way of supper, was, "It's been a bit too much like a holiday for my taste." And she went to her bedroom with her mind full of the thousand and one things which she had failed to get in.

"Still," she reflected, as she undressed, "Monday is always slack. We'll start working tomorrow."

118 *Hobson's Choice*

CHAPTER EIGHT

Education's A Wonderful Thing

Tubby Wadlow found nothing inconsistent in combining the stupid loyalty which held him bound to Hobson with a highly intelligent loyalty to the mutinous Maggie. At the shop, he held his tongue, worked faithfully for Hobson and deplored the falling off in the volume of made-to-measure trade which soon became apparent. Mrs. Hepworth let no grass grow under her feet. She meant to see her money back, and spared no efforts at the discreet "At Homes" in the Eccles Old Road to persuade her friends that her protege, William Mossop, was the only source in Salford of well-made boots. Where Mrs. Hepworth led, they followed gladly wondering a little at the crudity of the establishment in Oldfield Road, but leaving their orders with Maggie and being in a few days well satisfied with the result.

Tubby gave harbourage to Will. As a bachelor of means he had a bedroom and a tiny sitting-room to himself, and Will slept o'nights on three chairs in the sitting-room. When they had closed the shop in Oldfield Road, Maggie would go with Will to Tubby's room, for Maggie had her own ideas about propriety, and did not approve of sitting idle with her future husband in their future home. The working hours were different. Then they were partners, and laboured side by side, but when the books were closed and Will's tools tidily hung up, they left the premises and went to Tubby's room. But not for sweethearting. Maggie did not believe in idleness. She had the sense to know that change of occupation is the perfect rest.

Maggie was educating Will. The bank might pass his signature upon such cheques as Will had to sign, because it corresponded to the scrawl he had made in their books, but Maggie meant to change all that. She was the manager, but she foresaw the possibility of times when she might have to lay aside the reins and, if they came, she meant to know that Will was competent to take her place. And so, whilst she and Tubby chatted "shop," in a quite literal sense, Will Mossop bent his head above a slate and cramped his hand to unaccustomed movements of a pencil. She set a copy. And he copied it all down the slate. She made him read aloud to her from Tubby's books. She made him memorise the multiplication tables and drive his nails in working hours to their tune. Will Mossop should grow up.

In these pre-nuptial days, Maggie was growing, too, in confidence, and most of all, in happiness. Life deepend and took on a warmer, richer tone. Secretly she marvelled that a man so insignificant as Will could give her such a sense of vague, sweetly unutterable song. And here and now, though the lighter intimacies of courtship were few, he wore a halo in her eyes. She worked with triple energy, for him and for herself and for their shop, and all the while her dreams were with her and were generous, softening, enlarging, ripening. She understood the difficulty of her task, the prodigious contract she had undertaken - to succeed with Will. Therefore she laughed the more, and welcomed these nightly hours in Tubby's rooms. While Will contorted his body and laboured like a mountain to produce a pot-hook, Tubby talked, and Maggie found that Tubby in her father's shop was one man and another at his own fireside. With a pipe in his mouth and a jug of ale at his elbow, Tubby was turned philosopher.

"And so you're lifting Willie Mossop up a grade?" he said; "one of the lowers to the middles."

"If you like to put it that way, Tubby."

"Nay, lass, it's thou that likes. If thou wast owt but what thou art, it 'ud be t'other way round. He'd not go up to thee, but thou'd descend to him. It 'ud be a stitch dropped in the world's knitting."

"Why, Tubby, you're a democrat," she said. "You think of nothing but social grades."

"Grades are nowt to me," he said. "If a man's jannock, I say he's fit for any grade, and he'll none rule others till he's learned to rule himself. Dost not understand to every fibre of thy body, lass, that life is the great music, life is the music to the battered and the broken as much and more than to the whole and the sane. We hold the keys of life, my lass. Aye, you and I, the workers of the world, all grades and classes, we're the fighters, stripped clean and naked for the fight. The battle sings and calls, and we are at it underneath the smoke of Salford and our grimy clothes. It's there, the whistle of the sword, the clash and clang of the battle-axe; blood; wounds, and death and trumpets calling us to triumph and to thrones. It's humanity fighting for humanity in an everlasting fight on a field that has no bivouac, no camp, and no repose. That's life, my lass."

"You're a strange talker, Tubby," said Maggie.

"I am, and I know it. I'm proud of it, and all. It's all I am, and I'd rather have the voice of a trumpet than the bray of a jackass. Thou's a doer and I'm a talker, and they've both great places in the world. Life makes me drunk. It's marvellous. It's the great challenge. Aye, the force of life that we have here in Salford is a challenge, lass, for the hands of our renovation, and, I tell thee, I see the day when life on Irwell's banks shall be more wonderful, more majestic, and more radiant than the life of priests walking the the Temple of God at Jerusalem. God in the people, lass; and the People not one class, but all a Unity making and re-making all things nearer the similitude of perfection . . . Eh, lass, but I'm in form tonight."

"I'd think more of your ideas if they included a clean shirt once a fortnight," Maggie said, but repented and added: "Then does the world progress, Tubby?"

"No need to ask about the world," he said.

"Dost thou progress? That's all thou's asked or any one is asked."

"You're not altogether a fool," she said.

"I'm sixty and nigh spent. And that's too old to worry about a dirty shirt," he came back to her remark. "But," he went on with a flaming face and a gesture which filled the room, "But I hope in life and reason still."

"Well, Tubby," she said, "you've stuck to your last in Hobson's shop, and I see no reason in that for a man of your parts."

"I'm none ambitious, lass. Nay, I've taken a pride in standing still, in all ways but my tongue. And my talk's not for everybody's ears. It's none the sort they like. I take them down too much. I say my own grade's often wrong, and what I see is wrong I say is wrong. But thou's the other kind. Thou's practical. Thou'll take to thyself and Will the wealth of the world and make good use of it."

"That's my intention," she said dryly.

"Thy head's screwed on by a level hand and mine's a misfit. I was born to be a bishop and brought up a cobbler, but it's all one in the end, and I doubt that I'd have fitted the bench of bishops any better than I do my cobbler's bench. Eh, but I'm fond of talking, lass. It's like the drink to me. I cannot get enough of it. I talk yon lad to sleep most every night."

"He's good at listening," she said, wiping the copy off Will's slate and setting him a sum. "But he's progressing, anyhow."

Alice gets Promotion & Vickey gets Put On

But if the days of Maggie's short engagement were slipping by easily and profitably in Oldfield Road, it was more than could be said for the state of things in Chapel Street. Mr. Hobson had suffered, on that historic Monday morning, a shock to his complacency which only the entire day spent in the healing atmosphere of the Moonraker's was able to mitigate. But next day he took measures to cope with the situation. After all, the practical side of the matter was simple enough. As a father, Mr. Hobson was outraged, scorned, flouted, lacerated and appalled, but as the head of Hobson's boot shop, his course was clear. One woman was as good as another, and the punny responsibilities which he had fondly conferred upon Maggie could as easily be undertaken by either of her sisters. It did not matter which, but as Alice was the older, Alice should succeed the mutineer.

But the unaccountableness of women was such that he felt it desirable to approach the matter delicately. If Maggie, staid reliable Maggie, could throw her bonnet over the mill and take up with a shoe-hand after he had proved her out of her own mouth a permanent old maid, it was just possible that Alice was still dreaming of Albert Prosser.

"Alice," he said, coming into the shop, "this is a bad business. It shows what comes of Uppishness in women. Your sister's chosen to forget her duty to her family and her duty to me, and consequently I choose to forget your sister. Hence-forth she's dead to me, and I'll thank you not to name her. I abjure her and I wipe her out. She ceases to exist, and her office let another take. The question is, which other? And the answer to that question is another question. Are you fit?"

"Fit, father?"

"Aye, fit, my lass. A woman that's hankering after a husband is a woman unfit. She's lost control of herself. She's out of the bonds of reason. She's afflicted and unstrung, and she can't cast up accounts. She adds one to one and her sick fancy makes the total one, and I promote no woman to those books who's got a maggot in her mind and a man in her eye. I spoke some words of wisdom to you, Alice, and the question's this. Did they prevail, or are you hankering?"

"I'll do the books," said Alice.

"That's an evasion, lass. If love's still stirring in you, you'll take on no books of mine. If young men come in here when my back's turned and use my shop for the illicit purpose of corrupting and perverting my daughter - "

"He'll never come again."

"That's better, Alice."

"No, it's not," she said. "And I love him, father. And I'll go on loving him, but he'll not come again. Don't you see what Maggie's done for me?"

"I'm a bit at sea."

"Do you think a self-respecting man would look at us now? When Maggie's made Will Mossop our brother-in-law? That's what she's done. She's spoiled our chances, and I don't care if - if - " and she dissolved in tears.

The fact is, Albert Prosser *had* discontinued his morning call. Not, of course, because of Maggie and Will, of whom he knew nothing, but because of Maggie's feat of salesmanship. If half an hour's sweethearting was to cost him the price of a pair of boots, he decided it was too expensive. It was Maggie's presence in the shop, not her absence, which dammed the course of Albert's true but frugal love. He would not have welcomed Will Mossop as a family connection, but he would have ignored him quite pleasantly. He was playing truant simply because the burnt child fears the fire; but Alice, obsessed by the cataclysm of Maggie and Will, saw Will in everything, and Albert lost to her through him.

Her father contemplated her with satisfaction.

"Aye", he said. "That's the result of selfishness. You're suffering for the sins of your sister. She's guilty of disobedience to me, and she's put unseemly inclinations in front of her duty to her family. I quite agree with you, Alice, and I'll go so far as to say I'm sorry for you. But there's no doubt you're settled now for life as a single woman. You might find a man to accept you - nay, you did find one - but you'll never find a man to accept Will Mossop. He's a bar sinister. We're a disgraced family, but we'll hold our heads up, Alice, and I'll make you all the compensations in my power. I'll elevate you to the charge of the books. I appoint you head saleswoman, and if I happen to be called out of the shop for five minutes any time, the hands will take their orders from you. There now, my lass, cheer up, I can't do more than that, can I?"

Certainly he could hardly have used Alice's delusion about Albert to better purpose. And she did brighten up. Her promotion carried with it no material advantages, for you cannot increase a non-existent wage, but undoubtedly it is pleasant to be invested with authority; and honours, even though empty, are a sovereign balm for aching hearts. As to her capacity to stand in Maggie's vacant shoes, Alice had no more doubts that Hobson had. Maggie's methods had never been spectacular, and Alice imagined it was as easy to run the machine as Maggie had made it look.

Hobson departed to the Moonraker's very well content. There was good in everything, and, but for the nine days' wonder which he foresaw when Maggie's amazing marriage was published, the affair was positively turning to his advantage. The threat to Alice's virginity was disposed of, the lurking suspicion of restraint which Maggie's eye was apt to make him feel was now removed, he had a mouth the less to feed, a body the less to clothe, and as for replacing Will Mossop, that could wait a while. Since economy was in the air he would see if he could not dispense with a fourth boot-hand altogether, and let Tubby manage with three.

Alice installed herself at the receipt of custom in Maggie's place with an important air. Monday's takings were never large, but to Alice, who had to add them up, they loomed stupendous. She wrestled zestfully, a little puzzled by the varying total which the same column of figures was able to achieve, but hoping, if she tried long enough, to arrive twice at the same result. She was midway through the elusive sum for the fifth time when Vickey interrupted her.

Vickey was peevish. Owing to Alice's preoccupation in the shop, a double dose of the meaner household duties had fallen to Vickey's share. She had not only washed the breakfast pots, but wiped them. She had made the beds single-handed.

"I've had enough of the house," she said.

"You've not begun," said Alice. "You'll have to take it on altogether now, I'm busy here."

"You mind your own business, Alice Hobson, and I'll mind mine."

"I'm telling you what your business is. I can't sit here and cook as well."

"Cook!" said Vickey. "You don't expect me to cook?"

"I do," said Alice. "And I'm in charge. If I tell you to cook, you'll cook: so there. You'll go out and do the buying in. You'll arrange the dinners as well as cook them."

"I can't cook. You know that!"

"Then you'll learn."

Under the old regime, Alice had exercised her natural genius for cooking, and Maggie had organised the catering - no mean intellectual task where a gentleman of Mr. Hobson's capricious tastes was concerned. Vickey felt put upon.

"I can't help it, Vickey," said Alice, "Maggie's to blame. She's gone and the work's still here to be done. Father's put me in charge, and I've the shop to see to, and so you'll have to take on the house in the mornings and make your own arrangements there."

"I'll make my own arrangements," Vickey said, and went upstairs to put her hat on. She was a remarkable time doing it.

Usually the morning shopping, all of which could be done within a few yards of their own door, was accomplished in deshabille. A hat was superfluity. But Vickey dressed with care. She descended looking her best.

Alice was lost to time. Mathematics absorbed her, but she noticed Vickey's attire.

"My stars!" she said. "You have dressed up."

"I like to look dressed," said Vickey. "Give me four shillings for the dinner." And so went out to Chapel Street.

When Vickey said that she would make her own arrangements she intended that Mr. Frederick Beenstock should make them for her, and that in double quick time. If Maggie could hustle, Vickey would show that she could hustle too. The difference lay in the fact that Maggie did her own hustling whilst Vickey relied on Mr. Beenstock. Wherein she leant upon a broken reed.

As thus, Freddy Beenstock, as may have been gathered from a passing glimpse we took at him Peel Park, was a discreet young man. Vickey was perfection in his eyes, but Freddy had a father, whose business as a corn merchant he purposed to inherit, and that father was a Nonconformist and addicted to principles, whilst Vickey's father was a Churchman and addicted to drink.

There is, however, nothing in Nonconformist principles to prevent the Nonconformist from accepting a Churchman's cash, and though Freddy did not envisage the bargain he proposed quite so crudely as that, he counted upon receiving with the perfect Vickey a reasonable settlement from Hobson which, combined with Vickey's face, would overcome his father's scruples.

Money is always money, and nowhere more than in Lancashire. But a woman in a business office was a sensation in those days.

Vickey was aware of that, but she was still more aware of her face and its effect on the opposite sex.

Somehow it failed of its usual effectiveness with Mr Nathaniel Beenstock. From his desk in the corner he saw Vickey come into his office and rose to meet her at the counter. This was something too unexpected for an office-boy to meet.

"Is Mr. Beenstock in?" asked Vickey, very sure of herself.

"I am Mr. Beenstock, Madam," said Nathaniel, who had side-whiskers and a white tie.

"I - I meant Mr. Frederick Beenstock." There was less certainty now. Why *are* side-whiskers disconcerting?

"And who are you?" he asked.

Vickey made an effort. She smiled, and it was a winsome smile. She was prettily pathetic and should have melted a heart of stone.

"I should be so glad if you would let Mr. Frederick know that Miss Victoria Hobson is here," she said.

"And what is Miss Victoria Hobson's business with my son?" he said. Vickey blushed. He noted it. "This is a business establishment, and I have no intention of interrupting my son at his duties unless - "

At that moment it chanced that the duties of Mr. Beenstock's son brought him into the office.

"Vickey!" he gasped unguardedly.

"Indeed?" said Nathaniel. "You know this young lady?"

Freddy grasped the nettle boldly. He came to the counter, took Vickey's hand across it, and looked at his father.

"Vickey and I are going to be married, Father," he said.

"Dear me," said Mr. Beenstock, retiring from the counter and contemplating the picture, with his hands in his horizontal trouser-pockets and the blandest of smiles on his eupeptic face. "Dear me! And Miss Hobson is no doubt the daughter of Mr. Henry Hobson?"

"Yes," said Freddy.

"Of Chapel Street. Yes. A very sound business, I believe, Freddy. Mr. Hobson should do the handsome thing by his daughter."

It is thus that the Montagus and Capulets of Salford approach the marriage question, not by brawling in the street, fantastic potions and the tomb, but by a short cut to the heart of things. "And what did you want to see Freddy about my dear?"

"Oh, I just wanted a minute alone with him, please, Mr. Beenstock," faltered Vickey.

"Well, Frederick," the old gentleman beamed with benevolence," perhaps, in the circumstances, it could be allowed. Yes. Take your hat and don't be more than half an hour. Good morning, Victoria;" and Mr. Beenstock returned to his desk, there to occupy himself with a mass of figures designed to discover the amount of new capital to be introduced to his business by Mr. Henry Hobson in return for a junior partnership conferred on Mr. Hobson's son-in-law to be. Mr. Beenstock spent a pleasant half-hour. Something for nothing is an earthly Paradise, this time with the prospect of bleeding the unconscionable Hobson thrown in. No wonder Mr. Beenstock perspired with pleasure.

Vickey was delighted. She had conquered Mr. Nathaniel Beenstock, and the first tremors and doubts of the unexpected encounter were forgotten under the cares of his velvet-glove.

"I am so glad I came, Freddie," she said. "Your father's charming."

"Is he?" said Freddy, who was intimate with his father's iron hand and expected to feel its weight when he returned to the Office. "Why did you come for me, Vickey?"

She felt the disapproval in his voice. "Of course I should never have done such a thing if it hadn't been urgent, Fred. But as your father's been so nice, that doesn't matter now, does it?"

"Not now," said Fred, with mental reservations.

"No," said Vickey, as they turned into Peel Park, which at this hour in the morning was deserted, and found a seat. It was a dismal scene for a lovers' meeting, but the best they could do. They sat facing a forest of factory chimneys, which belched black smoke in defiance of the by-laws, and the Irwell ran suave and oily-black below.

Vickey saw it through rose-coloured glasses - the scene set for her triumph. She gurgled gladly and gave Fred's arm a little confidential squeeze. She thought him unresponsive, but, then, Fred did not know how near he was to happiness. She would tell him now, at once, and watch his face light up. He hadn't shaken off the office yet.

"Freddie," she said, "I came to tell you this. Let me

whisper in your ear. We're going to be married very soon!"

The light that never was on land or sea did not leap out of Freddy's eyes. Instead, he shuffled on their seat.

"I'm hoping for the best," he grudged.

"But, don't you understand? I've come to tell you that you and I - "

"Y-yes. I understand. But it's not just you and I. It's others and - "

"Yes." She interrupted. "It is others. It's Maggie, and Alice and Father." And so her tale came out, of Maggie and Will, of Alice's arrogance and the impossibility of Vickey's standing the new arrangements at the shop, and her confidence in Freddie to make all things right. "And," she added, "I know it was bold of me to come to see you at the office, but I simply had to come at once. And, of course, it turned out for the best. I think your father's a dear."

"I wonder if you heard him correctly," said Frederick.

"I'm sure he sounded very nice about it," Vickey said.

"Oh yes." Freddie gave it up. After all, his father had sounded very nice and how should poor Vickey understand? He faced his situation. The trouble was real enough, and he must do his best with Hobson. "All right," he said; "I'll come round to see your father today."

"Oh, but you mustn't do that," she said. "It's the last thing to do."

"No. It's the first."

"Do you mean because we'd be deceiving him if we were married behind his back? Because, as things are, I don't think that really matters, Freddie."

"It isn't that," he said. "But - " and he paused. How could he tell poor little Vickey the cold financial truth?

"Because Father's forbidden me to marry," she went on in her innocence. "He thinks everybody's after money."

"Money?" said Freddie, alert.

"Yes. Some of his nasty-minded friends told him people expect marriage settlements and he won't give any. Isn't it horrid, Freddie, to think of money in connection with a love like ours? As if we cared!"

Poor Freddie. "Vickey," he plunged," did you hear what my father said? That he expected Mr. Hobson would do the handsome thing? He meant exactly what your father's friends meant."

"Freddie!" she said.

"Well, it's the truth, and now you know it. Your father and mine aren't friends, but mine would consent at a price. Oh, I know it's beastly to have to tell you this, but there it is. I'll see your father tonight. I can but try Vickey!"

Vickey was weeping. So this - this was the result of her high enterprise.

"It's not good seeing Father," she wept, and Vickey was one of those rare miracles of women who weep prettily.

The Irwell attracted Fred's attention. It was said to be an easy death, and a very sure one. Its foulness poisoned you before you drowned.

"What can I do?" he said. "If I throw up my job it'll be years before we can marry. Can't you get round your father?"

"Not when it's money," she said. "You'll have to get round yours."

"I'll try," he said, as a matter of form. He knew it was hopeless.

"But till you've succeeded we can do nothing?"

"Nothing but love each other, Vickey."

"Yes, Freddy," she said. He put a consolatory arm around her waist. Gradually her sobs subsided. Silently, they surveyed the disconsolate landscape in a helpless communion of woe. A clock struck somewhere.

"I must get back to the office," he said.

"I'm supposed to be cooking," said she. Each contemplated the burden of the other. Each paid the tribute of a heavy sigh. Poor Romeo! Poor Juliet!

Smears, Blears & Erasions

Vickey ran back to Chapel Street with a tear-stained face, her Sunday hat awry and a tin of tongue in her hand. She arrived just ten minutes before Mr. Hobson returned from the Moonraker's. Alice had made no sales, but she had achieved the balancing of Monday's accounts about half an hour earlier, when she realised that Vickey was missing, and so far rose to the occasion as to peel potatoes behind the counter.

The meal awaiting Mr. Hobson on this first day of Maggie's absence consisted of cold tongue and insufficiently boiled potatoes!

Mr. Hobson did not see the potatoes, but his rosy Moonraker's face paled, and crimsoned again, more deeply crimson. There is a daunting solitude, a sense of concentrated inadequacy, about cold tinned meats.

"Is my house gone to rack and ruin in an hour?" he demanded.

"No," said the cook meekly.

"Then why is my dinner no dinner?"

"Say grace," interrupted Alice in a business-like manner. Mr. Hobson glared. He stared at Alice in amazement. She would rob him of his complaint? Then he remembered she had just been robbed of her young man and controlled his tongue, nobly. He muttered what the Scotch call "gude wordies," with his head down on his breast, but no one can guarantee the nature of his words, - they were badly pronounced. But he eyed the potatoes with clear eloquence. He ate one interestedly.

"Why is my stomach in jeopardy?" The girls could find no adequate answer to the terrible supplication. They said something unintelligible in their turn.

"Alice!"

"Yes, Father."

"I hope you have not been absent-minded this morning. I hope you have put such thoughts out of your mind.

"Yes," Alice was proud.

"Then why have I come home to this? Are you making a joke? Don't you joke about food; don't makes jokes about food, it's a form of wit I don't encourage." He eyed the table with wholehearted malevolence.

"I'm looking after the shop," explained Alice, with

dignity. Let every sister bear her share of the paternal wrath, she thought. "You don't expect me to fill Maggie's place and my own?"

"I left it to be divided amongst you." There was no leniency in Mr. Hobson; he had no food to soothe him. Alice glanced at the silent, self-effacing Vickey; it was her duty to confess at this point. And Vickey did confess, but not weakly, not foolishly, of the piteous meeting with Fred Beenstock. Wisely, she accused the Accuser.

"Alice made me cook," she admitted.

"She made you nowt of sort," shouted Mr. Hobson. "She put you in the place of cook, thou's none a made cook as yet my lass, not by no means."

"Nor likely to be." Since Father shouted Vickey would be defiant.

"Eh!"

"I have got all the other house-work to do. Do you expect two pairs of hands to do the work of three? There are beds to make if beds are to be comfortable; and floors to sweep if floors are to be clean. I was busy enough when Maggie was here, and I don't see how I can manage to cook the dinner over and above."

Mr. Hobson was bewildered. His daughters were past comprehension. He no sooner soothed the sorrows of one than the other had a grievance. He had expostulated with rare restraint about today's dinner, and behold he was flatly assured of a worse tomorrow. Further, he was accused of parsimony, of exacting the labour of three from the powers of two. Slave-driving, he supposed.

"Let me tell you, Vickey, my lass - "

"I know what you'll tell me," said Vickey delightfully at her ease; her quick wit had transformed an excuse for absence into a grievance and a possibility of further absences. "You'll tell me, Father - ". She ate a trifle of tongue with relish; it was a tasty tongue, so slight and nice as to be a refreshing change in this house of solid meals - "that you like to be economical, that girls who owe everything to you ought to be glad, pleased and eager, to give everything they have to you. It won't do, Dad, I've got other men to think of, I've got my looks to think of; I shan't catch a husband if I work till my face is haggard."

The audacity of the wench! She chaffed him, spoke easily of her own charms, and casually of a husband; she put her finger on his nicest notions, upset his frugal domestic weal with a smile. Where the devil did this new spirit come from? Girls were not like this when he was a boy; no, they were brought up differently when he was young. It was vain to roar, to shout, to threaten; you might as well threaten a lovely landscape as Vickey when she was in her perverse mood. He resorted to sarcasm, heavy pungent sarcasm.

"I had better hire a servant-girl," he hazarded, thinking the grotesque impossibility would silence the grumblers.

"No," Alice spoke firmly, and Mr. Hobson's face cleared prematurely. Alice had fallen in with Vickey's mood; she had accusations to make also, preparatory self-defence for the day when the shop books were inspected. "You had better let me hire the girl."

Mr. Hobson choked thunderously; a servant in his Salford household! Cock and hens! What were the daughters of men coming to?

"You would be taken in by the first draggle-tail that came along," went on Alice, leisurely. "And we must have a clean, capable girl. The work here to get through will take up all the time of any able-bodied woman, so we must have a very good girl."

Mr. Hobson jumped up; he could endure it no longer. His sarcasm had been taken as a genuine offer; such a dullness of brain in females made it dangerous for a man to be witty.

"Let me tell you, my ladies - " He choked. "What have you got for pudding?"

"Cheese," answered Vickey with real wit.

Mr. Hobson departed to the tune of a roar and a bang.

The young ladies smiled at one another and did justice to the tongue together.

"Shall we get one?" asked Vickey.

"No," said Alice, contentedly. "I'd rather keep a handy excuse than a servant any day."

"We've got out of this," Vickey indicated the cold feast, "very well."

Alice rose, and looked into the shop through the pane in the door. She saw her father look at the sales book. She shuddered; she was ashamed of the smears and blears, the erasions, the rubbings and scrubbings on every page at every total. She saw her father run his finger up the page as if checking a column. Tubby Wadlow stood looking on (he looked after the shop during the dinner hour now that the staff was reduced). He caught her anxious eye, and winked cheeringly back at her.

Mr. Hobson cast the book from him; hurled it to the far end of the shop. Undoubtedly that column was incorrectly added. But how had Alice achieved a balance? He paused irresolutely, Alice waited for the parlour door to open on her, and an explanation to be demanded of the balance, which she had arrived at by "trying," that is to say, altering a figure here and there without guile, and without reference to the origin of the figures. The method of the female balance seemed to strike Mr. Hobson miraculously. He turned on his heel, grabbed his hat from the counter, and vanished from the shop.

Alice saw him to the Moonraker's with a wonderful exactitude of imagination.

CHAPTER NINE

The Butting Ram Incident

The times were out of joint, troublous, stormy, irritating, full of perversity, disobedience, incompetence, bad cooking, weak saleswomanship and the illimitable vistas of feminine incorrigibility.

Mr Hobson got our of bed on Sunday morning in an unusual state of mind. he was clear-headed. Usually he was very dull indeed on Sundays. But accumulated anger dispelled all the mists. He had reached the stage where heroes suffer in silence. He found that cursing does not create cook, nor the gesticulation of man make a mathematician out of a daughter, nor the extremest resources of a father shake the matrimonial designs of a maiden with the capital equal to her intentions.

For a month the mind and the body of Henry Horatio had been disgruntled. The public proclamation in church of Maggie's approaching marriage gave the Moonrakers' opportunity to exercise their subtle and original wits on Will Mossop in Mr. Hobson's presence. He was no longer invulnerable. Maggie's was the offence, but his the head at which their keen-barbed shafts were launched. Will Mossop, the grandson of a bit of luck, the master fool of all the fools, the narrowest escape human nature ever had (in the opinion of Joe Tudsbuy) from reversion to its original type - this was his son-in-law to be.

And the envelope which awaited Mr. Hobson's descent to the breakfast table nauseated the already queasy stomach. The trollop dared to write to him! His younger daughters had examined the envelope inquisitively, he examined its contents miserably, but it was Sunday, and he put a Christian continence upon his fluent tongue. He merely informed Alice that he was ill, that he would not be at church, nor yet at home for dinner, whatever makeshift collation they had provided, that he would not be in to tea, and that unless the notions of females changed radically for the better he might very likely never return at all.

The two young ladies, who nursed secret sorrow even at breakfast, showed little sympathy. They were callously unmoved when Mr. Hobson stated that his corpse would be found in the Irwell mud one of these days. They were aware of the value their father set on his life. A dead man neither eats nor drinks nor talks nor sleeps, and they could imagine no evil sufficiently great to drive Mr. Hobson into voluntary renunciation of these functions of the body. They made good breakfasts.

The churchwarden came out of his house in full external splendour of churchwardens. What the internal effulgence of churchwardens may be is totally a matter of luck, but there was nothing splendied inside Mr. Hobson this morning. He had no zest for himself. He suffered depression. He held terrific animosities. He must blaspheme or burst. He desired to do both. For him, to walk any considerable distance implied both, involved both.

He had no poetic delusions about walking. He was not in search of solitude, or rusticity, or the visible works of God; but he felt that streets were too confined to hold his anger, and that by doing outrage on himself might find inspiration to cope with the outrageous conduct of his daughters. He went out to indulge his rage in open spaces where there was room for a man to let himself go, to walk until he had worked himself up into a state of mind equal to and greater than their state of mind. He was bent of taking measures, violently successful measures. There was a horrible savagery in the ruthless beat of his feet on the pavement, the pavement that leads to Agecroft Bridge. He followed his route mechanically, he desired a vast open space to swear in luridly, a mountainous high place from which to curse pigmies, male and female pigmies, with intense cordiality.

"I have stood hearing the banns called twice, 'cause or just impediment,' and I'd to sit and hold my tongue while the parson beamed and called their names as if he liked it. But I'll impediment Maggie Hobson. I'm none clear yet, but I'll impede her some road," and the letter that had wrought the painful mischief came out of the churchwarden's pocket.

"Dear Father," muttered Mr. Hobson savagely. "Aye," he whispered to himself sentimentally. "I was 'dear father' whiles I could spank her. But the sincerity has gone out of the words since Maggie grew independent. Aye, females intelligent and unintelligent, both sorts are preposterous." He read again.

"Will and I are to be married tomorrow at a quarter to twelve at St. Philip's." A paternal groan, an uncontrollable sob, of anger, desperation and baffled rage, escaped him. Maggie was so diabolically sure of herself. "I expect to see you and the girls there, and - "

Mr. Hobson studied the houses on the roadside blindly. Choking wrath stifled his eyes, his mouth and ears. He was a smothered volcano, and smothered volcanoes are not inclined to go to weddings. "And to supper at the above address in the evening."

The magic of this line of Maggie's letter preserved Mr. Hobson from explosion. He became pure wrath, a simple opalescent body of wholesome fury. He regretted nothing, he chafed at nothing. He was happily, heatedly himself. He studied the address with a clear eye.

WILLIAM MOSSOP
Practical Boot and Clog Maker,
39A Oldfield Road,
SALFORD

He realised the cunning of the address, the beautiful direct-ness of Maggie's ideas. All were fish that came to her net and she dropped her net in the right spot. But he was not out to admire his daughter's brain: the admirable in her was fuel to his fire. Briefly he said to himself as he crossed the river and climbed towards the fields of Prestwich: "I'll poison their supper for them."

He repeated the statement to himself several times. The hill was steep, and he panted heavily, but rejoiced in the notion. He did not wish the death of the bridal party on their bridal night, but he would be grateful, heartily grateful if they were put in two boxes and buried under the ground. As long as they were forgotten and out of sight and mind till he himself rode into Heaven on a triumphant cloud - that was all he desire.

Mr. Hobson discovered that walking was not good for him, despite the energy of his temper. Walking was an evil, a mechanical stretching of legs till one arrived at some place and a mechanical stretching of legs till one got back again and ceased to stretch one's legs. He realised that he was out for the day by himself and that it was no use turning back, for the dinner reorganized by two females for their own consumption would certainly make himm ill to look at, he did not want to turn back. He no longer wanted to poison the bridal pair, but he wanted to discover how to prevent their wedding, to pulverise Will Mossop and destroy Maggie, to restore him to his eighteen shillings a week servitude, and her to her wageless servitude. They were objectionable asses, but useful asses.

It seemed to him to be necesary to walk, but resented walking. He had no one to lash with his tongue and this leg-stretching was a thankless occupation. He struck across country for Besses-o'-th'-Barn, where the bands come from. Mr. Hobson cared little for the music of the band. It was the public-house frequented by the band that he cared for.

He stood awhile upon the track. His eye ranged backwards over his tormented path and located the house of Hobson. He did not curse his children. He remembered still the old-fashioned ways of the baby Maggie, the shy impetuosity of Alice, and the gay wheedling of infantile Vickey. His was a great household then, a noble middle-class house without peer in the width of the world. But age and uppishness play the devil with the temper no less than with the faces of females. And he cursed the actions of his grown-up daughters, he rolled out the long indictment.

140 *Hobson's Choice*

WALKING TO BESSES-O-TH' BARN.

Pride, vain glory, and hypocrisy, malice and all uncharitableness: these were the least of their sins. He wasted a great deal of breath, but he rose to eloquence - and eloquence restored him. His nose set towards the inn, his complacent paternity returned. Always after fluency, he understood how easily he could overcome the devil and his own daughters.

He entered the front door of the Butting Ram and put his head inside the bar. He withdrew it hastily. The bar contained a class of people who, he was certain, used profane language for no reason whatever, who drank more down their waistcoats than was good for their waistcoats, and whose criticisms of a churchwarden's external spendour would not stop words. He knew these Lancashire colliers. Their idea of a comic entertainment suited to the day would be: firstly, to kick his top hat into shreds; and secondly, to make a football of his frock-coat. Mr. Hobsob was no snob, but he was frugal, and he had objections to his attire being butchered to make a collier's holiday.

He entered the parlour, where sat a solitary man smoking an unlighted pipe and drinking out of an empty pot. But this man was quite respectable. He was, in fact, a decayed coachman, imported from London by a merchant prince of high ambitions, and now left derelict through his employer's death, a perfect blend of decay and dignity. He wished Mr. Hobson good-morning in the high pipe of a London West End mews, thereby earning Mr. Hobson's complete contempt. To speak with the tongue of Park Lane in the neighbourhood of Salford is to make yourself more unpopular than a sewage rat.

Mr. Hobson shouted. The incorruptible landlord appeared, exchanged landlordly remarks with Mr. Hobson and took an order for a quart and bread-and-cheese.

The decayed coachman looked at Mr. Hobson with dignified expectancy. Mr. Hobson saw the look and, remembering the accent, ignored its appeal.

"I'll go back to London termorrer, demmit," asserted the cockney.

Mr. Hobson grunted.

"Hi've been in this Gawd-foresaken Lancashire twenty years. Filthiest place in creation is this Lancashire. No association for a gent like myself obteenable. Demmed lonely. The men are low-mannered brutes, and the women, begad, they speak a langwidge no fair creature should if she desires the regard of a gentleman."

Mr. Hobson made no remark. The landlord entered with his order. He was requested to bring another quart in five minutes.

"And cheese?" he asked, pointing to the twin slabs.

"Nay, lad," quoth Mr. Hobson. "This is broad enough foundation to build my liquor on."

The landlord departed. Mr. Hobson drank and eyed the eyeing coachman malevolently.

"I'm a Lancashire man," he said.

The uninvited one eyed the vanishing quart.

"I judged you were Lancashire."

"Are you sorry for me?" demanded Mr. Hobson truculently.

"Demmit! Hi'm sorry for the animals wot 'ave to live in this Gawd-foresaken desert."

"Aye, I'm sorry for thee." Mr. Hobson classed his antagonist with the animals and chuckled at his score. Silence, broken only by the long draught and the stout mastication of Mr. Hobson, descended on the bar-parlour of the Butting Ram.

The landlord reappeared with nice calculation. He was desired to bring a third quart in a quarter of an hour and departed, cheerfully landlordish. Mr. Hobson raised the second quart to his lips, but, in the act of drinking, he glanced over the top of the mug. He saw the curl of contempt on the lip of the aristocrat from London, and rose suddenly, crossed the parlour floor and pulled the aristocratic nose vigorously and very effectively. With a squeal of rage, the Londoner sprang to his feet, grasped Mr. Hobson's nose and danced as he pulled. Mr. Hobson got a second grip on the nose of the face he detested and tugged with wild energy and wilder resentment. There arose yells and kickings, breakings and crackings. Tables rolled over, Mr. Hobson's full quart and the coachman's empty half-pint fell; the spittoons side-tracked and the sawdust flew whilst the splended churchwarden and the decayed but dignified coachman pulled each other's noses. They used both hands in the nasal tug-of-war, but weight was telling and the coachman changed his tactics. They plumped for fisticuffs and battered each other with an intensity of zeal remarkable in two such comparative strangers. It was loose fighting, but heartily murderous. They grew tired of battering and buffeting. They closed in a deadly embrace, and the coachman endeavoured to squeeze the breath out of Mr. Hobson by clasping his neck, while Mr. Hobson endeavoured to squeeze the breath out of the coachman by clasping his middle. They rolled on the floor, but Mr. Hobson, contrary to the laws of nature, fell on top of the coachman. He allowed the aristocrat to hang on to his neck while he freed his own legs and arms. Then he most dexterously contrived to obtain a seat on the stomach of his adversary. It was all up with the man who despised Lancashire. Mr. Hobson weighed twenty stone, solid concentrated stuff. He pinned the coachman's wrists and settled down for a prolonged sojourn on the stomach.

Now that the victor was too content to triumph audibly, and the vanquished too heavily handicapped to expostulate, and the calm of the parlour suggested that the murder was over, the landlord appeared full of threats and summonses.

With magnificent self-possession Mr. Hobson desired the landlord to bring a fresh quart and to hold it to his lips till the contents disappeared. Further, if the landlord wanted to be kicked as far as the middle of next week he had only to make himself a trifle more objectionable in Mr. Hobson's opinion.

Vickey & Freddie are Caught

It drew towards dusk as Mr. Hobson got outside the front door of the Butting Ram, that early hour of dusk when the shadows are kind and the spirit of earth most gentle to the children of her womb. But this child of earth was mightily indifferent to her consolations. He required none. He had patronised the landlord all the afternoon, since the saddened driver of carriages had been ejected with the well-learnt lesson that it is wise to keep criticisms of Lancashire for home consumption only. He had filled himself with the contents of many quart jugs and flattered himself more fully than was good for him.

"Eh!" he declared. "But I feel better for that dust-up."

And he was better. Inspiration had followed exercise and he broke away for Kersal Moor with great, strong strides, bland, confident and free. He had originated a great scheme with all the greatness of simplicity. He would visit 39A Oldfield Road tomorrow morning, he would disguise his feelings and show a content and generous disposition. Then he would lure Will Mossop out on the pretext of selecting a wedding-present for Maggie. He would next invite the bridegroom into the Moonraker's, overpower him with the aid of Sam Minns and Jim Heeler and lock him up in the 'drunks' room" - the shuttered cell where Sam stowed brawlers till the police came. Mr. Hobson thought of his scheme and saw that it was good. He crowed, he marched on singing jovially, making his way by Kersal Moor to concert measures with Sam Minns for the abduction of Will Mossop.

The young moon came up and hung over the black frontage of the distant Crescent. Mr. Hobson was grateful. He blessed the moon in genial condescension. He complimented the Creator. But, little by little, he ceased to sing and to praise God. Walking grew mechanical as the liquor grew less potent. He no longer flew on wings. His feet grew leaden and his admirable boots too small for their new bulk. He deplored the necessity for dragging them about with him wherever he went. The flying pace of five miles per hour dropped to the walking pace of two miles per hour. He loitered in the moonlight and gazed sentimentally across the moorland breaking gently to the circumference of the towns: Kersal, Broughton, Salford, Pendleton.

Their lights appeared, dulled through the faint mist which lingers always on this upland, but not dulled in the appeal they made to Hobson's heart. Something terribly genuine, mercilessly soft, compelling, mastering, arose in him: it was the feeling for his own city.

"Eh!" he muttered, stricken almost to tears. "I know thou's ugly, but I'm fond of thee. There's summat wonderful about Lancashire other places haven't got. Same as my wife had. She had strange notions and awkward ways, and so has Lancashire; but women and places lay a stronger hand on your heart for having such perverse habits and notions. Nobody will ever build a city like ours again, and no race will ever put such people in the streets of a city like ours again. There's ugly mugs in Lancashire, and rum women and rummer men. We're a tough lot, but we're wholesome. It's a gradely place to live in if you're tough and wholesome; and I'm glad I leathered that London coachman. He laughed at Lancashire. He from London, and I've never met a Londoner yet with sense enough to give away to a cocksparrow. London!" Mr. Hobson regarded the struggling lights of his native town. "London is not like us. It's a poor place after Salford."

Having praised the place of his birth as a patriot should, Mr. Hobson considered his whereabouts. He sighed. It was still far to the Moonraker's and the cheerful conversation of Sam Minns on locking up bridegrooms. By now loverly couples were wandering out from the streets, seeking the sweets of love in the solitude. They took little note of Mr. Hobson, but his eye dwelt on them with melancholy benevolence. He pardoned the frank embrace of certain blurs upon the ground. He knew that love was sweetest when the clasp was closest. Here had he brought his wife when love was young, but always, and unlike the truants he now saw, after church. Still for him, the elderly burgess, the restrained ardours of the young sweetheart lived and persisted in his memory.

He halted suddenly, jogged from his reminiscent mood by an astounding sight. A lenient eye on love in general on

Kersal Moor was one thing, this was another. In his mellow reverie he mechanically and all unsuspiciously scanned the passing couples. He stopped. He made noises in his throat and stamped his feet. The couple halted too: they had to halt for Mr. Hobson raised his stick in a manner that threatened smashed noses.

"Oh!" gasped Vickey, clinging to her swain.

"What is it?" he inquired, not yet awake from dreams.

"I'll show you what it is, my lad," said Mr. Hobson, seizing Mr. Frederick Beenstock by the ear. "It's trouble for you."

Freddie didn't think so. He spoke quite coldly and clearly. "If you don't leave go of my ear." he stated, "you will lose your front teeth, Mr. Hobson," and his tone was such that Mr. Hobson believed him.

He let go of the young man's ear and turned on Vickey instead with full confidence and no female could or should baffle his punitive intentions. No sooner had he mentally settled Maggie's hash than the spectre of a daughterly disobedience confronted him again in the shape of Vickey. But he could deal with Vickey in his stride.

"Vickey," he said, "I'll none enlarge here on the enormity of your conduct and the immodesty of this place and the advantage that's taken of my absence. I'll keep my remarks for your private ear and I'll none waste words here. I've one word now. It's home. Home," he repeated, taking her arm. "And as for you, my lad, you've the Beenstock eye and the Beenstock nose and I'll take trouble in the morning to address a few remarks at the place you got them from. Aye, I'll call on Mr. Nathaniel Beenstock in the morning."

Freddie was suddenly unwell. He could face Hobson, but the thought of his father was too much for him. Hobson perceived it. His grip tightened on Vickey's arm. He swelled with reassurance and it hurt him badly when Vickey twisted from his grasp and said -

"I shan't. I shan't go home."

She had endured too much in the weks since Maggie left the shop. Tonight's experience filled up the measure of endurance. She scarcely knew what she did, but she broke from her father's grip and cried out her defiance, her virgin right to liberty.

Mr. Hobson stood stock still and his inside turned to water. He was voiceless, breathless, witless, overtaken by the last enormity of all. Vickey, the daughter he had cherished above all his daughters, she, too, defied him, frankly, nakedly, and unashamedly. Freddie moved to his lady's side. She fired him and he did the gallant thing. He challenged poverty and disownment by his parent. he knew it, he counted his loss and he supported Vickey. Immediately he rose to greater manhood and the future was to profit him.

They seemed a resolute pair to Mr. Hobson. They pleased his paternal eye, but they crucified his paternal heart.

"You mean," he said hoarsely, "you disobey? You will go on walking and hugging on Kersal Moor when I bid you to come home?"

Vickey nodded. She could not speak, but she was resolute. He looked at Fred. Fred showed respectful defiance, but unmistakable defiance.

Mr. Hobson did the only thing. Without another word he turned and left them. He thought his heart was broken, but he found the Moonraker's parlour without experiencing any indications of premature death. He sat there in a great silence, forgetful of the plan against Will Mossop's liberty which he was come to mature, consuming vast quantities of Sam Minns's best. Occasionally he murmured "daughters," and "Vickey, my Vickey." The company was sympathetic. They left him alone with his grief and their loyal fellowship was grateful to his troubled soul. He made much use of alcohol, and the weight of sorrow was lifted from him.

And, after all, Vickey went home, though the night was young, and sweethearting but begun. Not out of weakness did she repent of her defiance, but from that pure unsearchable instinct which requires the child to defy the parent and to repent the defiance. She had a gentle heart beneath the little affectations of her years, and Freddie grudged the loss of kisses for that night, but saw that Vickey Hobson was even better than his dreams of her. And he had dreamed she was a great many things.

Clog Dancing on Sunday

If it is respectable for a churchwarden to come out of a public-house at eleven o'clock on a Sunday evening, as near to insobriety as sobriety will allow, then Mr. Hobson was respectable. In the abstract and in appearance Mr. Hobson was a churchwarden of churchwardens, rigid, unwinking, unbending; in reality and in practice he was a latitudinarian. He would have deceived the incurious eye of his vicar, but would have made a sad mess of Melchizedek, if he had been questioned regarding the parentage of Abraham as he left the Moonraker's. As for "Shibboleth" he would have been wary enough to raise a side-issue.

He was a redoubtable liquor-reservoir and liked himself very well. Instead of haunting pictures of rebellious daughters, a pleasing vacancy filled his mind. Pure instinct made him watch the kerb with one eye and the next lamp-post with the other. He felt that lamp-posts had increased in Salford. There was a magnificent conglomeration of lamp-posts about his path, even after he had allowed, in a spirit of honest candour, for the exaggerative imagination of his state. The Lighting Committee of the Council were decidedly too zealous.

Steadily, with scarcely a perceptible sway, the burgess travelled homewards. His eye was glassy, virtuous, rebuking. He was enormously content with himself, only he knew, with his wondrous perception of the rightness of things, that a churchwarden should find his own door handle without fumbling on a Sunday. He came to a quiet by-street and was highly pleased when he stepped into the roadway with no more than a slight lurch and relieved his eyes of their steadfast occupation with the lamp-posts. There was room to roam in the road.

Suddenly, there came steps, quick steps, tapping,

dancing clogs, rhythmical and regular. Mr. Hobson stiffened himself. He listened with profound attention to the noise of clogs coming nearer to him along the solitary by-street. It occurred to him that this was wrong. It was the sound of dancing, clog dancing, and on Sunday! And, as Mr. Hobson realised, very capable clog-dancing, too. He could discern the form of the dancer dimly and more clearly as the moments passed. It reminded him of a gnat dancing over a light. It was great dancing.

And now the performer danced within ten yards of him, halted and exhibited his foot-play to the spectator. It was Mum Ned, the Salford champion. No doubt he was out practising for some dancing competition while people were out of the way, and nobody in Salford complained if they were wakened by the noise of Ned's clogs. He was worth hearing, and as for broken sleep, a champion is a champion, and how was Ned to uphold the honour of Salford in competitions if he didn't practise?

Mr. Hobson seemed to interest Mum Ned. He gave him a private exhibition on the side-walk. Mr. Hobson frowned, struck his stick on the ground and opened his mouth.

"Tha knows Sunny," he said severly.

Mum Ned sweated and tapped.

"Sunny," repeated Mr. Hobson. "I shall call police," he communicated with awful dignity.

Ned kept beautiful time. His eyes were bright, his face was white and he paid no regard to the Sabbatarian.

"Ish nor 'speshable." said Mr. Hobson angrily, examining Mum Ned like an incensed magistrate. He eyed him up and he eyed him down, and as soon as his eyes fell on the twinkling feet of the dancer he was entangled, fascinated. Never were fairest lady's pretty feet more witching to a lover's eyes than this clog-dancer's feet to Mr Hobson's. They ensnared his imagination, complicated his morals, lured him into a morass of perplexity.

The feet were so nimble, so clever, so vital. They hammered out life and liveliness. They were the one sign of life about Mum Ned: they were Mum Ned. Herein broke out the soul of Lancashire, its frustrate desires, its vigour, elasticity, craft, humour, daring, joy, its challenge to all the Graces. Where but in Lancashire would men attempt to dance in heavy, rigid, wooden-soled clogs, deliberately handicapping grace and, in spite of the self-imposed handicap, achieving it? The Morris Dance survives in Lancashire, a real traditional survival, not an anaemic revival fostered in schools and fanned to languid life by the patronage of folk-lore enthusiasts; but for the stronger growth, the dance which expresses for the people whom one might misjudge the least joyous of Englishmen, the clog-dance of Lancashire embodies still the great qualities of the English spirit, the high romance, the gallant chivalry, the far adventure, the colour and the gaiety of the English man and the English countryside.

The gladness of the dance, the one real dance of his county, laid hold of Mr. Hobson.

"Eh!" he cried, blundering on to the pavement. "Lemme do it, too." He hopped wildly, he lurched fantastically, but he meant well. He had forgotten all about Sunday and Sunday garments. He cared for nobody's opinion. He was bewitched by the glorious intensity of his desire to outshine Mum Ned. He found his legs and feet intricate, but he tried to fall into step with his silent exemplar.

Suddenly the magician slipped off, side-dancing swiftly with feet like leaves that patter in the wind. Mr. Hobson stumbled after him, fascinated. Mum Newd waited till the pupil came up and then, like an elusive Will o' the Wisp, darted on again, unsmiling, busy, grimly busy, with Mr. Hobson in pursuit, like a little tug with a huge clumsy cargo-boat. Through narrow streets and wider streets, up back-lanes, side-alleys, courts, pathways to respectable streets and immodest streets, clean streets (a few), dirty streets (these the majority), passed public buildings and private buildings, good men's houses, bad women's houses, doctors houses, doss houses, spinsters' houses, and sluts' houses, workhouses and out-o'-work houses - Salford was a maze and a haze to Mr. Hobson. Ned danced delirious fantastic dreams, he was a lure, a graal, a golden fleece, a heart's desire, and Mr. Hobson followed him, doggedly, tenaciously. He sought after the clog-dancer though weariness unmanned him and he wept, sobbing profanity, though hope deffered made his heart sick and his head was a cannon-ball, and his mind was too slow and his eyes too dull to notice the carelessly open cellar-flap which the dance-immersed magician avoided neatly. The pursuit ended abruptly. The pursuer disappeared.

Mr. Hobson alighted softly. He was immensely gratified. Deliverance had come from all his troubles, release from the mirage of Mum Ned, the end of brain-fag, feet-fag, tongue-fag. His mind was clear. Here was a downy couch and here himself, fit for a downy couch, sleepy as sleep itself. He closed his eyes.

Mum Ned returned when he noticed the loss of his follower. He peered into the dark abyss. A happy snore saluted him and he danced a lullaby.

Chapter Ten

Seth Finds A Lodger

As the reluctant light of a Salford dawn filled Cross Lane on the morning of Maggie Hobson's wedding day, Seth Newbigging began his duties by unlocking the door of Beenstock's corn warehouse. Having performed that function with exemplary punctuality designed to impress bed-loving porters, Seth rested from his labours. There was time enough for energy when his efforts could be observed by his employer. Labour unseen was labour unrecognised, and Seth was not the man to waste his strength on fruitless toil. He knew of a divan in the cellar where elderly limbs could recuperate after the strain of getting up and carrying their owner so virtuously to work and anticipated a pleasant hour before Mr. Beenstock would arrive.

Seth found his couch in occupation. Mr. Hobson slept in his unregistered hotel as soundly as any bewitched princess in her enchanted castle. The fairy prince approached with foot itching to kick the interloper, but Mr. Hobson's appearance gave him pause. These clothes, that silk hat, did not denote a tramp. Seth changed his mind and let his itching foot descend to mother earth. He scratched his head, which caused his thoughts to turn from the effect to the cause. He raised his eyes and saw that the cellar flap, which it was his duty to fasten, was wide open. It became a matter of urgency with Seth Newbigging to expel the trespasser before the arrival of Mr. Beenstock.

Had Seth been large and Mr. Hobson small, the problem would have been easy, but the reverse was true. Had Mr. Hobson been poor, his clothes an outcast's, again the solution would have been obvious. A bucket of cold water would have met the case. But Mr. Hobson was plainly a man of means. He had a gold watch-chain. Seth considered that chain, but decided that his position was already precarious enough.

He prodded Mr. Hobson, gently at first. There was no response. He doubled the dose. The patient merely snored the louder, so loudly, in fact that Seth feared the porters upstairs would hear the noise and come to confound him. He refrained from prodding. It was a dangerous pastime. He preferrred to watch and pray.

A pile of empty flour-bags in a cellar is undeniably less comfortable than a feather bed garnished with blankets, but Hobson slept on, and that, too, although the dawn was very cold. In other places other bodies felt the cold. Little sisters Peg and Meg snuggled up closer to one another in bed, each thinking how much warmer the other was than herself, and how nice it was to have a sister who was as good as a warming-pan; determined wives hauled back their proper share of the bed-clothes from unfeeling, snoring husbands, acquisitive even in sleep; young men in lodgings stirred uneasily and rolled up tighter as if to squeeze more heat out of the cheap blankets.

But Mr. Hobson stirred not, neither did he feel the cold. He was self-heating. And the clock went round.

The worst of watching and praying, considered as a practical policy, is that you never know what is going on behind your back whilst you are doing it. What went on behind Seth Newbigging's back was that Freddy Beenstock arrived at the office and, wanting Seth, came to look for him. And, though Seth did not suspect it, Freddy knew enough of Seth's habits to come straight to the right place.

"I want you, Seth," he called from the stairs, but stopped as he turned, arrested by the sight of Mr. Hobson on the sacks, and Seth like a heathen worshipper in contemplation of the monstrous form. "What's this?" he said, and came into the cellar. "Good Lord! It's Mr. Hobson."

"I don't know what it is," said Seth, "but it spells

trouble for me if the master hears about it. What shall we do, Mr. Fred?" Seth had sound instincts, and saw in Fred a fellow-conspirator.

"Is he asleep?" asked Freddie stupidly.

Mr. Hobson's snores left no room for doubt, but Seth made assurance doubly sure. He prodded the unconscious ribs again.

"Yes, he's asleep," said Seth; "and I reckon from the way you came out with his name that this here gentleman's a friend of yours. Well, you know, young fellow, my lad" - Fred's palpable distress gave Seth self-confidence; he grew familiar in language; his thumbs were in his arm-pits; he, the delin-quent, the cause of the accident, posed boldly as accuser - "we can't have your friends sleeping here, and if you want to know what I think, Mr. Fred, your friend's drunk and I'm going for a bucket of water."

"No, don't do that," said Fred.

"Well, I'll fetch the master, then, and he can do as he likes."

"No, no," Fred positively pleaded.

"Then what am I to do?" Seth hectored. "You tell me, and I'll do it. I'm here to do as I'm told."

"Do nothing. Don't tell my father, whatever you do." Fred had an awful vision of Mr. Beenstock's benevolent eyes gazing at his fallen enemy. Hobson would get short shrift from him, and Fred had optimistic dreams of a grateful, settlement-providing Hobson, rescued by him from the perils of Beenstockery. "Father never comes down here. Just keep about and let me know quietly when Mr. Hobson wakes."

"It'll cost you a bit," said Seth.

Fred gave him half-a-crown. Virtue is its own reward, but Seth preferred cash down.

"All right," he said, "I'll keep an eye on him." And, lest any one else should do the same, he covered Mr. Hobson tenderly with a couple of bags. The sleeper snored affably. "As peaceful as a child," said Seth.

Frederick Beenstock performed his morning duties with an absent mind. He discovered himself singularly fertile in the invention of excuses to leave the office in order to inspect the sleeper in the cellar. To his amazement, no one remarked his restlessness. He saw detection in every eye, and knew guilt was written on his face for all who ran to read; but nobody commented on his blushes, none called him to account. Astonishing indifference of a hard-worked office staff to the apprehensive agonies of self-conscious youth! And eleven o'clock arrived. The seconds were minutes and the minutes hours, but still the hour of his release miraculously came at last, and his father had seen nothing unusual in all the eternity. It was incredible, but the office dinner hour (in practice an hour and a half) had come and he was free to act, or at least, if not to act, to take his troubles where he could rely on good advice.

He took them to Maggie. One last inspection of the placid sleeper, and he fled. The sight of Mr. Hobson lent wings to Freddy's feet, for Hobson had stirred and the crisis might now be at hand. But Hobson had no intentions of precipitating it. Some half-hour earlier, he opened his eyes just enough to let a glimmering of light into them. He believed in taking shocks gradually. To see daylight abruptly and thoroughly is bad for the breakfast appetite. He lay awhile, prone on his back, taking stock of his surroundings. They seemed his usual surroundings at his waking hour. He might have slept in cellars regularly for all the difference he noticed this morning.

"Eh" But I am comfortable, proper comfortable. I like comfort. Comfort is good for me," he murmured in a lazy haze of succulent happiness, happiness not to be lightly forsaken by a man who knows what is good for him. Still only half present in mind, his eye took in the overhead grid. "But my ceiling has not had an easy night of it," he declared; "all the plaster has fallen down on me, and I've been sheltered from the adversity of the elements by nowt but laths. I'm surprised at Maggie. My mother would have done better. She'd have had the plasterer at work before this. But it's quiet in the house and Maggie 'ull be out after him now. I'll none disturb myself till he comes.

With which confused thinking of his dead mother and his transplanted daughter, Hobson settled himself amongst the sacks and slept again the sleep of innocence.

Freddy, post-haste, arrived at Oldfield Road. "She'll none rule me," he had said of Maggie, yet in his trouble and his hope it was to Maggie and not to Vickey that he bore his tale. And no Christian ever felt his pack grow lighter more certainly than did Freddy Beenstock as he turned the corner of Liverpool Street and reached William Mossop's shop. But alas for human hopes! The tribulations of Frederick were not yet over. On the closed door of the shop he read the astounding words, "Business suspended for the day."

Help Please Maggie

Maggie listened to Fred's despairing knocks with serene indifference. "If that's Will," she thought, "he's early and he can wait. If it's customers and they can't read, it's their look out, not mine." This was Maggie's day for getting married, and consequently not her day for worrying about the shop. With her usual thoroughness, she had pinned her notice on the door when she got up, and banished shop cares from her mind. For a month she had concentrated on the shop, turning from it only to direct Will's studies at Tubby Wadlow's, but today was set apart for domesticity.

Having written to tell Hobson she expected him and the girls to supper, she expected them. No other possibility occurred to her, and, as a Lancashire woman expecting guests, she rose early with the consciousness of having a busy morning before her. She had no objections to Will's working on his wedding day, but she wanted a clear field for her preparatory operations, and so had told him not to come till he called to walk with her to church. She was busy with soap and scrubbing-brush. The cellar was a cellar and a temporary resting-place at that, but those sisters of hers should see it clean and polished or she would know the reason why. There was a table to lay for supper, too. Supper was a long way off, but a wedding day was a wedding day and anything might happen. However early those sisters came, they should not find Maggie napping.

And so she laid the table now with cold viands, with a great pork pie at the table's head ("They needn't starve," she thought), and a wedding cake in the middle, and all her store of cups and saucers at its foot, for, of course, they would drink tea. And then she paused, and if the word aghast was ever rightly used of her, its time is now. She had two chairs! And needed five at least. Moreover, she had finished spending money on furniture for Oldfield Road. Next time she put hand to pocket for that purpose would be when William Mossop, bootmaker, was a going concern, and then her furniture would be "somthing like." Meantime - "Oh, well," she concluded, "it'll cost me the hire of a handcart and Will 'ull have some work to do this afternoon. And now I've got to dress."

She gave a last criticisng glance at her apartment's shining morning face, and was turning satisfied to her bedroom, when a carriage stopped outside and the cellar echoed with a commanding knock. Maggie meant to ignore knocks that morning, but she had heard the carriage stop and made a concession. She opened the door.

"Mrs Hepworth's compliments," said that lady's footman, handing Maggie a choice bouquet from the Hope Hall hot-houses.

"My stars!" she said, jerked out of all composure. The footman sniffed; then wilted under Maggie's eye. "My compliments to Mrs Hepworth," she announced with dignity, "and tell her I'm much obliged." She closed the door.

"Well!" she said aloud. "Well!" Further words failed her, but the depth of her emotion is to be gauged by the fact that she nearly, very nearly, went out to buy a flower-vase. But she decided that the slop-basin would do. The flowers themselves were decoration enough, and her luxury account was closed.

She was dressing when Freddie Beenstock knocked, and she continued to dress. She was to be married in the Sunday dress which had done service for a year; a plain, straight-fronted dress, with the waist nowhere in particular, pleated a little in the skirt, with a sash tied in a bow behind and a little white lace about the neck. Black shoes were strapped over her white stockings, and her hat lay flatly on her head. Long pendant ear-rings, once her mother's were her one adornment. It was simplicity iself, but simplicity suited her, and as Maggie looked into the second-hand mirror on the deal dressing-table she was pleasantly aware that many a satined bride had seemed less suitably attired. For all her thirty years, Maggie was good to look upon today, with the new-born softness in her face and the love-light in her eyes.

Fred hurt his knuckles on the door, and suffered in soul when Mr. Pratt issued from his shop and inquired if he could read, but he wanted Maggie, and he waited. He felt conspicuous, observed of every passer-by, horribly conscious of the suspicious eye of Mr. Pratt watching from behind a pile of shirtings in his shop, imagining dire happenings to Mr.Hobson in his father's cellar; but he had no hope but in Maggie, and waited for her while the minutes of his dinner hour ticked tragically on and black despair engulfed him.

Will Mossop crawled along the street moving like an automaton, rigid with resolution. he had the air of a man who has faced and discounted all, and now walks calmly to his doom. He reached the door before he realised Fred's presence. But he saw Fred before Fred saw him.

"What's up?" asked Will.

Fred recognised his rescuer. Will did not look Olympian, but he was Providence to Fred.

"The devil!" he replied, referring not to Will but to the general situation. "Where's Maggie Hobson?"

"Inside."

"She's not. I've knocked."

Will spared his knuckles, but the whole of Olfield Road could hear his voice. "Maggie!" he roared. She heard, and Will being due, came.

"Hullo!" she said to Fred. "Are you coming to my wedding with a face like that?"

"Let me come in," he said. "And perhpas your face will look like mine."

"I doubt it," Maggie said. "But I'd rather take no risks today, and so - "

"No," said Freddie, in desperation defying her eye. "You've got to hear me."

"Is it Vickey?" asked Maggie.

"No. It's your father. He's asleep in our cellar."

"Come in," she said. "That won't upset my face."

Fred told his tale while Will gaped and Maggie thought.

"Go and get a handcart, Will," she said, when he finished.

Will rose obediently. He asked no questions, but went.

Fred asked, "For Mr. Hobson?"

"Don't be an idiot," she said. "Now, listen to me. I don't know that I'm bursting to worry with other people's troubles today, but happen I can work this in. How do things stand with you and Vickey.

The settlement difficulty came out. "I thought as much," she said.

It was an irrelevancy on her wedding day, but, after all, she had put her family completely out of mind for a month, and, now that her own aim was about to be accomplished, she could perhaps spare a moment or two to arrange her sisters' lives for them. The main thing was that she, as she had promised, was to be married first and, after that, they had their claims, and "The Lord knows," she thought, "they'll get no forrarder by themselves; and I've closed my shop for the day, so I might as well have something to do. I never did believe in idleness.

"All right, Mr. Beenstock," she said aloud. "You'd better come with us. We're going round to Hobson's now."

"My time's up at half-past twelve, and I'm on pins lest Mr. Hobson should awake and show himself."

"We have to chance that, but I'll see you're back by half-past twelve."

Then Will came in. "I've got the handcart outside," he said.

"You can push it round to Chapel Street. Come along, Mr. Beenstock." And she took a final approving look at her preparations. "Will! Come here. Just so as you'll not forget you're a bridegroom today." She choose a buttonhole from Mrs. Hepworth's flowers and pinned it in his coat, then, looking at him as a mother scrutinises the child she has dressed to do her credit at a party. "You'll do," she said.

Getting Used to Kissing

Alice and Vickey were in the shop, and Tubby Wadlow, with a twinkle in his eye and a general air of suppressed gaiety, was enjoying himself at Alice's expense. He had come up as usual for the day's orders, but knew very well that Alice had none to give. Maggie's competition and Mrs. Hepworth's interested canvassing for Will had already told a devastating tale on Hobson's "good-class" trade, not to mention that Mr. Hobson's unprecedented all-night absence from home had reduced Alice to the verge of imbecility. She or Vickey would have gone to Maggie long before this hour had Maggie ever told them where she was, and it didn't occur to them that to ask Tubby was the way to find out.

Nevertheless, they were less astonished at Hobson's escapade than they would have been a month earlier. He had never concealed the fact that he was no ascetic, but though Maggie had regarded the shop as her prime concern and refrained from the kind of caustic comment on his habits which her mother used to utter, her presence and her knack of expressing a strong opinion by a passing glance had exercised wholesome restraint. The Moonraker's was lately seeing more, and Alice less, of Mr.Hobson, and his present conduct was merely the unwelcome development of a recognised tendency, not the unexpected outburst of a Puritan. he would return when he was ready, and, meantime, Alice's job was to run the shop. She did not like her job.

"There's nothing at all to start on, Miss Alice," Tubby said. "We're worked up."

"Well,father's out, and I can't help you."

"He'll play old Harry if he comes in and finds us doing nowt in the workroom."

Vickey came to Alice's assistance. "Then do something," she contributed intelligently. "We're not stopping you."

"You're not telling me, either, Miss Vickey. And I'm supposed to take my orders from the shop."

"I don't know what to tell you to do," said Alice in despair. "Nobody seems to want any boots made."

Tubby agreed. "The high-class trade has dropped like a stone this last month. Of course we can go on making clogs for stock if you like."

"Then you'd better." Any suggestions was better than none, and Alice felt relieved.

"Well," said Tubby, enjoying himself, "you know what's got by selling clogs won't pay the rent, let alone wages, but if clogs are your orders, Miss Alice, clogs it is." And he moved to the ladder-head.

"You suggested it."

Tubby corrected her. "I made the remark. But I'm not a rash man, and I'm not going to be responsible to the master, with his temper so nowty and all since Miss Maggie went."

"Oh, dear! What would Miss Maggie have told you to do?"

"I couldn't tell you that, miss, I'm sure. I don't recollect things being as slack as this in her time." Which was very true.

"You don't help us much for an intelligent foreman," said Vickey.

Tubby adjusted their relations. "I have my place, miss, and you have yours. When you've told me what to do, I'll use my intelligence, and see it's done properly."

"Then go and make clogs," ordered Alice sharply.

"Them's your orders?"

"Yes."

"Thank you, Miss Alice," he said with infinite politeness, and descended to the cellar chuckling.

"I wonder if I've done right," said Alice pathetically. She got no sympathy from Vickey.

"That's your look out."

"I don't care. It's father's place to be here to tell them what to do."

"Maggie used to manage without him, and you're supposed to be doing her work."

This was hardly a sedative for fretted nerves

"That's right," said Alice. "Keep it up. Blame me that the place is all at sixes and sevens," and she moved with dignity to her seat of honour at the book-keepers's desk.

"I don't blame you," said Vickey. "I know as well as you do that it's father's fault. He ought to look after his business himself instead of wasting more time than ever in the Moonraker's, but you needn't be snappy with me about it."

"I'm not snappy in myself," apologised Alice. "It's these figures. I can't get them right. What's seventeen and twenty-five?"

"Fifty-two, of course," said Vickey promptly. Women are optimistic mathematicians.

"That's what I make it myself and it doesn't balance right. Oh, I wish I was married, and out of it."

"We're further off than ever. What with Maggie queering our pitch with Will Mossop and father turning so mean, I don't fancy our chances myself. Oh, it's a horrid world." and the ready tears leapt into Vickey's eyes, while Alice swallowed hard.

Maggie came into this damp sisterhhod like a north wind chasing a shower. She had talked busily to her attendant squires all the way from Oldfield Road, and Freddie Beenstock was feeling

"Like some watcher of the skies

When a new planet swims into his ken."

Will had received his less exciting instructions with his usual stolidity.

"A nice sight you'd have looked if I'd been a customer," Maggie greeted her sisters after a month's absence.

"Maggie, you here!" said Alice.

"I thought we'd just drop in to see if your young man was here this morning."

"My young man! No, if you mean Mr. Prosser, he isn't, and what's more, he - - " she stopped.

"Yes?" encouraged Maggie.

"He's not been here so often since you and Will Mossop got - - " Then she changed her mind. Maggie was looking at her. "Since you made him buy that pair of boots he didn't want."

"I see," said Maggie. "He didn't like paying to take his pleasure in our shop. Well, if he's not expected somebody must go for him."

"What's he got to do with you?" asked Alice jealously.

"I'm none selling him boots this time, Alice. Prosser, Pilkington & Prosser, of Bexley Square. That's right, isn't it?"

"Yes, Albert's the 'and Prosser'."

"Is he? Quite a big man in his way. Then will you go and fetch him, Mr. Beenstock? Tell him to bring the paper with him."

"You're ordering folk about a bit," said Vickey, as Fred turned smartly to obey Maggie.

"I'm used to it," she said.

Freddie reassured Vickey. "It's all right," he said. "In fact, I think it's spendid."

"Is it?" asked Alice. "It won't be if father comes in and finds you all here."

"I've a crow to pluck with you about father, Alice. What have you been doing to him since I went? He never stayed out all night in my time."

"How did you know?" gasped Alice.

"The fact is, he's at our place," said Fred; "er - he's asleep."

"Now you can go for Albert Prosser," said Alice, "and don't be long."

"I won't," said Frederick, thinking of his father.

"Don't," said Maggie, thinking of a little job she had for him when he returned.

"And if you wanrt to know about father," said Alice, as the door closed, "it's your fault, Maggie and not ours at all."

164 *Hobson's Choice*

GOING TO BEXLEY SQUARE.

"Indeed?"

"He had a letter from you yesterday, and it upset him. He put it in his pocket and went straight out, and we've not seen him since."

"Did he read you the letter?"

"No."

"Then - Will, they don't know." Will gave a loud guffaw, then, finding he laughed alone, was silent suddenly. Maggie was watching Alice quizzically.

"I don't know what you're aiming at, Maggie," said Alice, "but - "

"The difference between us is that I do. I always did."

Vickey tried her strength. "It's a queer thing you aimed at," she said, pointing to the still embarrassed Will. Maggie took Will's arm and faced her sisters proudly.

"I've done uncommon well myself and I've come here to put things straight for you. Father told you to get married and you don't shape."

"He changed his mind," said Alice.

"I don't allow for folks to change their minds. He made his choice. He said get married, and you're going to." Assertions in that tone from Maggie carried conviction, and it was the measure of her sisters' hopelessness that they still had doubts.

"I'm sure we're willing," said Alice, "but I dunno that you've made it easier for us so far," and she looked at Willie.

"It wasn't my fault, Miss Alice," he said; "really it wasn't."

"You call her Alice, Will," said Maggie quietly.

"He doesn't," said Alice; "not much."

"He's in the family or going to be," said Maggie.

"And I'll tell you this: if you, Vickey, want your Freddy, and if you Alice, want Albert, you'll be respectful to my Willie."

Alice sniffed. "Willie Mossop was our boot-hand," she appealed to history.

"He was, and you'll let bygones by bygones. He's as good as you are now - and better, too."

"Nay, come, Maggie." Will was modest, but he was interrupted.

"Better, I say. They're shop assistants. You're your own master, aren't you?"

"I've got my name wrote up on the windows," Will agreed so far. "But I dunno so much about being master."

"You're William Mossop, Boot and Shoe Maker of your own shop. You're a master bootmaker, Will, and you're the man they've privileged to call by your Christian name. Aye, and I'll do more for you than let you call him in his name. You can both of you kiss him for your brother-in-law to be."

Will backed in terror. Then he smiled. It was only a joke. Finally he perceived she meant it, and a prickly heat assailed him

"Nay, Maggie, I'm no great hand at kissing."

"I've noticed that," she said dryly. "A bit of practice 'ull do you no harm. Come along Vickey."

Alice attempted to change the subject. "But, Maggie, a shop of your own - "

"I'm waiting, Vickey," said Maggie grimly.

"I don't see that you ought to drive her into it," said Will hopefully.

"You hold your hush," said Maggie, "and stand still. She's making up her mind to do it."

"I'd just as lief not put her to the trouble."

Maggie vouchsafed an explanation. "You'll take your proper place in this family, my lad, trouble or no trouble."

"I don't see why you should always get your way," said Vickey querulously.

"It's just a habit," Maggie said. "Come along now Vickey. I've a lot to do today, and you're holding everything back."

Vickey looked at her fellow-victim. It was obvious that he liked the idea less than she did. In that case, she had not so much objection. She was going to annoy Will Mossop, anyhow. So she approached him. "It's under protest," she said.

"Protest, but kiss."

Will shrank from her, so Vickey kissed him heartily, and found he rather like it.

"Your turn now, Alice."

Alice saw no escape, but she hoped to make a bargain. "I'll do it if you'll help me with these books, Maggie."

"Books?" said Maggie. "Has father given you the books to do?"

"Yes."

"Then he must take the consequences. Your books aren't my affair."

"I think you might help me, Maggie."

"I'm surprised at you, Alice, I really am, after what you've just been told. Exposing your books to a rival shop. You ought to know better. Will's waiting. And you're to kiss him hearty, now."

"Very well," said Alice. Will was no shirker this time. His lips met hers in a resounding smack.

"There's more in kissing nice young women than I thought," he said.

"Don't you get too fond of it, my lad," said Maggie.

Chapter Eleven

Second-Hand Furniture

Alice parted from Will after her forced share in the ordeal of initiating him into the bosom of the family with stiffened resentment against Maggie. She knew Maggie had come with a purpose, for Maggie never went anywhere withhout reason, but it was obvious to her that Maggie had at the moment time to burn and was simply amusing herself. Alice objected to be the cause of Maggie's amusement.

"Well," she said, "I hope you're satisfied, Maggie. You've got your way again. And now perhaps you'll be good enough to tell us if there's anything you want in this shop." Alice was supremely business-like - a reproduction in plaster-of-paris of Maggie's selling attitude.

Maggie laughed at her. "Are you trying to sell me something?"

"I'm asking you what's your business here," said Alice, with great aplomb.

"Oh, Will and me are taking day off to put you two in the way of getting wed."

"It looks like things are slow at your new shop if you can walk round in your new clothes on a working day," said Vickey.

Will could hold it no longer. "It's not a working day with us," he said. "It's a wedding day."

"You've been married this morning!"

"Not us," said Maggie. "It's at a quarter to twelve at St. Philip's. That's what I told father in that letter, and I don't see nowt in it to upset him either. Are you coming?"

"We can't leave the shop," said Vickey.

"Why not? Is trade so brisk?"

"No, but - "

"Not so much high-class trade doing with you, eh?"

"I don't see how you know that," said Alice.

"I'm good at guessing," said Maggie. "I'll have my sisters there when I get wed. You'll miss no trade by coming with us to church, and we'll expect you at home tonight for a wedding spread. Tubby can see to the shop. And that reminds me, Alice, you can sell me something. There are some rings in that drawer to your hand, Vickey."

Vickey pulled out the drawer. "Yes. Brass rings," she said, wondering.

"I know they're brass. That's the size," she said, trying one on her wedding-ring finger. Alice and Vickey stared horrified.

"That!" said Vickey. "But - - "

"It's a good fit," said Maggie, feeling in her purse and extracting fourpence. "Will and me aren't throwing money round, but we can pay our way. Gather it up, Vickey."

Alice turned up her eyes and apostrophised the ceiling. "Married with a brass ring!"

"Alice," said Maggie, "you haven't entered that sale in your book. No wonder you're worried with the accounts if that's the way you see to them."

"I'm a bit to much astonished at you to think about accounts. A ring out of stock!"

"Come to think of it, you know, Alice, they're always out of some one's stock, and I don't see that it makes any difference who's stock it is."

"Well," said Vickey, "I'd think shame to myself to be married with a ring like that."

"When folks can't afford the best, they have to do without," said Maggie, with a humility which ought to have warned her sisters of breakers ahead.

Vickey tossed her head. "I'll take good care I never go without."

"Semi-detached for you, I supose, and a houseful of new furniture?" asked Maggie, producing her bait.

Alice sniffed nicely. "Haven't you furnished?" she asked.

"Partly what," said Maggie, using a local idiom. The "what" is added after the "partly" much as "like" qualifies the adjective in "lonesome-like."

"We've made a start at the Flat-Iron Market."

That finished Alice. "I'd stay single sooner than have other people's cast-off sticks in my house. Where's your pride gone to, Maggie?"

"Nay," said Maggie serenely; "I'm not getting wed to help the furniture trade along." She turned to Vickey. "I suppose you're of the same mind as Alice? You'd turn your nose up at second-hand stuff as well?"

Vickey was very sure. "I'll start properly or not at all."

"Oh," said Maggie, very contentedly. "Then you'll neither of you have any objections to my clearing out the lumber-room upstairs. We brought a handcart with us."

Will caught her eye and took his coat off. His wits were growing sharper. Alice and Vickey gaped at one another. They perceived too late to where they had been led.

"Wait a bit, Will." said Alice. He hesitated for a fraction of a second.

"Get upstairs," said Maggie. "I've told you what to bring." She spoke tartly and he leapt to obey. Maggie, in fact, was a little disappointed in him. After the past month, he ought to have known better than to let any one's voice check him, even momentarily, in doing her behest. Still, the lad was coming on, and here was Alice talking and, by natural consequence, calling for repression.

"Let me tell you this," Alice was saying, "that if you claim that furniture from your old room, it's my room now, and you'll not budge one stick of it."

Maggie smiled sweetly. "I expected you'd promote yourself, Alice. But I said Lumber-room. There's a two-three old broken chairs in the attic; and a sofa with the springs all gone. You'll not tell me they're of any use to you."

"Nor to you, either."

"Will's handy with his fingers. He'll put in his time this

afternoon mending them up, and they'll be secure against you come to sit on them at supper tonight."

"And that's the way you're going to live!" said Vickey with biting scorn. "With cast-off furniture."

"Aye," said Maggie meekly. "In two cellars in Oldfield Road."

"A cellar!" screamed Alice.

Maggie protested humbly. "Two of 'em, Alice. One to live in and the other to sleep in."

ST. PHILIP'S CHURCH, SALFORD.

"Well, it 'ud not suit me," said Alice, hoping Maggie would see how much more she meant than she deemed it politic to say.

Maggie saw. "It suits me champion," she said. "And when me and Will are richer than the lot of you together, it'll be a grand satisfaction to look back and think of how we were when we began."

Will returned from the attic with a couple of superannuated chairs and made for the door. Vickey pounced on him.

"Just a minute, Will," she said, examining his burden. "You know, Maggie, mended up those chairs would do very well for my kitchen when I'm wed."

"Yes, or for mine." Alice supported her.

"Put the chairs on the handcart, Will," said Maggie; "and as for your kitchens, my girls, you've got none yet, and if you want my plan for getting you some work, you'll just remember that all I'm taking off you is some crippled stuff that isn't yours, and what I'm getting for you is marriage portions. And if you don't go upstairs this minute and put your hats on in a hurry, you'll be late at the church, and it's not allowed."

Pompous & Circumlocutory Precision

Prosser, senior, was the representative of a dynasty of lawyers dating back to the days when Salford was a village. He was more than a respectable family solicitor: he was a Personage. He was Prosser every bit as much as Hobson was Hobson, and it was a greater thing to be. Had the legal profession possessed anything equivalent to the Bench of Bishops, Prosser would certainly have won an apron. As it was, he was either president, treasurer, or secretary of half a dozen worthy committees for as many impeccable objects. But most of all, he was a lawyer. There are lawyers who contemn the law, regard it lightly as a means to an end, and that end mere livelihood, there are even lawyers who evade the law, are intimate with it only that they may dodge it, and assist others to sail ever so near the wind without capsizing their ships, and there are lawyers who are legal, who reverence the law, look at it almost (if one may push the matter to extremes) as a devout clergyman regards the Bible. Prosser reverenced the law, and his son Albert, sat at his father's feet. Never had the shadow of a shady transaction crossed the office threshold of Prosser, Pilkington & Prosser. And as for abusing the law, invoking its assistance without serious intentions, in fact, jesting with the law, which was what Maggie's messenger now required of the scandalised Albert Prosser, earthquakes could shake Bexley Square to dust before such a blasphemy should occur in that dignified office.

Fred's troubles were not yet over. Himself completely at Maggie's command, he forgot that there were people still in the world who could say of her, as he once rashly did, "She'll not rule me." Albert had two reasons for saying it. The first was the excellent pair of boots he was wearing, and the second was his profound reverence for the majesty of the law. He sat in his arm-chair with the light behind him amongst the great array of real (not dummy) deed-boxes, facing Fred, pressing his finger-tips together, looking twice his age and immovably professional.

"You won't do it for me, and you won't do it for Maggie, and you won't even do it for Alice. Then do it for yourself."

"Eh?" Albert was certainly interested now.

"If you want Alice, and want a settlement from her father, here's the way to get one. Damn it, Prosser, he is trespassing in our cellar. I'm not lying to you. The man's there and he's committed trespass."

"Undoubtedly," agreed Albert. "Am I to take your instructions then to - - -?"

"I've told you it's Maggie's idea."

"I'm not concerend with that. If Nathaniel Beenstock & Co. instruct me to proceed against Henry Horatio Hobson, I am willing to proceed. But as you put the matter first - that it was Maggie's idea and - - "

"Oh!" Fred saw the point. The legal lawyer wanted to

save his face. Besides, it was getting late, and Fred had no time to spare. He took the plunge. After all, his father couldn't eat him. "Certainly," he said formally. "My firm does ask you."

"Very well," said Albert. "I will draw up the papers, and, as you're an acquaintance, I will do it at once and bring them with me."

Fred watched the clock while Albert put some legal language on blue paper. He was annoyed with Albert. Why couldn't the fellow be a sportsman and enter into the spirit of Maggie's entertaining and profitable scheme? As it was, here was Fred saddled with the responsibility of taking his father's name in vain - and Fred was uncomfortabley aware of the probable consequenceds to himself should Maggie's plan miscarry. He knew her plans had the habit of success, but it was a ticklish situation. Anyhow, the thing was done, or at least was in the doing. He had formally authorised Albert in the name of Nathanial Beenstock to go ahead, and Albert was elaborately going ahead. He set forth with pompous and circumlocutory precision that the very fabric of the firm of Nathaniel Beenstock had been so directed, torn and rent by the utterly inexcusable and unwarrantable trespass of Henry Horatio Hobson as only to be made whole by the mulcting in heavy damages of the aforesaid H. H. Hobson and, further, the aforesaid H. H. Hobson having plainly entered the premises of the aforesaid Nathaniel with the felonious intention of spying upon the trade secrets of the aforesaid Nathaniel, such malfeasance and wicked conspiracy against good faith and the principles of honest trading were to be condoned only by the recovery in compensation of supplementary damages from the aforesaid H. H. Hobson to the aforesaid Nathaniel Beenstock.

Albert leant back in his chair and contemplated his document approvingly. Freddy was on his feet.

"Come on," he said.

"I'm not in the habit of serving personally," said Albert, with dignity.

Fred was considerably larger than Albert, and apprenticeship amongst the corn bags had made him muscular. "I dare say not," he said. "But you're coming along to Maggie with that paper if I have to drag you there. I'll do the rest."

"I might stretch a point that far," said Albert, taking his hat. And the remarkable fact is that, once free of that edifice of legal austerity, the offices of Prosser, Pilkington & Prosser, Albert manifested an irresponsible levity and a fine indifference to the piece of legal chicanery on which he knew very well he was engaged. That boot purchase rankled and he did not love Maggie for it, but he wanted Alice and he had adroitly shuffled all responsibility on to Fred's shoulders. He needn't worry, and he didn't.

They turned into the shop just as Alice and Vickey had gone upstairs and Will had put the dilapidated chairs on the handcart. Albert observed Will's occupation with contempt, and it was unfortunate for him that Maggie, having for the moment nothing else to do, made a mental note of his attitude. People were apt to pay for contemptuous observation of Will Mossop. But his punishment would keep.

"Freddy," she said, "I told you I had a job here for you. You go upstairs with Will. There's a sofa to come down. Get you coat off to it."

"But - the time - - "

"The time is the time I need to talk to Mr. Prosser, and you needn't stand idle. If that sofa isn't here in two minutes, I'll leave the lot of you to tackle this yourselves, and a nice hash you'll make of it."

Freddie took his coat off and went upstairs with Will.

"Now, Mr. Prosser, let me see that paper."

Albert produced his masterpiece with proper pride, but Maggie was unappreciative. "Do you call this English?"

"Legal English, Miss Hobson,"

"I thought it weren't the sort we talk in Lancashire. What is it when you've got behind the whereases and the aforesaids and to wits?"

"It's what I was instructed. Action against Henry Horatio Hobson for trespass on the premises of Nathaniel

176 *Hobson's Choice*

COUNTY COURT, OLD OWENS COLLEGE, QUAY STREET.

Beenstock with damages to certain corn bags caused by falling on them, and further damages claimed for spying on the trade secrets of the aforesaid Nathaniel Beenstock."

"Well," said Maggie, holding out the paper derisively. "I'll take your word that this means that. I shouldn't have thought it, but I reckon lawyers are like doctors. They've each a secret language of their own, so that if you get a letter from one lawyer, you've to take it to another to get it read, just like a doctor sends you to a chemist with a rigmarole that one one else can read so he can charge you what he likes for a drop of coloured water."

"I've made this out according to instructions, Miss Hobson, and it's well drawn, but I'm far from saying it represents a good case, and I'd not be keen on going into court with it."

"Nobody asked you to," she said. "It'll not get into court."

Will and Freddy returned carrying an ancient horsehair sofa, whose springs had long ago succumbed beneath the weight of Mr. Hobson. A look from Maggie, and Albert was sent flying to open the outer door for them. Albert was feeling the spell of Maggie's eye.

"Girls," she called up the stairs, "if you're late for my wedding I'll never forgive you. Put your coats on," she added to Fred and Will as they returned from the street. "Now then, Freddy, you can take that paper and put it on my father in your cellar. If he's wakened, and gone, come back and tell me, and remember anyhow that you and Vickey come to my wedding party tonight. So do you and Alice, Albert."

"Thanks," said Fred, clutching the precious talisman and sprinting for the door. He'd done with taking chances, and further words could wait.

"We're getting on," said Maggie, with a compelling eye on Albert. "But there's that handcart. Are we to take it with us?"

"To church?" asked Albert, horrified. "You can't do that."

"I'll take it home," Will volunteered.

"And have me waiting for you at St. Philip's? That's not for me, my lad."

"You can't very well leave it where it is," said Albert, with an officiousness for which he was to pay.

"No, there's only one thing for it. You'll have to take it to our place, Albert."

"Me!"

"There's the key," she said coolly. "It's 39a Oldfield Road."

"I say! To push a handcart through Salford in broad daylight." The office behind him, Albert was more or less out for a lark, but this was really a little too much of a good thing. Supose he met a client!

"It won't dirty your collar, and I'll tell you this, Albert, if you're too proud to do a job like that, you're not the husband for my sister.

"It's the look of the thing. Can't you send somebody from here?"

"No. This isn't my shop now. You can think it over." She left him thinking while she raised the trap in the floor. "Tubby!"

"Yes," said Tubby, coming up the ladder.

"Come up, Tubby," she said. "Your're in charge of the shop. We'll all be out for a while."

"I'll be up in half a minute, Miss Maggie," he said, and disappeared below with a Gargantuan smirk on his face. If Tubby was not to go to the wedding, he meant to express his feelings somehow, and old boots found their way to Hobson's for repairs.

"Well, Albert Prosser?" Maggie asked sharply. It wasn't policy to offend the ruling power, and he certainly could not find inoffensive words in which to express his opinion of her. Surrender seemed the only thing.

"I suppose I must," he said.

Maggie was gracious. It was a victory and she appreciated it. "That's better, and I like you more now. We'll call this your wedding gift to me, and I'll allow you're putting yourself out a bit for me." She saw him to the door pleasantly, and watched him start with the handcart. "Well, Will," she said returning. "You've not had much to say for yourself today. Hows't feeling, lad?"

"I'm going through with it, Maggie," he announced, with gloomy resolution.

"Eh?"

"My mind's made up. I've got wrought up to point. I'm ready," and he stood erect, facing the fearful future.

"You're not making a mistake, are you? It's church we're going to, not dentist's."

"I know," said Will. "You get rid of summat at dentist's, but it's taking summat on to go to church with a wench and the Lords knows what."

"Sithee, Will," said Maggie earnestly. "I've a respect for church. Yon's not the place for lies. The parson's going to ask you will you have me, and you'll either answer truthfully or not at all. If you're not willing just say so now, and - - "

"I'll tell him 'yes'"said Will.

"And truthfully," she persisted.

"Yes, Maggie," he assured her. "I'm resigned."

She left it at that. Alice and Vickey came down, dressed in their Sunday clothes - those same new dresses, so artificially prominent behind, which had excited Mr. Hobson's patriotic wrath when first he saw them.

"We're ready," said Alice.

"And time you were," said Maggie, surveying her bridesmaids. "It's not your wedding that you're dressing for. Come up, Tubby, and keep an eye on things.

"Have you got the ring?" Vickey asked Will.

"Not he," said Maggie, tucking his arm in hers. "Do you think I'd trust him to remember?"

Tubby came up with a battery of slippers and bombarded them heftily from the trap. So Maggie Hobson went to change her name.

Liquor and Lawyers

Freddie Beenstock was in time. If running could do it, he meant to be. But Mr. Hobson still slept on his jute divan in Nathaniel's cellar, and the sight of him was balm to Freddie's anxious eyes. Just, however, to give Freddie a final sensation, that of seeing the cup slipping from his lips, Hobson stirred dreamily and settled again with a sack clutched tightly to his breast. Freddie took his chance, and with fingers trembling from anxiety and the distress of his running inserted the writ between Hobson and the sack and into the first pocket he came to, which happened to be that in which Hobson kept his handkerchief. Faint murmurs of complaint, strangled in drowsiness, proceeded from the sleeper as Fred fled like a guilty thing upstairs. True, he was dinnerless, but he was in time, and no more satisfied young man than Fred sat on an office stool in Salford. The aftermath was still to come, but the supreme rightness of things so far

FROM THE CRESCENT, SALFORD.

inspired confidence, and he began devoutly to believe in Maggie and her lucky star.

Mr. Hobson hovered on the brink of consciousness as a balloon descending to earth from the empyrean will coyly kiss its surface twice or thrice, finally settling. There are uncomfortable people in the world whose idea of getting up is to rise briskly at the call of duty and make one movement of it from unconsciousness to their trousers. They will even make a virtue of necessity and pretend to an enjoyment of the sunrise. Insensibles, to miss life's greatest joy, the languorous lingering in sleep-warmed sheets, the luxury of doing nothing, thinking nothing, simply being, in care-free indolence! The body in repose, the mind at rest, the nerves at ease, why -

"Angels alone, that soar above,
Enjoy such liberty."

Mr. Hobson was not an angel, but he was a hedonist and fond of what he liked. He liked his bed and especially he liked those last few moments, elastic as the finest rubber of Para, when soliloquy itself was banished from his blissful mind and all was perfect joy.

It was Seth Newbigging who disturbed his felicity. Seth was a man who looked ahead and kept a careful eye on closing-time. In about three hours Seth would be at liberty to go home, whereas Mr. Hobson's capacity for sleep appeared to have no relation at all to the march of time. So, by way of forcing events, Seth dropped a half-stone weight on the cemented floor and dodged behind a pillar. Hobson woke with distressing suddenness and realised with a nasty jar of his internal machinery, comparable only with what happens when the speed-gear of a tired motor-car is abruptly changed, that he had a bad headache, was exceedingly hungry, and was not at home. Where he was hardly troubled him. The trouble was that he, a churchwarden, had passed a night unbedded, and from home. His questing eyes caught sight of the cellar door, obligingly left open by Seth Newbigging, and Hobson's departure from the cellar of Nathaniel Beenstock was hardly more dignified than his entrance had been.

Home and a wash occurred to him, but he decided they could wait, and followed his natural inclinations into the parlour of the Moonraker's. Sam Minns was polishing glasses in the bar. He was angry with Hobson. If Hobson was not in the Moonraker's that morning, it followed as the night the day that Hobson was in some other tavern. Hobson in no tavern was inconceivable; and Sam was hurt at his desertion. Then Hobson passed through the bar on his way to the parlour.

"Well, I'll be hanged!" said Sam. "Thought better of it?"

"What's time?" asked Hobson, whose watch had curiously stopped.

"Close on five," said Samm. "Tha doesn't look so rosy, lad," he added, growing sympathetic.

"Don't twit me, Sam. I'm none up to it today. Close on five! And that wedding was before noon."

"Wedding?" said Sam, offering his friend a glass of double ale of wondrous strength which he kept for the hardy drovers from the cattle-market. "What's trouble, Henry? Daughters again?"

"Aye, daughters and - - What's that?" he shrieked. Sam was alarmed. Was Hobson "seeing things"? He was, but they were real things. Having drunk at a gulp the cordial Sam offered him, Hobson's hand sought his handkerchief in order to wipe his mouth, and found the masterly document inscribed by Albert "Lawyers!" he yelled "Lawyers!"

Sam felt relieved. Lawyers were pests, but they existed, and the document in Hobson's hand, if ominous to him, was reassuring to Sam.

"Help me to read this, Sam."

"Brandy?" suggested Minns, whose ideas of assistance were strictly professional.

"No," said Hobson. "Let's know the worst." They read it together. Hobson had no secrets from the Moonraker's.

"Looks like trouble, to me," said Sam judicially.

"What shall I do, Sam?"

"Nay, don't ask me. Liquor's my subject, not lawyers.

I'm out of my depth in this, and I don't mind owning it. Of course, Henry, if you like to pay up and look pleasant, there's a short road out of trouble."

"Pay!" said Mr. Hobson. "Never!"

"Well, I put my hands up, then. I daren't advise. I'm sorry to fail you, Henry, but lawyers are beyond me. What worries me is how you got into that cellar. How did it happen? I could see you weren't yourself last night."

"Could you? Then I reckon that's how it happened, Sam. I can tell I've had something that wasn't fit for Christian drinking."

"Henry, my liquor's sound." Sam was severe. Professional honour was concerned in this.

"I know I went for a walk to get rid of some trouble I had, Sam."

"I'm against walking for that purpose. They keep bad beer in the country. If you have trouble, Henry, bring it to the Moonraker's. Don't take it where you risk meeting bad beer and worse trouble than you've got already."

"No," said Hobson meekly. "I won't again. But Moonraker's isn't helping me now."

"There's trouble and trouble - ordinary trouble and extraordinary trouble, and when it's got to lawyers, it's reached a point where common standards don't apply. You're welcome to anything the house contains, and I've the oldest brandy in Salford, but advising a man what to do when lawyers are after him is a responsibility I'll not accept. What will you drink?"

"Nothing," said Hobson, rising.

Sam stared at him incredulously. "Nothing!" he repeated.

"No," said Hobson, with tight lips. "I'll happen see you in the morning, Sam, but I can see you're no use to me today."

"I've done my best," said Sam.

"It's a poor best," said Hobson, "and I've got to find a better." He left the Moonraker's and the broken reed, Sam Minns, and struggled with his pride in Chapel Street. He wanted to ask Maggie. He'd be damned if he would ask Maggie. Maggie was a rebel. He disowned her. Was her letter still in his pocket, and if so, what was her confounded address? He wasn't going to eat humble pie to Maggie, but where was she? He found her letter. Oldfield Road, was it? No, not at any price. Curse the people in Chapel Street. Couldn't they let a man think without bumping into him? He decided that the spaces of Peel Park were necessary. He required largeness of vision. Maggie was his daughter in spite of all. It was her duty to advise. But she had defied him. How could he go to her? He sat thinking it out on a hard bench in Peel Park.

CHAPTER TWELVE

Riding Elephants

The dancers, the airey light-footed dancers who dance at other's joy and not merely for their own joy, have arrived. The musicians, also, who play not for money nor for praise, but are the voluntary and eternal sprites rendering into beauty the experience of the world. For this is a wedding, and though it is a walking-party of half-a-dozen, you may be sure the fairies are out along the pavement of Salford. The Land of Faery is not dead. It has but slept a while, rather than recognise the ugly images of truth man has worshipped these many years under the titles of Commerce, Progress, and Religion. And the fairies re-awaken, they have grown in their sleep, they are as beautiful and quaint as ever, but their persons are larger, their instinct to dance and trick are wider and wilder. And to our Maggie's wedding they come, in default of Hobson and the society of Salford. The gentle habit of our former wiser poets was to welcome and invoke the fairies to a wedding, but *sans* welcome and *sans* invitation to glad marriages they come; to wrongful marriages they come, to utter curse and malison; but for the folk who make their human bond in righteousness they have naught but songs and harmless dance and unstinted blessings. For these immortals recognise the mystery and the goodness of the pact. Not only the possession of one by one, dear as this is, but they believe in beauty and all their errand is to increase it and to harmonise in deeper harmony the one soul of the pair till shall recreate the beauty they desire.

And though Maggie Mossop, wife of William Mossop, thought very little about such unsubstantial things, she rose

ELEPHANT RIDERS AT BELLE VUE GARDENS.

to the hour in her magnificent fashion. She rode on an elephant. It is an observance we recommend to the newly married as a worthier than riding in motor cars or in reserved first-class compartments. Pooh! these are vulgar, and the great flow is not born of steam and sparking plugs. Ride elephants, in the sight of the world and a fig for travelling costumes and such-like unholy contraptions.

There are no elephants in Salford, but a four-penny tram-ride is a pardonable luxury on your wedding day, although you are going to make your fortune at boot-selling inside twenty years; and at the corner of the street where the horse-trams used to go, and stop where you waved your hand (so much more courteous were the days of simple traction), Maggie struck an attitude and challenged her party.

"If you can't play the fool on your wedding day, when can you play the fool?"

Nobody quarrelled with her obvious intentions, although Alice thought her language rather free.

"See you all to-night," said Maggie, lugging the church-bewildered Will towards an advancing tram. He obeyed willingly when he saw she meant tram-rides. In fact, he was quite glad he had been married if the honeymoon were going to be all tram-rides. But Maggie had mightier visions. True, Will thought he had hold of her idea when they got out of the tram at Manchester and boarded another for Belle Vue.

"I suppose they've" (he dare not yet refer familiarly to Alice and Vickey) "gone back to the shop."

"Aye," said Maggie, producing the coppers to the fare-collector.

Will enjoyed the contrast between his luxurious locomotion and their dull occupation.

"We're going to Belle Vue, my lad," quoth Maggie presently. "So thou must try to patch up a holiday face."

"Belle Vue," Will gasped, half-alarmed at the unknown place, and half-excited by the romantic legends he had heard of the unknown place.

"Aye; Belle Vue, not the cemetery. That's why I'd like a grin, even if it's only a daft grin."

Will grinned obligingly.

"That's better," complimented Maggie, and most mischievously clutched his arm like any half-witted bride, and exhibited her smiling face to one draggle-tailed wife and two pompous old men who looked as if they knew how to behave in a tram-car. Will squirmed and muttered that tram-rides weren't undiluted joy if this sort of thing was to be the rule. He would rather take his honeymoon on a day when familiarity was more modified. The draggle-tail wife who seemed to have more of the world's worry than was fair, leant across the car, and with the clear frankness of the Lancashire breed addressed Will.

"Hast had back luck?"

"Aye," answered Will, with guiltless eyes.

"Ah've been married today."

The woman did not laugh, the answer was too much within the bounds of possibility for laughter. But she looked at Maggie as if to ask whether she were the newly acquired bad luck.

"Aye, it's me," said Maggie, brightly.

The woman examined Maggie, and then got up to to. "Eh, he's like a lad I keep at home myself. He doesn't know when he's well off."

Tram-conductors are still a happy race, but they were still more genial when their permanent company was increased by two horses. Thenadays, they took a family interest in their fares, discussed domestic experiences and politics, and looked for a tip at Christmas from their regulars. The conductor on Maggie's car was young, but not so young as not to relish other people's conversation and a share in it himself. He was old enough to know a smart wench, but he was not old enough to know better than to chaff a smart wench.

"Bright day, miss," said he, from the doorway.

"Ma'am, if you please," Maggie turned a dangerous eye on the cheerful young man.

"Aw, just done it," said he admiringly.

"Aye," said Maggie placidly.

"Y' have 'ad a day for it," went on the imperturbable one.

"We've been lucky," admitted the bride.

"First show of sun in Manchester for a year," the young man exaggerated, but not very much. "Ah'm fro' Bowton maself. It's a grand spot, Bowton, allus dry to yonder. Company weather is Bowton's weather.

"Eh!" marvelled Maggie. "Then they cannot keep ducks at Bowton?"

"Ducks?" said the unseeing youngster. "Nay, there's no ponds in our streets."

"Well," Maggie was able to converse sensibly although she was a bride, "tha doesn't need to."

Still the door-leaner could not see it.

"Bowton folk can do their own quacking," explained Maggie, looking at him very steadily.

And that is the way they got to Belle Vue. The conductor looked after them as he conversed with the driver. "Eh, there's another smart wench wasted on a gawk."

"Aye," quoth the driver, after he had hitched his horses and gazed his fill. "Aye, thee and me, Jim, us has been done in again." Which must be wit, inasmuch as the tram-driver had a wife as big as a wheat stack in his own four-and-sixpenny. Meantime our well-matched couple in spite of the ignorant opinions of tram-conductors, have put their money down and are rapidly putting down the equivalent of more money. They feed. They have had very little breakfast and no dinner. Maggie felt like a shilling's-worth and took it; Will felt like it also, but the dimensions of the room, its magnificence, and the consciousness of other folk's eyes, overawed him, and regrettable as it is, Will encouraged his emotions at the expense of his banking account.

"Well," said Maggie, as soon as she felt satisfied, "we're not here for eating; we can do that at home, and there's a large-sized supper tonight."

"Aye," said Will hopefully. The small boy from Harpurhey made him very despondent, he had such an inquisitive stare.

"Up, lad." Maggie was on her feet. "You'll eat better than this come a month."

They went out to explore Belle Vue.

The Southerner in Lancashire is startled by Belle Vue. Empty, it is a muddy wilderness, a ram-shackle town of wooden huts and quaint erections. On a wet day it encourages suicidal tendencies; is the sort of place a new Edgar Allan Poe might frequent for the higher development of the morbid and bizarre in his nature. But Lancashire people are used to their climate and Bell Vue when it is full, in wet or dry weather, is a pugnacious paradise. The Southerner is still shocked, there is something so vehement in the enjoyment of these Northerners. There is a Zoo at Bell Vue, perhaps not so scientific as the London Zoo, but much more admirable in Lancashire's opinion. Further, at Bell Vue there are dancing halls, merry-go-rounds, a steamer on the lake, and grand illuminated displays. Are these things at Regent's Park? London is frigid even in its debauches, but Belle Vue is the place where Lancashire enjoys itself when it hasn't time to go to Blackpool.

Mrs Maggie Mossop, then, took her half day's honeymoon not in a sentimental solitude with her lad, but in the uplifting company of the multitude. The cockatoos which talk, the lions which roar, satisfied their thirst for sensation until the dinner was digested. But with stomach-ease comes a desire for delirium. A brass band contest was the supreme thing, but this afternoon only ran to a hand-bell ringing competition. They decided that was luck enough and made ado to get into the hall, which was, as the papers say, crowded to its upmost capacity.

Now, to hear the same set piece of music interpreted by team after team of hand-bell ringers may strike the outsider as a monotonous form of entertainment. Thoroughly to appreciate it one requires, perhaps to have an interest in one or more of the performers. But that is the sporting, not the musical excitement, and if you have an ear you can judge the various renderings as justly as the judges themselves who sit screened off and hear but do not see the ringers. The bells, of course, are tuned to various notes and stand on tables. Behind the tables are the ringers, and, as it is strenuous work, and Belle Vue is not a formal place, they doff their coats and waistcoats and tackle their job like men. It is spectacular because each man rings several bells and their busy hands must flash from bell to bell with the speed of a conjurer's; and it is musical because the clear notes of the bells are beautifully modulated; and it is exciting because the slightest slip in timing is a point against success; and each band has its local supporters in the audience to cheer it on to victory or to mourn defeat.

The audience listened with the self-abandonment of connoisseurs. They were all that a classical concert audience ought to be. Will was absorbed. He sat in silent ecstasy, utterly forgetful of his surroundings, the ordeal he had survived at church, of Maggie herself. This was seeing life, this was doing the gay things he had heard about.

After two hours, Maggie touched his arm. She was as reluctant to leave the hall as he was, because she had not yet heard all she had paid to hear, but those chairs were to be mended by supper-time, and there was still a lot to do before she had finished with Belle Vue. They fed the bears and marvelled at the giraffes. Reassured by the keeper, they rode together on an elephant. They had a steamer trip round the lake and swung on hobby-horses round the merry-go-round, and, finally they danced. The hand-bell contest was over, the benches cleared from the hall, a brass band playing on the platform, and Will Mossop danced! That is to say, Maggie, who could manage everything, steered him securely through the rapids of a polka. She meant to do it and she did, but it was a tumbled Maggie and a panting Will who climbed the tram for home after that crowning victory of hers in the dancing-hall of Belle Vue. Something more than an ear for music and a sense of rhythm is needed for the execution of a polka, and Maggie's feet had felt the weight of Will.

But "it's a sad heart that never rejoices, and I favour a bit of fun sometimes," said Maggie.

"Well, by gum," said Will, who had not seen this side of her before, and concentrated in his mild expletive all the emotion of his crowded afternoon. They rode in silence, side by side, and as they descended at the corner of Oldfield Road from their fourth tram, "Well, by gum," he said again. Beyond that, it was inexpressible.

The Wedding Supper

Mrs. Mossop sat in her elegant parlour awaiting her guests. She knew she was Mrs. Mossop, because her marriage certificate was in the top left-hand drawer of her dressing-table and Will was sitting stiffly on the extreme edge of a mended chair; and she knew her parlour was elegant because it contained all she meant it to contain. She was self-conscious because a wedding-party is a unique occasion, and she was a little anxious about Will. Her sisters had been put in their places, but if those young men of theirs failed to show a proper respect to her husband, she saw herself forced to take measures regrettable in a hostess.

But Freddie and Albert were affability itself. Maggie

held their future happiness in her capable hands; and Will, as her consort, might be queer, but had to be accepted. They all came down the stairs with a starched formality and Maggie greeted them politely. Everybody recognised this as a ceremonial occasion and played up to it with a rigorous regard for etiquette.

"Good evening, Mrs. Mossop," they said, and "Good evening, Miss Hobson," "Good evening, Miss Victoria," said Maggie. Will, on his mettle, got through very well, and, with the first cup of tea, the ice was thawed. Will carved the pork pie as skilfully as if he was cutting leather, and Maggie cut the wedding-cake amongst cheers. They were hungry and made no pretence about satisfying appetite. It was a hearty, homely party, and Will found himself getting along famously. But his trial was at hand.

Freddie Beenstock rose solemnly with an unconscious imitation of his father addressing Hope Sunday School, and proposed the health of the bride and bridegroom. He spoke

IN BELLE VUE GARDENS.

at length, mouthing the usual platitudes with gusto, and sat down with an unmistakable wink at Albert. "Now," said the wink," we shall see some fun."

But Freddie counted without his hostess. Maggie rose too early in the morning to be caught napping by Freddie Beenstock. She merely nudged Will and watched him stand up quite complacently. Will was not complacent, but he had rehearsed his speech with Maggie, and the sooner it was off his chest the more pleased he.

"It's a very great pleasure to us to see you here tonight," he said, reciting rapidly; "It's an honour you do us, and I assure you, speaking for my - my wife" that came with an effort - "as well as for myself that - the - "

"Generous," prompted Maggie, without a qualm.

"Oh, aye, that's it. That the generous warmth of the sentiments so cordially expressed by Mr. Beenstock will never be forgotten by either my life-partner or self. And - and I'd like to drink this toast to you in my own house:

"Our guests and may they all be married soon themselves."

"Our guests," said Maggie, rising and drinking from her cup. She took Will's hand because she couldn't help it and squeezed appreciatively. Will had done well. But Albert meant to go one better. As Will and Maggie sat, he rose and assumed an oratorical aspect.

"Sit down," said Alice, tugging at his coat tail.

"I know men fancy themselves when they're talking, but I've heard enough. You'll not do better than Will."

"Oh, but - - - " said the would-be orator.

"You're quite right, Alice," Maggie said. "I'm sorry to disappoint Albert, but our supper's settled nicely, and I'm for something more lively than speeches. Where's that jew's-harp of yours, Will? We'll have some singing now."

Albert accepted this as a personal invitation. He was an up-to-date man, and he took the floor at once with a song which was new to the rest about "The Ruler of the Queen's Navee" from an operetta by Mr. Gilbert and Mr. Sullivan, which had been produced in London during the previous year and was just filtering through to Salford. They liked the song, but it wasn't quite what Maggie meant. A soloist divides a party into a majority and a minority of one. Maggie was for union that night; social, companionable, collective song was what she wanted, not the hazard of the unfamiliar or the private gratification of Mr. Prosser. She struck into "Johnny's so long at the Fair" and had them roaring with her lusty chorus and a jew's-harp accompaniment from Will, went on to "In her hair she wore a bunch of roses," and finished, on ground more solid still, with some of the good tunes which the devil hasn't got like "Onward, Christian Soldiers" and "the Old Hundredth." There was nothing implied by her choice of hymn tunes beyond that she like them as tunes, and that they were well know to all so that there could be no shirkers. And, indeed, there weren't. The cellar echoed and re-echoed with good fellow-ship made vocal. No passer-by need read the announcement on the door to know that business was emphatically suspended in Will Mossop's shop.

"I'm sure we ought to be getting home, Maggie," said Alice.

"Oh no," cried Will aghast. Was he to be left alone with Maggie at this hour? Maggie thought he was.

"You'd better," she said, candidly scorning polite lies. "I reckon Tubby's a bit tired of looking after the shop by now. You'd better take him this along," she added parenthetically, cutting a solid wedge from her wedding-cake. "If Father's wakened up and gone in home, I'm not envying Tubby, nor you neither when you get there."

"That's it," said Alice. "I'm a bit nervous."

"He'll have an edge on his temper," said the comforter. "Come and put your hats on. Will, you can be clearing the table while we're away." She turned to follow Alice and Vickey to her bedroom, but Albert laughed too soon. If he and Freddie had been content to put their opinion of Will into a glance, they might have escaped humiliation. As it was, Maggie heard and froze the laugh on Albert's lips.

"And you and Freddie can just lend him a hand with the washing up, Albert."

Vickey heard. This was to outrage all convention. "Maggie! We're guests."

Maggie admitted it. She knew the code as well as Vickey. To ask a guest to raise hand to anything was an offence against the social law. To ask, nay, to command, a male guest to wash up was a gross insult. But Maggie was not insulting. She was only punishing.

"I know," she said. "But I noticed them laughing at Will, and washing up 'ull maybe make them think on that it's not allowed."

"Well, I'll be hanged," said Freddie, as the door closed behind the girls, and Will began to remove the cups. Albert winked at him confidently, and took a parcel from his pocket. In Maggie's absence he could enjoy himself with Will.

"By Jove, Will," he said, "I was nearly forgetting this. I bought you a little present. Something you need.

"That's good of you," said Will, opening it and discovering Albert's little jest, a packet of preserved ginger. "Eh, by gum, that's champion. How did you know I've a sweet tooth? Wilt have one now?"

Albert and Freddie gazed at each other helplessly. What are you to do with an unsophisticated creature who won't see the point of a jest as old as the hills? Will in his primaeval innocence was grinning blandly, pleased as Punch with his present, holding out a great paw for Albert to shake. Albert shook it. There was nothing else to do.

The impervious Will continued to remove pots. Albert consulted Freddie's eye, but saw no hope in it.

"Are you going to wash up pots?" he asked.

"Are you?"

"I look at it like this myself. All being well, you and I are marrying into this family and we know what Maggie is. If we start giving in to her now she'll be a nuisance to us all our lives."

"That's right enough, but there's this plan of hers to get us married. Are you prepared to work it for us?"

The lawyer in him shuddered. "I'm not, anything but - " A pregnant pause ensued. They watched Will silently.

"What would you do in our place, Will?" tried Freddie.

"Please. yourselves," said Will. "I'm getting on with what she told me."

Freddie explained the difference. "You're married to her, we aren't."

"What's the hurry for the table, anyhow?" asked Albert.

Will stopped short. "Nay," he said, with earnestness, "I'm not in any hurry myself."

"She is," said Freddie.

"It 'ull be for my lessons, I reckon. She's schooling me."

"And don't you want to learn them?"

"T'isn't that. I - I just don't want to be rude to you, turning you out so early. I don't see you need to go away so soon."

"Why not?"

"I'm fond of a bit of company."

"Do you want company on your wedding night?" persisted Albert.

"I don't favour your going so soon," Will said obstinately.

Illumination came on Freddie. "He's afraid to be alone with her. That's what it is. He's shy of his wife. This was compensation for the jest that failed. At last they had Will on the raw. Let him deny it if he could.

Will tried no denials. "That's a fact," he said, "I am. You see I've not been married before, and I'm new to it. I've not been left alone with her, either. Up to now, she's been coming round to where I lodge at Tubby Wadlow's to give me my lessons. It's different tonight, and I freely own I'm feeling awkward-like. I'd be deeply obliged if you would stay on a bit to help to - to thaw the ice for me."

Albert's eye met Freddie's. There was derision in their glances, mingled with mighty relief. This was simply a gift. What better excuses could two young men possibly have? They lost no dignity now by washing pots. On the contrary, the nimbler they were, the worse Will liked it. They weren't washing pots to please Maggie, or because she told them to. Not at all: they did it to please themselves and to displease Will. They flourished towels briskly.

"You've been engaged to her," said Albert, "and if you didn't thaw the ice then, it's your own fault for not making use of your opportunities."

"Well, you see, we weren't engaged for long," said Will. "And Maggie's not the sort you get familiar with. You needn't be in such a desperate hurry with those pots, anyhow."

"Hurry!" said Albert facetiously, "this is nothing to our usual pace. We're the champion pot-washers of Salford."

"It's that being alone with her that worries me, and I did think you'd stand by a fellow-man to make things not so strange at first."

"That's not the way we look at it," said Freddie.

"Hurry up with those pots, Albert."

"Have you broken anything yet, Albert?" said Maggie, returning from the bedroom with her sisters.

"Broken!" he repeated indignantly. "No."

"Too slow, I expect," she said.

"I must say you don't show much gratitude. Aren't you at all surprised to find us doing this?"

"Surprised!" she said; "I told you to do it."

Consulting Mr. Shugwell

To sit revolving many memories is a glorious occupation when one is young, and memories are short and sweet. It is a morbid affair when you have a head, a hard park seat and very little inside you. And when you have been served with a writ and see the horrors of publicity in front of you, perhaps you begin to consider whether the Irwell is as filthy as it is painted. You have still a preference for a clean death, which shows you mean to go on living, albeit miserably, until you are more miserable. Pride dies hard, prejudice dies hard, but pride dies last. And Mr. Hobson was not yet prepared to bow the knee to his daughter Maggie. He would sooner face a lawyer. So pitiful is his strait. Let no one think Mr. Hobson hated his daughter. Only Mr. Hobson had ever been the Pattern in his own household, the Dictator, Arbitrator, Autocratic Source of all Good. He had never been humble before his offspring, and no genuine parent can ever watch the rising generation faithfully and not be moved to humility. It is not that sons and daughters have more than we had. Very likely they have less, but we did not see ourselves in our youth, and in our age we must surely marvel, and reverence, this free uprising of life in our own house. But Mr. Hobson had refused to see; the audacious capacity, the fine business ingenuity, and the clear devotion of Maggie to some purposes, did not stir him to pride outside himself; rather it alarmed him; he saw one, a woman, overtaking him, reaping admiration from customers, praise from envious tradesmen their neighbours, as if he was played out. He wasn't going to Maggie yet.

Mr. Hobson arose and looked evilly upon Peel Park, which is quite excusable. Peel Park is at times an unlovely depressing spot, unless you have the self-sufficient temperament.

At the first corner Mr. Hobson looked about him. He was dissatisfied. He stalked away into Chapel Street, and there saw what he desired, a policeman. He went up to the uniformed human.

"Does thou know a lawyer?" he demanded.

The official saluted. "I do, several, and all sorts."

"One that's less like a lawyer than all the rest put together?"

The policeman considered Mr. Hobson and gathered that Mr. Hobson was unwell. But he said nothing about that. He considered the practical information he was to give by request.

"First on right, third on right, round by the Pothouse and two doors up from the Pothouse, Mr. Isaac Shugwall is your man." The policeman saluted Mr. Hobson to intimate that the audience was finished. Mr. Hobson knew the Pothouse, so that any repetition of the directions was unnecessary. He remembered nothing but the Pothouse, and thither he went his troubled way. There they told him the name of the lawyer he was seeking, and directed him two doors up and two stairs. He obeyed, without purchasing a drink in return for the information, but the landlady did not murmur. She knew very well if the gentleman had business with Mr. Shugwall, business would be also done with her. Mr. Shugwall was made that way.

Mr. Hobson recovered his breath after the stair journey, and plunged into the abhorred office of a lawyer. He pulled up rather sharply, finding himself in a compartment already largely occupied by a cane-bottomed chair. He knocked loudly on a shelf, and waited. Nothing stirred, except the air, by reason of some nasal performance in an adjoining room. The office-boy, whose occupation was divided between self-amusement and beer-fetching errands, was within, but unfortunately deeply immersed in a ticklish game of noughts and crosses with himself. For all the stillness Mr. Hobson felt humanity about him and banged louder.

"Chuck it," said the absent-minded office boy.

Mr. Hobson did chuck it; he burst open the top door of the partition and gazed at the subtle juvenile with awe-inspiring gaze. But the youth had seen some curious clients in his time, and was not one bit abashed.

"Nowt," he said, as to an importune commercial traveller.

"Nowt," ejaculated Hobson. "Isaac Shugwall I want, my lad, or I'll dust they breeches."

The lad came up to the door and drummed his fingers idly on the ledge. He looked at Mr. Hobson casually.

"Nowt," he repeated.

"Is Mr. Shugwall inside?"

The boy shook his head.

"Pothouse says he is, and they know. What's that snoring next door?"

"Parrot," lied the boy, almost cheerfully. "Mr. Shugwall's parrot having a snooze by itself."

There was an irrefutable note about that nasal performance, and Mr. Hobson was a man of vast knowledge of the world. "It's Shugwall sleeping off morning. I have got some business for him, a job that lawyers like, my lad, court work."

"Eh! why didst tha not say so at first? Ah thowt tha was a new soort of bum. Come in," said the wary youth, hospitably. "I'll give Mr. Shugwall a souse wi' water can."

He left Mr. Hobson in the clerk's office, a place of smut-laden papers, foul ink-pots, and unleashed floors. Inside the private room arose splutterings, murmurs and then silence.

"What name?" inquired the boy, when he reappeared.

"Mr. Hobson," said the owner, aspirating heavily.

"Mr. Robson," announced the boy mellifluously but inaccurately.

Mr. Hobson found himself in the presence of a gentleman very busy at a table, with much sealed parchment and antiquated law-books conspicuously open, making an impressive litter about him. But the illusion was not maintained when the eye dwelt on the gentleman. He was small and sly, with a pretty facial colouring, rose-tipped promontory on a chalky background.

"Hobson of Chapel Street," said the consultant, as he sank on to a rickety chair, which sagged alarmingly, and then steadied at a leg extension, which seemed quite natural to its condition.

"What can *(hic)* do for *(hic)*?" asked the legal man, somewhat involuntarily.

"Got the hiccups pretty bad," grunted Mr. Hobson suspiciously.

Mr. Shugwall nodded with closed lips. And really, although Mr. Hobson was too far gone in bitterness to worry about trifles, Mr. Shugwall was entirely capable of attending to business. He was most acute when recovering. He looked at his client.

"That!" snorted Mr. Hobson, throwing down his writ.

The lawyer picked up the blue damnation and appeared to study it with interest and acumen. In reality, he read nothing at all beyond the name of the solicitors serving. He was in that condition when one has to be very careful of one's reading, otherwise the mind is hopelessly bewildered.

"Wonderful people," sneered Mr. Hobson.

Mr. Shugwall did not reply. Instead, he studied Mr. Hobson carefully, with an observation of detail he had not yet had time to collect. He noticed the silk hat and the Sunday garments, the white shirt and the gold watch-chain. He made no mistake in thinking this anything but Mr. Hobson's Sunday costume, but he did think the man who put on his Sunday costume to visit a lawyer was good for heavy costs. And it was the custom of Mr. Shugwall with his peculiar class of clients to bargain for his fee before he did any thinking about the case at all.

"Fi' pounds if you lose," he said thickly, but intelligibly.

"Lose!" shouted Mr. Hobson, "I don't come to a lawyer to lose, my lad. I'll get dangerous if you open your mouth to that tune."

"Seven guineas and a half if I get you off," concluded the gentleman imperturbably.

"It's a lot of money," said Mr. Hobson cautiously.

"'S a heavy case. Prossie and Pikieton 'n Prossie, nothin' they touch is unsound.

"Thankee! The fact that Bexley Square has taken up Beenstock's suit is as good as a verdict, ha! Fines me, ah! damages, ho! Sets the judge against me!" Mr. Hobson was very grievously angry. It seemed to him justice in England was what it had always been, rank and corrupt, only a thousand times more foully rank and corrupt now that he had occasion to appeal to it.

Nr. Shugwall noted that his expenses might be doubled. This client was of the shouting order, and consequently of the ignorant order who are most liable to be robbed for the enlargement of their experience.

"Will you get me off?" repeated Mr. Hobson.

"Show up Beenstock, show the town what a swindling, sniffling, bog-cheeked, sanctimonious stealer they've got for a Councillor? I'll put fifteen pounds in your waistcoat pocket, Mr. Shugwall if thou can souse Beenstock in his own sewer he had digged for me."

"Come Pothouse," said Mr. Shugwall, rising and lurching very friendly. But the lurch was only temporary. Any man may lurch when he is half dead with sleep.

"I could do with a corrective myself," allowed Mr. Hobson, and they descended the stairs in happy unity of mind, but with little unity of action.

Mr. Shugwall drew Mr. Hobson into a partitioned recess, with the sort of table that stretches so far both ends as to make your entry into the recess a distinct effort, and convinces you that you will depart most easily when you are in the condition which implies indistinct efforts.

"Rum," said Mr. Shugwall, to nobody in particular.

M. Hobson paid for rum to the landlady, and Mr. Shugwall brightened up considerably. He pulled the writ out of his pocket.

....."Saw you do it?" He was quite unaware of what Mr. Hobson had done.

"Eh?"

"Saw - do it?" repeated Mr. Shugwall.

"I done it by myself," retorted Mr. Hobson, rather irately. The question was a delicate one for a churchwarden.

....." Swear alibi," quoth the ignorant adviser.

"Hah?" grunted Mr. Hobson ignorantly.

....."Never done it, wasn't there, witnesses plenty." Mr. Shugwall roared airily.

Mr. Hobson looked at Mr. Shugwall. Was this the legal adviser he had been recommended to take? Was this the sort of a resource that got one off with a caution? "My lad," he said, sternly, "I woke up where I was, on what I'd done, with that writ in my pocket."

"Ha!" said Mr. Shugwall, with rum profundity.

"Aye!" said Mr. Hobson, with sober sarcasm.

In flagrante delicto," stuttered Mr. Shugwall.

"Is thou going to yap, numskull?" said Mr. Hobson, infuriated. He got up suddenly, and upset his own rum and the empty glass of Mr. Shugwall. He also upset the table with a terrible din. The landlady appeared, and cried "Damages." The word still further maddened Mr. Hobson.

PEEL PARK, THE IRWELL, AND PENDLETON, FROM THE CRESCENT.

Had he not eaten his full of the detestable word? He choked, he fumed and boiled, the sight of his apoplectic face silenced the landlady. He recovered, and, without hesitation, he grabbed the writ, turned and ran out of the Pothouse, leaving an amazed Shugwall and an aggrieved landlady, who presently started a squabble on the theme of damages with the lawyer.

The unfortunate use of a Latin tag had given Mr. Hobson a sudden devastating vision of a law court, with himself in the dock, surrounded by lawyers and judges in wigs and gowns, condemning him to prison in this unintelligible language. It was monstrous injustice, and degradation of an Englishman's rights. Therefore he fled.

Chapter Thirteen

Father Comes Round

Will's hour of agony was upon him, irritable and fearful he looked upon the sisters of Maggie with a resentful eye. They were dressed for departure, and would depart. They did not consider him, and would not consider him, even if he protested and explained. No doubt the females were of the same opinion as Freddy and Albert, no doubt they thought the bride likes to be left along with the bridegroom on her wedding night.

But the torment was deferred. Mr. Hobson arrived, to the temporary relief of Will Mossop. Thus it ever is - the poor help the poor.

Mr. Hobson did not come in, he felt himself an Ishmaelite, a forlorn waif, a stray dog for all men's brutal sport. But it was his own daughter's cellar, and he therefore knocked very loudly. But again he was kept waiting; which was the best thing that could have happened to Mr. Hobson. It gave him a grievance, and a grievance was as good as an Army Corps. He would charge any stubborn position now. He was not longer a mongrel wondering lonely gutters; he was a parent outraged by his daughter.

Inside the cellar they seemed to be mysteriously endowed with powers of divination. Everybody knew, on the strength of a tap, that "Father" had come.

"I've been expecting it," said Maggie coolly.

"I didn't," said the fluttering Vickie.

"Or I wouldn't have come," said the terrified Alice.

The circumstances, or the male attachments of the two young ladies were incriminating. Also, the defiant revolt on

Kersal Moor was, as yet, an unpunished breach of domestic laws. With one accord the unwedded pairs turned towards the bedroom again.

"Hullo," said Maggie cheerfully; "what's to do?"

"Well....." hesitated Alice.

"All things considered..." said Vickey, considering last night.

"All right," agreed Maggie. "We'll consider all things. And the bedroom is the best place for people with nerves."

Will thought this included himself naturally, but his better half stopped his flight. "Nat, lad, I'm curing your nerves. Sit you down, Will, and try to look twice as big as my father. You're gaffer here and you can stick your chest out." Will grinned foolishly, moderately foolishly, since Maggie's eye was on him.

"Now," said Maggie, very unlike a ministering angel. She glanced round her room, and went up the cellar stairs.

"Well, Father," she said. It was not an encouraging tone of voice, but it was the right diplomacy.

"I'll come in," said her father, but without much confidence. The half-opened door was not inviting.

"I don't know about that."

"Eh!" The right diplomacy was right enough if Mr. Hobson had remembered his situation. As it was, he only remembered his grievance, and he glared, brilliant eyed.

"I'll have to ask my husband."

Mr. Hobson snorted. "Husband? Cod-fish! Stop-gap! Discount!"

Maggie pushed the door to; it is the least you can do when your husband is called a cod-fish. But the fluent stormer set his foot against the door and there was no dynamite in Maggie's cellar.

"Sithee, my lass! Does thou think because thou's wedded, the golden chains of daughterly duties are snapped, broken asunder for evermore because thou's forged the bond of matrimony? No, I say. Unnatural, that's your nature. I am kept waiting, in my hour of distress. I am refused entrance to make my statement. Lass! Lass! said Mr. Hobson in dispassionate reproach. "The years have much to teach you. Your edifice is founded on reason. It is error, simple fundamental error. Life is not reason, it is the summit of perversity, absurdity - - "

"Come inside," said Maggie happily; the invitation did not spring from a dislike to her father's eloquence. Not at all. She knew him through to the basement as they say of houses. He was talking loudly to drown the louder voice, the voice of the writ. Over her shoulder she cried, "Will, it's my father," with warning in her voice.

The information was quite unnecessary, but the warning successfully recalled to Will that he was to swell gafferwise. "I'll be glad to see him," with the condescension a humble person achieves when he tries to live beyond his limits.

Mr. Hobson snorted again. It was a foolish thing to do. Maggie counted the snorts and they went to the reckoning Mr. Hobson was to render tonight. The sins of the fathers are sometimes visited upon the fathers - by the children!

"Uppishness!" quoth Hobson eyeing Will; "catching disease is uppishness, and it's not taken thee long to catch it. I've seen thee in places, Will Mossop, where thou wasn't glad to see me." Will quailed; it takes a long time to wear off the marks of the shackles. Maggie looked invigorated and Will revived, and put out his hand, and said, with some dignity in the welcome: "Eh, I'm glad to see you, Mr. Hobson."

Mr. Hobson shook, after deliberation. He was really a visitor in distress.

And the other distressful one recognised a stronger ally than know-all young men and crush-all young ladies. "Eh!" he beamed, "I hope thou'll make a night of it with us. I hope you'll stop with us to air the house." . . . Will was wammering . . . "Good luck, thou knows, first-foot like, all the night is more lucky . . . I'll sit up with you in here."

Mr. Hobson stared, a good deal puzzled. But Maggie took the upper hand in her own inimitable style.

"That's enough, Will," she said. "I was married this morning and Father's a bit late in turning up. But seeing you're here at last you can sit down for five minutes. That sofa 'ull bear your weight. It's been tested."

Mr. Hobson sat, and sitting, remembered all his woe. Will with the cloak of gafferdom upon him made made an attempt to play the host. He apologised for the absence of Hobson's usual stimulants.

"There's nobbut tea to drink and I reckon what's in the pot is stewed." He offered to make new tea, but Maggie thought not.

"You'll do nowt of sort," she said. "Father likes his liquids strong," and poured black liquor into a cup. "Will, cut port pie."

It was hardly invalid's fare for a distressed sinner, but Maggie expected him to eat it. "You'll be sociable now you're here, I hope.

Hobson groaned. "It wasn't sociability that brought me, Maggie. I'm in disgrace. A sore and sad misfortune's fallen on me."

"Happen a piece of wedding-cake 'll do you good," she suggested cheerfully.

He shuddered. "It's sweet."

"That's only natural in cake."

"Eh, lass, I've gotten such a head."

"Aye, have you? But I reckon wedding-cake's a question of heart. There'd be no bride-cakes made at all if we thought first about our heads. I'm quite aware it's foolishness, but I've a wish to see my father sitting at my table eating my wedding-cake on my wedding-day.

Hobson fenced. "It's a very serious thing I came about, Maggie."

"It's not more serious than knowing that you wish us well," she retorted.

He cheered up slightly. If words were all she wanted he was ready to oblige. "I wish you well, my lass. You know my way. When a thing's done, it's done." He glanced at Will casually. "I'm none proud of the choice you made and I'll not lie and say I am; but I've shaken your husband's hand and that's a sign for you. The milk's spilt and I'll not cry." As far as words went this was handsome, but Maggie was implacable.

"Then there's your cake," she said, "and you can eat it."

"I've passed my word there's no ill-feeling, lass."

"Aye, so you have," said Maggie cheerily; "and now we'll have the deed."

She had no mercy. "You're a hard woman, Maggie," he said, eating his cake. "You've no consideration for the weakness of old age."

"Finished?" she asked.

"Pass me that tea," he said, and drank. "That's easier."

"I'm glad," she said. "Now that I know all's right between us, Father, you can come to what brought you here. I daresay I can find something to do in the bedroom while you talk it over with my husband."

"Eh?" said Hobson, in amazement.

"You'll not be wanting me," she said. "Women are only in your way."

"Maggie," he said, "you're not going to desert me in the hour of my need!"

"Surely to goodness you don't want a woman to help you after all you've said? Will 'ull do his best for you, I make no doubt. Give me a call when you've finished, Will," she added, rooting that unfortunate to his seat with a glance and turning briskly towards the bedroom. Hobson stared in bewilderment. Will Mossop as confidential adviser to him, Hobson, was a little too much to swallow, but Maggie meant it. At least she said it and she didn't turn, and there was Will sitting expectantly.

"Maggie," he appealed, "it's private."

"Why, yes," she said; "you needn't fear I'm going to intrude. I'm off now and you can discuss it privately with Will, as man to man, with no fools of women about."

"I tell you it's private form him."

She abandoned her comedy with the door. This was the root of the matter. "That's where you're making a mistake," she said, coming back to the table. "Will's in the family now, and you've nowt to say to me that can't be said to him."

"I've to tell you this with him sitting there?"

"Will and me's one," she said.

"Sit down, Mr. Hobson," said Will, encouragingly, rather proud of joining in with a practical suggestion.

"You call him Father now," said Maggie.

"Do I?"

"Does he?" said Hobson, daring Will to do it.

"He does," Maggie decided placidly. "Sit down, Will. Now, if you're ready, Father, we are. What's the matter?"

"That," said Hobson, with concentrated bitterness. "That's the matter." He handed Maggie the blue paper, which she accepted with curious innocence, and, like a gentle wife, passed it on to Will. Will took it, and she went behind his chair to read over his shoulder. She found it easier to read when she had reversed it. Will was endeavouring to read it upside down.

"What is it, Will?" she asked with artless curiosity.

Hobson saved Will the trouble of explaining that legal English was Greek to him. "Ruin, Maggie, that's what it is in English. Ruin and bankruptcy. Am I vicar's warden at St. Philip's or am I not? Am I Hobson, of Hobson's Boot Shop in Chapel Street, Salford? Am I a respectable ratepayer and the father of a family, or - - "

Maggie did not reply. "I see it's an action for damages for trespass," she said very quietly.

He corrected her. "It's a stab in the back, it's an unfair, un-English, cowardly way of taking a mean advantage of a casual accident, and no one but a grasping, clutching, filching, pinching, narrow-gutted scarecrow of a Nonconformist miser would have stooped to set lawyers on a Christian man that has met misfortune. I tell you, Maggie, I though I knew the world. I fancied I was acquainted with its ways and its wickedness, but I'd none plumbed the depths till this. Nathaniel Beenstock! He's something new in my experience of human nature. He's - - "

But Maggie spared the listening Fred further opinions of his father's character. She brought the orator back to his muttons.

"This says trespass. Did you trespass?"

"Trespass? I'd a lodging for the night in Beenstock's

cellar. You don't suppose I wanted to lodge in Beenstock's cellar, do you?" Will Mossop, I've a word in season for you at the beginning of your matrimonial career. Take my advice, my lad, and don't be the father of daughters. Avoid them, Will, or you'll regret it."

Will blushed crimson.

"We'll take what comes, said Maggie. "But I thought you came in here to ask advice, not give it. Was it an accident, or did you trespass?"

"You leave cross-examination to the lawyers, my lass, and I'll thank you. I'm none so clear what happened if you want to know. I can give you the cause in a nutshell - and the cause is daughters, and uppishness, and that's enough for you. I had an accident, I don't deny it. I sought oblivion in strange places instead of sticking to the Moonraker's. I rambled in search of peace and I fell on worse trouble than before. It's an accident. As plain as Salford Town Hall, its's an accident; but they that live by law have twisted ways of putting things that make white show as black. I'm in their grip at last. I've kept away from lawyers all my life. I've hated lawyers and they've got their chance to make me bleed for it. I've dodged them and they've caught me in the end. They'll squeeze me dry for it."

"My word," said Will, gazing at Mr. Hobson's full-blooded form with his guileless eyes.

"That's summat like a squeeze and all."

"I shouldn't wonder if you didn't lose some trade through this," said Maggie.

"Wonder! it's as certain as Christmas. I told you it was ruin. My good class customers aren't going to buy their boots from a man who's stood up in open court and had to acknowledge he was over-come. It'll begin with the parson and run through the whole Church connection. They'll not remember it was private grief that caused it all. They'll only think the worse of me because I couldn't control my daughter better than to let her go and be the cause of sorrow to me in my age. That's what you've done. Brought this on me, you two, between you."

"Do you think it will get into the paper, Maggie?" Will

suggested blandly, in perfect simplicity. He merely wanted to measure the catastrophe.

"For sure it will," she said. "You'll see your name in the *Salford Reporter*, Father."

Hobson chose to be insulted. After all, if one is in trouble there is a sort of satisfaction in feeling that one's troble is the "greatest ever," and consequently any annoyance if people make light of it. The *Salford Reporter* was a weekly paper of limited local circulation.

"*Salford Reporter*," he said, "and more. When there is ruin and disaster and outrageous fortune overwhelms a man of my importance in the world, it isn't only the *Salford Reporter* that takes note of it. The awful cross that's come to me will be recorded in the *Manchester Guardian* for the whole of Lancashire to read."

"And, possibly, it would have been. The *Manchester Guardian* is read in Lancashire because it is the best commercial paper in the North of England; and outside Lancashire because it is the best literary paper in the provinces. Londoners have heard of it, and Londoners are rarely aware of the products of the provinces. "Surprising what a craze there is amongst you cultured people for the *Manchester Guardian*", says Mr. Arnold Bennett's Napoleon of the Press in "What the Public Wants."

But it was not because of the cultured people that Mr. Hobson had a chance of figuring in the *Manchester Guardian*. It was because it was a Liberal paper, and politics lead the best of editors into strange company. They led the *Manchester Guardian* into the company of the teetotal wing of the Liberal Party. As brewers are to Tories, so teetotallers are to Liberals, and it was therefore just conceivable that the case of Henry Hobson, if brought to court, might figure obscurely in a short paragraph amongst the police court reports as an awful example of the results of intemperance.

"Eh, by gum, think of that!" said Will, tremendously impressed. "To have your name appearing in the *Guardian*. Why, it's very near worth while being ruined for the pleasure of reading about yourself in a printed paper."

"It's there for others to read beside me, my lad," said Hobson grimly.

"Aye, so it is," said Will, developing the theme with gusto and entirely without malice. "I didn't think of that. This 'ull give a lot of satisfaction to many I could name. Other people's troubles is mostly what folks read the paper for; and I reckon it's twice the pleasure to them when it's troubles of man they know themselves."

"To hear you talk it sounds like a pleasure to you."

"Nay, indeed it's not," said Will sincerely.

"You've ate my wedding-cake and you've shook my hand. We're friends, I hope, and I were nobbut meditating aloud like a friend. I always think," went on the Job's comforter, "I always think it's best to look on the worst side of things first, and then whatever chances can't be worse than you looked for. There's St. Philip's comes into my mind now. I don't suppose you'll go on being vicar's warden after this to-do, and it brought you a powerful lot of customers from the Church."

"Have you got any more consolation for me, Will?"

"I only spoke what came into my mind," said Will, rather aggrieved. He'd meant so well.

"Well, have you spoken it all?"

"I can keep my mouth shut, if you'd rather."

"Don't strain yourself for my sake," said Hobson.

"When a man's mind is full of thought like yours, they're better out than in. You let them come out, my lad. They'll leave a cleaner place behind.."

"Have I said summat to upset you?" said Will.

"I'm sure I didn't mean to. It's a fact I'm not much good at talking and I always seem to say wrong things when I try. I'm sorry if my well-meant words don't suit your taste, but I thought you came here for advice."

This was Will Mossopm as he ought to be, apologetic, a worm for Hobson's hoof to crush. And Henry, after his humiliation, was in the mood for crushing somebody.

"Advice from you," he roared, "you jumped-up, cock-a-hooping - - "

"That'll do, Father," said Maggie very quietly. "My husband's trying to help you.

"Yes, Maggie," he said, collapsing like a pricked balloon. A longish pause ensued. Maggie intended the lesson to sink lower.

The End of Uppishness

Mr. Hobson shuffled uneasily on the sofa. Maggie's eye was on him and she prolonged the silent, penitential pause to the limits of his endurance. It was Mr. Heeler who had advocated silent strength to Hobson in the Moonraker's a month ago. Hobson was now given an opportunity of testing the efficacy of that policy, though the roles of coercer and coerced were not in the hands intended by Mr. Heeler. In the space of three minutes Mr. Hobson found himself carried back fifty years. He was a small, boy again and Maggie was his mother. The silence was intolerable.

She considered his state and judged it time to come to business. "Now," she said, "about this accident of yours."

"Yes, Maggie," he said thankfully.

She summed it up. "It's the publicity that you're afraid of."

"It's being dragged into a court of law at all: me that's voted right all through my life and been a sound supporter of the Queen and Constitution."

"Then we must keep it out of court."

Because Maggie said it, it sounded possible at first blush. He face lightened, but the shadows fell again. Maggie was not omnipotence, and the nature of pigs is to grunt.

"If there are lawyers in heaven, Maggie, which I greatly doubt, they may keep the cases out of courts there. On earth a lawyer's job is to squeeze a man, and to squeeze him where his squirming's seen the most - in court."

"I've heard of cases being settled out of court, in private."

"In private? Yes, I daresay, and all the worse for that. It's done amongst themselves in lawyers' offices behind closed doors, so that no one can see they're squeezing twice as hard in private as they'd dare to do in public. There's some decency of restraint demanded by a public place, but privately - - . It'll cost a fortune to settle this in private, Maggie."

Maggie knew very well what it would cost. It would cost exactly the sum which she considered could be withdrawn from Hobson's business without crippling it, and as keeper of the books she had had full opportunity to compute that sum. And she computed it with moderation. She was going to be fair to her father. If he could run his home and his business better without his daughters than with them he should have a chance to try, and no chance of telling her that she had left him with insufficient capital. All she wanted to secure was that Alice and Vickey should be married; and further, that, should Hobson's business (as she anticipated) now go to ruin, the younger girls should first have some share out of it in return for their years of labour. For herself, who had worked without wages for twice as many years as they had, she was taking nothing - except Will Mossop. She was doing justice all round, and if any one was dissatisfied with her ideas of justice, so much the worse for them. Meantime there was no need to tell Hobson that he was to get off far more lightly than he deserved.

"I make no doubt it's going to cost you something," she said grimly, "but you'd rather do it privately than publicly?"

"If it were only not a lawyer's office."

"You can settle it with the lawyer out of his office. You can settle it with him here," and before the astonished eye of Mr. Hobson there filed out from the bedroom, in procession, Albert - looking so different in his present professional mood from that unfortunate victim of Maggie's salesmanship that no wonder Mr. Hobson had but the haziest recollection of having seen him before; Fred, who was only too conscious that Mr. Hobson remembered him very well; and the girls who followed after an interval in a state of dithering nervousness.

Maggie introduced Albert: "This is Mr. Prosser, of Prosser, Pilkington & Prosser."

The attacking party had all the advantages of surprise:

a surprise, too, administered to one already reduced by Maggie's eye and the experiences of the day. Hobson retreated as Albert advanced.

"A lawyer!" he said, precisely as a beliver in a personal devil might have apostrophised a satanic apparition.

"Yes," said Albert firmly.

"You're a lawyer! At your age!"

But Maggie gave him no time to contemplate the natural malignancy of a man who took to evil courses in the flower of his youth. She introduced Freddie: "This is Mr. Beenstock."

Hobson had his back to the wall. He could retreat no further. "What! Here!" he gasped.

"Family gathering!" said Maggie, as Alice and Vickey emerged. "When you've got a thing to settle, you need all the parties to be present."

"But there are so many of them," he said, helplessly. "Where have they all come from?"

"My bedroom."

"You - - ! Maggie, I wish you'd explain before my brain gives way."

"It's quite simple, Father," she said. "I got them here because I expected you."

"You expected me!"

"You're in trouble, and I knew you'd bring your trouble to me."

It was bitingly true, and perhaps not more outspoken than was Maggie's habit with him, but he resented her candour before an audience. Some one should suffer for it; not Maggie, for his hope was in her; nor Albert, for there was no health in him; nor Fred's dauntless attitude on Kersal Moor. He turned to Alice and Vickey.

"What's it got to do with you? Why are you here? What's happening to the shop?"

But, plunge as he would, Maggie could deal shrewdly with him. "You can let them be," she said. "They came out because it's my wedding day, and that's quite reason enough. Will and me 'ull do the same for them and more. We'll close this shop and welcome on their wedding days."

"Their wedding days," he snorted. "That's a long time off. It'll be many a year before there's another wedding in this family, I give you my word. One daughter defying me is quite enough."

Vickey wondered what her part in the Kersal Moor encounter could be called if it was not defiance. However, the lawyer in Albert was chafing at delay and he interrupted: "Hadn't we better get to business, sir?"

Hobson welcomed the diversion. He was in a tight corner, but no spawn of the devil was going to ride roughshod over him.

"Young man," he said, "your're abusing a noble word. You're a lawyer. By your own admission, you're a lawyer. Honest men live by business, and lawyers live by law."

"In this matter, sir," said Albert, countering the blow, "I am followilng the instructions of my client, Mr. Beenstock; and the remark you have just let fall, before witnesses, appears to me to bear a libellous reflection on the actions of my client."

It was bad sense, worse law, and a thousand miles from the precise traditions of the firm of Prosser; but Albert had left Bexley Square very much behind him today and this had the merit of effectiveness. It visibly impressed Mr. Hobson.

FLAT IRON MARKET, SALFORD.

"What," he roared, "so it's libel now! Isn't trespass and - and spying on trade secrets enough for you? You bloodsucking - - "

"One moment, Mr. Hobson," interrupted Albert; "you can call me what you like - "

"And I shall," he declared. "You - - "

" - but I wish to remind you, in your own interests, that abuse of a lawyer is remembered in the costs. Now, my client tells me he is prepared to settle this matter out of court. Personally, I don't advise him to, because we should probably get higher damages in court. But Mr. Beenstock has no desire to be vindictive. He remembers your position, your reputation for respectability and - "

"How much?"

"Er - I beg your pardon?" said Albert, brought up all-standing by the brusque question.

"I'm not so fond of the sound of your voice as you are, my lad. What's the figure?"

"The sum we propose," said Albert smoothly, "which will include my ordinary costs, but not any additional costs which you may incur by persisting in the use of defamatory language towards me, is one thousand pounds."

"What!" roared the burgess.

"It isn't," said Maggie, quietly.

"A thousand pounds for tumbling down a cellar! Why, I might have broken my leg."

"That is in the nature of an admission, Mr. Hobson," said Albert. "Our flour bags saved your leg from fracture, and I am therefore inclined to add to the sum I have stated a reasonable estiamte of the doctor's bill we have saved you by protecting your leg with our bags."

The assurance of the fellow left Hobson speechless. Maggie had followe Albert's arguments with some admiration, but she felt it time to put him in his place. Evidently a sanguine discussion of the settlement question had taken place in her bedroom, but the figures were predetermined, by her, and she didn't believe in avarice.

"Albert Prosser," she remarked, "I can see you're going

to get on in the world, but you needn't be greedy. That thousand pounds is too much."

"We thought - " began Albert.

"Then you can think again," she said.

"But surely - " said Freddie.

"If there are any more signs of greediness from you two," she said, "there'll be a counter-action for personal damages due to your criminal carelessness in leaving your cellar-flap open."

A great light leapt to Hobson's eyes. Maggie had only played with him. Now she was saving him, being his daughter, turning the tables on these despoilers of his house.

"Maggie you've saved me. I'll bring that action. I'll show them up."

Maggie smiled. But it was not what Hobson would have called her pleasant smile. "You're not damaged," she said, "and one lawyer's quite enough. But," she added, withering Albert with one of her incomparable glances, "he'll be more reasonable now. I know perfectly well what you can affort to pay, and it's not a thousand pounds, nor anything like a thousand pounds."

"Not so much of your can't afford, Maggie. You'll make me out a pauper."

"You can afford five hundred pounds," she stated calmly, "and you're going to pay five hundred."

"There's a difference between affording and paying, my lass."

"That's true," she said. "And you can go to the courts and be reported in the papers if you like. Five hundred's less than the value of the trade you'll lose in a year."

He knew it was. The fight, in fact, was over, but Hobson surrendered with difficulty. He looked sullen while Albert produced papers for his signature. That brought the light of battle to his eyes again.

"Those things aren't needed, Albert," Maggie said. "My father's word's enough." Unspoken word, at that, but Maggie knew, and Hobson nodded his assent. It was Vickey who put the majority sentiment into words. She clapped her hands. She danced.

"It's settled! It's settled" Hurrah! Hurrah!"

"Vickey," said Mr. Hobson, with dignified severity, "I've none forgot last night, it you have. And I'll remember this night to the end of my days. I'll remember that a daughter of mine could clap her hands and show unseemly joy at the sight of her father robbed by a gang of footpads who deserve to be hanged for it. But I'll bring it home to you, my lass. I'm not to be dragged to public scorn, but you can just consider this before you cheer again. Five hundred pounds 'ull none break me, but it's a tidy sum of money to be going out of the family."

Vickey looked contrite, but, her aim achieved, Maggie was for making an end of it all without more ado.

"It's not going out of the family, Father," she told him, and in the moments to come she used her eye on him as never before. "Their wedding day is not so far off as you thought now there's the half of five hundred pounds apiece for them to make a start on."

And Albert, with a sense of situation, put his arm round Alice, while Freddie followed his example with his Vickey. They were a melting sight, the girls at any rate like humble supplicants. But the moment had its danger and Maggie exerted herself.

"You mean to tell me - " he began.

"You won't forget you've passed your word, will you, Father?" said Maggie.

"I've been done, It's a plant. It's conspiracy. It's - "

But Maggie explained what it did and passed over what it was. "It takes two daughters off your hands at once and clears your shop of all the fools of women that used to lumber up the place."

Alice tried to help, and for once effectively. Hobson resolved to cut his loss. He was not hit harder than he could afford, and, as Alice said, "it will be much easier for you without us in your way, Father."

He agreed. "Aye, and you can keep out of my way, and all. Do you hear that, all of you? I'll run that shop with men and - and I'll show Salford how it should be run. One smart young man 'ull do, and he'll cost me less in wages than it took to clothe and feed the three of you. It's a release this is. It's the end of uppishness. And don't you imagine there'll be room for you when you come home crying and tired of your fine husbands. I'm rid of you and it's a lasting riddance, mind. I'll pay this money that you've robbed me of amongst you and that's the end of it, for all of you. You especially, Maggie. I'm not blind yet and I can see who 'tis I've got to thank for this."

"Don't be vicious, Father," she said.

He turned upon the shrinking Will, the silent, scared - but, at the bottom of his heart, grateful - spectator of the stupendous scene. Will flinched, but held his ground, and after all it was pity he was to receive.

"Will Mossop, I'm sorry for you, married to the likes of her. Take you for all in all, you're the best of the bunch. You'r backward lad, but you know your trade, and it's an honest one."

"So does my Albert know his trade," blundered Alice. It was loyal, but obtuse. Hobson paused as he climbed the stairs. It gave him dominance, and he felt elevated.

"I'll grant you that," he said. "He knows his trade. He's good at robbery." Albert permitted himself a smile and Fred was so indiscreet as to follow suit. "Aye, you may grin, you two, but you'll laugh on the other side of your faces soon. You're taking trouble on board, my lads, and I'd none be you for forty times five hundred quid. Those wenches don't eat air, and your penny buns 'ull cost you tuppence now. Aye, and more. Wait till the families begin to come. Don't look to me for help, that all."

"Father!" protested the crimson Vickey.

"Aye, you may Father me, but that's a piece of work I've finished with. I've done with fathering and they're beginning it. They'll know what marrying a woman means before so long. They're putting chains upon themselves and I have thrown the shackles off. I've suffered thirty years and more and I'm a free man from today. Lord! What a thing you're taking on! You poor, poor wretches! You're red-nosed robbers, but you're going to pay for it."

He had the honours and he flung open the door with a majestic air and stalked out to Oldfield Road mightily content. Fluency, as usual, exalted him, and he made for the Moonraker's with a firm step. He was himself. He ordered steak. He ate largely of steak. He suffused the bar-parlour, wielding the sceptre as in the days before the feminine revolt grew burdensome, haranguing masterfully of the defeat and expulsion of daughters, the revolution in the shop, and the palmy, viril days to come.

Come to Bed Willie Mossop

"That's that," said Maggie, as he closed the door; "but if you'll take advice from me, you'll arrange to get married quick. Alice and Vickey won't have a rosy time with him."

"Can they go home at all?" asked Fred, "after what he's said."

"He'll not remember half of it. He's for the Moonraker's now - if there's time. What is the time?"

"Time we were going, Maggie," said Albert.

"You'll be glad to see the back of us."

"No, no," said panic-stricken Will. "I wouldn't dream of asking you to go."

"Then I would," said Maggie. "There are your hats. Good-night." She had done with ceremoney, and Albert found himself taken very much at his word.

The sisters followed their lovers. One quick kiss and Vickey was gone. Alice took things more leisurely. "Good-night, Maggie," she said, "and - thank you."

"Oh, that," said Maggie, lightly. "I was pleasing myself. I'll see you again soon; only don't come round here too much, because Will and me's going to be busy, and you'll happen find enough to do yourselves with getting wed. Send us word when the day is."

"We'll be glad to see you at the wedding," said Alice, and it was obvious that the bride of Albert Prosser did not intend to see much of Mrs. William Mossop after that event. Maggie agreed with her.

"We'll come to that," she said. "You'll be too grand afterwards."

"Oh, no, Maggie," came with repentance, but half-heartedly.

"Well, happen we'll be catching up with you before so long. We're only starting here, and I reckon I know which of our husbands 'ull be thought most of at the bank in twenty years from now. Good-night."

Alice departed, and Maggie turned to Will, who was gaping incredulously at this roseate vision of his financial future.

"Now, you've heard what I've said of you tonight. In twenty years you're going to be a bigger man than either of your brothers-in-law."

"I heard you say it, Maggie."

"And we've to make it good. I'm not a boaster, Will. And it's to be in less than twenty years, and all, so just think on."

"Well, I dunno. They've a long start on us."

"And you've got me." His look of dog-like admiration conceded it. She went on briskly: "Your slate's in the bedroom. Bring it out, and we'll get a move on. My father was right when he called you a backwrd lad, but he'll none be right for long."

He produced his slate and pencil.

"Off with your Sunday coat now. You don't want to sit making your mess in that. I'll set you a short copy for tonight, because it's getting late, and we've a lot to do in the morning." She sat and wrote on the slate in fair round copy-hand: "There is always room at the top." Maggie believed in training Will's mind as well as his fingers.

She stood awhile, till he settled down to his task. Her mind ran over the events of the day. She agreed with herself it had been an eventful one, full, sweet, lively, triumphant. She was not afraid of triumph, nor did any false humility enter her thoughts. Only, satisfaction is a pleasant sensation, and she sat down to enjoy it. There was a corner of the table between herself and Will, so that the bridegroom was not nervous. For the moment he was absorbed in the familiar routine of a month, tracing the faithful imitation of her letters in the presence of the teacher. Not every wife has taught her husband the alphabet. The majority of men are more advanced by the time they fall in love. But Will was backward, and every little step that is taken in the growth of the unified life had to be shown to him. Nay, he had to be compelled to take it. Love may teach all things, but that is only when the spirit of the lover is bold, confident of his love, and possessed by his love. Will Mossop was not at that happy stage. Shy, fugitive and terrified, that was the nature of his heart, as though it loved best to hide in the dark wood, and peep like a wild coney on the allurement of the meadows of sunshine. The month of Maggie's tuterage had changed him little, but she knew the slender growth had begun. He had begun to wonder, and to wonder is to grow. At Belle Vue today he had dared to dance with her. Confidence in her had bred confidence in himself. He permitted the magic of joy to overcome his distate for doing anything but hide. Assuredly the child grew, and despite his unflattering appearance, the unflattering compliments of her father, and the tolerance of her smarter sisters and her smarter sisters' young men, Maggie Hobson enjoyed her selection. This plodding speller was the pick of Salford's matrimonial market. And her eye dwelt on his simple, steadfast face with the kindest, dearest expression that had ever come into it. He was hers, and while she rejoiced in her possession her spirit knelt to him, adoring him. How good it was to sit along with him by lamplight in this poor cellar! How rare! It was her hour, and many morrows could not obliterate it and its richness. There was a little cry in her for fondling, for kisses, and the thousand endearments of more impulsive kinds. True, these would come in time as her man gathered manhood, but this present was very well. It was quiet, it was holy, the best of her life, her wedding night.

Her face was soft and serene, there was something dove-like, folded in peace within her, as she rose to her task of cleaning up.

The flowers from Hope Hall, exotics in that cellar, drooped heavily, and she took them from the slop-basin. Unconsciously she spoke aloud. "I'll put these flowers of Mrs Hepworth's behind the fire. We"ll not want litter in the place come working time tomorrow." Then, as she fingered them, she stopped, looked half askance at Will, and swiftly salved a flower from the bunch. Cremating the rest, she turned quickly to the bed-room, a shade too rapidly. Some consciousness of her slight perturbation communicated itself to Will.

"You're saving one?" he asked, looking up.

Maggie was caught in an act of sentiment. "I thought I'd press it in my Bible for a keepsake, Will," she said; then, brazening it out with fine candour, added: "I'm not beyond liking to be reminded of this day."

But that was as far as she meant to go. She had been detected and she had confessed. Now Will Mossop's hour was come. There was no more respite.

"Lord, I'm tired," she said. "Pleasuring does take it out of you. I reckon I'll leave clearing up while morning. It's a slackish way of starting, but I don't get married every day."

"No," agreed Will, suddenly absorbed in his task. But a slate has limitations. It could not last for ever, but - Furtively he took his handkerchief and moistened it.

"What are you doing?" Maggie asked sharply.

"I made a bloomer and I was washing it out," he said.

She came to see. "Bloomer? I can't see it. Your writing's getting better every day. There's nothing wrong with that. Finish that copy out and it'll do for tonight. I'm for my bed."

"Yes, Maggie," said the procrastinator.

She took the flower with her and the bedroom door closed. The clock ticked on and Will's slate-pencil scratched laboriously. He was notably careful tonight. Care takes time. But he dared not attempt again his delaying tactics with the handkerchief. He spaced his copies closely, got extra lines upon the slate, but in the end resources were exhausted and his task helped him no more.

He rose reluctantly. With a faint glow of proprietary

pride he went upstairs to try the locking of the door. As Maggie had locked it, it was naturally secure. His roving eye alighted on the fire. Oh, there was occupation. He raked it out with care. Not till the embers ceased to glow did he desist. Perhaps he was thinking of economy.

He laid the poker down and glanced shyly at the bedroom door. There was no sound. Discouraged, he sat on the sofa, and took his boots off. Curiously enough there were obstinate knots in both laces. It took Will Mossop as long to quit his boots as Mr Hobson occupied with the opposite operation of putting his on. And when they were off, he did not know where to put them, and tried place after place in turn. He put them down at last, temporarily, and took his collar off. He sat tugging his tie, eyeing the closed door for quite a long while. Then with cold despair he rose, picked up his boots and went to the door.

His hand was on the handle when it occurred to him that he had not put out the gas. He sighed. He almost sobbed with relief, and came slowly to the gas. He turned it out.

In darkness, panic came. He could find the bedroom door, for the cellar of Will Mossop was not entirely dark at night. A street lamp cast a pallid light through the windows. But he found the sofa first. He gave a last terrified look in the direction of the door and buried his face in the friendly horsehair.

Maggie opened the door. She was attired in a plain calico nightdress of a strictly utilitarian description, and in her hand was a lighted candle. Maggie wasted no words. She came to Will and watched him cringe more closely to the horsehair as the candle shone upon him. Her face was grim. She took him very firmly by the ear and drew him to the bedroom.

226 *Hobson's Choice*

CHAPTER FOURTEEN

Column And A Half In The Salford Reporter

Long before the day when Alice and Vickey were both married at St. Philip's, with full ceremonial honours due to the daughters of a churchwarden. Mr. Hobson had persuaded himself that their settlements were no more than voluntary thank-offerings. He smiled, as he added a generous sum for expenses, and expanded his smile to positively luscious benevolence when a photograph was taken of the wedding party. That was because his fluency had had full scope, and in the oratorical contest after the wedding breakfast he had challenged and defeated the rival orators Beenstock and Prosser.

For once these incompatibles met on common ground. There had been awkward interviews between each bridegroom and his parent, but the money, if less than expected, was at least ready cash, and ardour plus prompt settlement had prevailed. A nicer point had been to find a place for the breakfast where such opposing elements as Hobson and Beenstock could meet without offence to either. The shop was ruled out as unsuitable; political club-rooms, which could be hired for such occasions, were - political; and Sunday-school rooms were sectarian. Maggie solved it for them by suggesting the Oddfellows' Hall as neutral ground, and the employment of a caterer circumvented the domestic problem of a household now bereft of daughters.

It was a great occasion, and the *Salford Reporter* celebrated it in a column and a half, little guessing what spicier "copy" might have swollen its circulation had it not been for the compelling eye of Maggie Mossop, who with her obviously ineligible husband sat unregarded at this banquet of Olympians.

Vainly did Beenstock address the table as if it were a Sunday-school, vainly did Prosser argue as if it were a bench of magistrates. Hobson talked to it as if it were the Moonraker's (which by strong representation it was), and the human touch was all. "A racy speech" the reporter summed it up; "a Salford man at home amongst his friends." It was not for the reporter to observe that the departure of the couples - one to North Wales, the other to the Lake District. - was followed abruptly by a break-up of the party. Clan Beenstock went to the right, Clan Prosser to the left, and Mr. Hobson, a clan in himself, to the Moonraker's, taking with him his supporting adherents and the representative of the *Reporter*, whom he favoured with a sketch of his life-history, and so impressed that ingenuous youth that of the column and a half, one column was devoted to Henry Hobson; and his daughters, their bridegrooms and their bridegrooms' eminent fathers had to share half a column amongst them.

"By gum," said Willie Mossop, who could now read without spelling out each word, "he's got his name in paper after all."

Maggie nodded towards her Sales Book. "It's all right," she said. "I'd rather have Mrs. Hepworth for my advertising any day than the *Salford Reporter*"

Maggie was perfectly satisfied. Things were going well at Oldfield Road, and her father's business was bound to suffer from the loss of its leading craftsman, its persuasive saleswoman, and the considerable proportion of its better-class *clientele* which came under the influence of Mrs. Hepworth; but even supposing that Hobson held his ground, her sales-book already promised a bright future for the shop of William Mossop.

Indeed, it could hardly do otherwise. Hobson's was really quite vulnerable, and Maggie was there to supply the intelligent competition which had been lacking hitherto. Though it was not the only large boot shop in Salford, she could safely omit the other two from her calculations, because one was the Nonconformist and the other the Catholic establishment. These were the colossi of the trade, and punny men of each religious persuasion poked about under their huge legs to find a livelihood.

So far the punny men had been punny. Now there was a competitor in the department spiritually controlled by the Established Church who was not satisfied with the crumbs which fell from the rich men's tables. Clearly, Hobson's was in jeopardy, but as long as Mr. Blundell, the vicar, was willing, for old times' sake, to turn a blind eye on Mr. Hobson's Moonraking propensities and to retain him as warden, so long woulda valuable share of the church connection continue to patronise the shop in Chapel Street.

Mrs. Figgins Gets Invited Back

Hobson returned to the shop on the afternoon of his daughters' weddings after a long sitting at the Moonraker's. He had impressed the reporter much but himself more. He overflowed with words and geniality, but, towards tea-time, Jim Heeler and Joe Tudsbury, who had sympathetically made an afternoon of it with him, decided that their business could no longer get on without their personal attention, and Mr. Hobson left the inn with them.

He entered his shop happily, and gazed with satisfaction at the spruce young man whom he had engaged at the weekly wage of five-and-twenty shillings to do the work of his departed daughters.

As usual, in the afternoon, there had been little doing, and his report was brief. Mr. Hobson made a few complacent remarks and a little joke at which the youth laughed very heartily, and went into the parlour for his tea.

There was no tea. The table was bare, unlaid. Forgetfully, he roared for Alice, and then remembered. Mr. Hobson was annoyed. He had a fancy for crumpets, hot, richly buttered crumpets, and there was no one to toast them for him. The spruce young man whom he had engaged to take his daughters' places seemed suddenly unsatisfactory. His daughters' places included the house, and he could not ask the young man to make his bed. Were things to cost him more now he'd kicked his daughters out (for "kicking out" was how he now thought of their going)? He sat on the table with his hat on the back of his head, and took from his pocket a paper which had given him extreme satisfaction earlier in the week.

	£	s.	d.
Food for three daughters at 7s a week.	54	12	0
Cloth same by contract with Tudsbury	30	0	0
Church donations for same at 6d a week each	3	18	0
Total annual expenses of daughters. .	88	10	0
Less wages of shop assistant at 25s weekly	65	0	0
Total annual saving . . .	£23	10	0

He wanted to save twenty-three pounds ten, but he wanted his tea. It was a nighty predicament. It assumed the proportions of a national crises. He had demanded the consequences, and an empty stomach confronted him. He thought imperially. The brain declares woman is intolerable, the stomach declares woman is inevitable. He decided and got off the table. He discovered the possibilities of Mrs. Figgins, the "decent woman" of his skilfully flattered imagination. Say five shillings a week, that would leave him a margin. But she would require feeding, which endangered the margin. It came to this, then, that he would not replace Will Mossop, and the other men must work the harder and do something for their wages.

    Things were slack just now - one of those passing depressions which came unaccountably, and as unaccountably go, and certainly need not trouble an old campaigner. In fact, a little slackness was of advantage till the shop assistant knew the ropes, and the cellar-men, when it passed, accustomed themselves gradually to increased output per man.

"Eh, that'll settle it," he thought. "Of course I said 'no woman,' and Mrs Figgins might be reckoned a female of a sort; but I regard her as a machine for making my bed and cooking my dinner, and I'm none forsworn in using Mrs. Figgins. I'll send for her."

He sent for Mrs. Figgins, and, apprehensively, she came. Had Maggie told Hobson about the clock? Knowing something, and guessing more, of Maggie's relations with her father, she doubted it, but she came in fear and trembling. For professional reasons Mrs. Figgins did not desire to go to prison. But she fervently desired to be revenged on Maggie, and if Maggie was beyond her reach, then on Mr. Hobson, who begat Maggie.

She inclined a favourable ear to Mr. Hobson's proposal. It appeared to her one which she could turn greatly to her personal advantage. She anticipated a profit on the housekeeping, and foresaw great opportunity for the acquisition of Mr. Hobson's household goods. She sat more firmly on the horsehair seat in the parlour. Its bare edge had been support enough for her trepidation, but now - why, the chair itself, or some more portable theft, was as good as hers.

"Of course I sleep here," she said.

Mrs. Figgins belived in asking for all she could get. She had sized up Mr. Hobson with rapidity by no means complimentary. She knew his hazy man-mind, knew his grasping, domineering intentions, and smiled inwardly.

He had not thought of her sleeping on the premises. That meant extra food, but there was plenty of room, and he might as well have the machine handy. "All right," he said.

"And I've a daughter," she reminded him.

"Get rid of her," said Mr. Hobson tersely.

"She's my flesh and blood, Mr. 'Obson. I can't 'ave my Ada any worse off than her mother. It would tear my heart to pieces and particles."

"I've done with having daughters here." Mr. Hobson was red with wrath, which told Mrs. Figgins all a woman of her intelligence required to know.

"I'll have to lodge her somewhere," she said.

"I'll come for seven-and-six a week."

He considered it. His first idea had been to have her for the mornings only, and with the assistance of the Moonraker's to "manage" the rest himself; but a hired, servile, bulliable machine available at any hour of the twenty-four for seven-and-six a week was tempting, and he took her offer.

Mrs. Figgins was delighted. The advantage of lodging Ada elsewhere was that she would have at her disposal a reliable storage for the odds and ends she expected to pick up. She was an adept at picking up, and, with Ada's room as a depositary could dispose of her hoard at her enlarged leisure. Hobson should pay for Maggie's insolence!

She took her shawl off on the instant, brought crumpets from the shop next door, toasted them to admiration, and buttered Mr. Hobson and the crumpets with equal zest. Mr. Hobson ate, purring with satisfaction. It was wonderful how readily life's problems yielded to the manipulation of a master mind.

He leant back in his chair and spat accurately in the fire, thrilling at the thought that his parlour was his own and his manners what he pleased. There was no Maggie to object on grounds of hygiene, no Alice to protest that expectoration was a *common* habit, no Vickey to inform him that spitting was not pretty. It was a man's abode at last. A delirious thought; the crowning achievement of the immortal master mind.

But Mr. Hobson was a gregarious animal, and it began to strike him that the house was empty. He could hear the friendly chink of china as Mrs. Figgins washed up, and was presently inclined to call her to him. He like somnolent soliloquy in the afternoons, but preferred an audience at other times. Still, now that Mrs. Figgins was established in his house, he would have lots of opportunity for impressing her with the grandeur of his intellect. She would be a useful stand-by at odd moments when the shop became busy again and he was detained from the Moonraker's. Tonight the shop was not busy, and the bar parlour invited. Mr. Hobson accepted the invitation.

It was an invitation which in the days to come he was to accept with increased frequency, till even Jim Heeler shook his head and wondered whether Hobson was not overdoing it. Hobson's business did not increase, but the business he did with Sam Minns increased steadily.

Mrs. Figgins walked warily at first till she was assured that no blow impended from Maggie. She agreed wonderfully with Mr. Hobson's opinions. She flattered his mind and flattered his stomach. He liked rich foods and she provided them. Maggie used to insinuate an occasional day of Lenten fare, but it was not Mrs. Figgin's policy to deprive her employer of what he like. Her policy had not precise aim. It was oportunist, but Mr. Figgins saw no sense in mortifying Hobson for his own good. The good of Mrs. Figgins was all that interested her.

She found that he had no eye for cleanliness, and as cleanliness for its own sake was no part of her creed she abstained from wasting soap. Ada Figgins was living far better than she had ever lived before on the surplus of rich, fragrant food from Hobson's table. Mrs. Figgins as a domestic machine had made herself indispensable to Hobson; and Mrs. Figgins as a thief was filching less perishable goods than food with an audacity which increased with immunity, till Ada's room became a treasure-house and its walls could have been papered with pawn-tickets. She accumulated, Hobson degenerated.

Maggie knew. Her lips tightened, but she bided her time. Tubby went to her with a pitiable tale of "the mater's blindness to the 'goings on' of that there Mrs. Figgins," but left her with a considerable flea in his ear.

"He's brought it on himself," she said, "and he'll get out of it best way he can."

"It's not a laughing matter, Mrs. Mossop," said Tubby. "She's a thieving slut and she drinks gin."

"I thought it wasn't vinegar," said Maggie, puzzling Tubby with her allusion to the bottle she had seen in Mrs. Figgins's room. "But he can lie on the bed he's made for himself."

"Art quite heartless, lass?"

"No, Tubby, but I'm busy here."

"It's more than we are yonder."

"I could have told you that," she said. "I'll maybe spare an hour to come and settle Mrs. Figgins one of these days, but I'll be very sure he's learnt his lesson before I stir a hand to pull his chestnuts from the fire for him."

"It goes to my heart to see the old master put upon like this."

"Tubby, you're a sentimental idiot. You've got no work to do and your mind's wandering to things that don't concern you."

"They ought to concern you."

"Aye! Well, they do and they don't. You tell me my father doesn't know it yet - "

"Sithee, lass," he interruped, "I'll be honest with you. He's drinking too much to know anything."

"Well, he's got to know it before I interfere Tubby, and when he knows it good and hard you can come round here again and I'll fall on Mrs. Figgins like a ton of bricks. But till then you can just think on I've a business here that's growing every day and takes me all my time to run, and I want to see no faces from Hobson's in this shop while I'm in opposition. Good-night."

"Tubby," called Will Mossop from his bench, "do you want a job? You can have one here if you do."

The loyalist stared at his old assistant. "I work for Mr. Hobson," he said, and marched out proudly.

Giving Advice To Henry

But it was not Maggie who fell on Mrs. Figgins, Mrs. Figgins tripped herself up, and brought down Hobson with her. It was not entirely her fault. She drank gin, and gin is said to wing the imagination. She honestly misunderstood the situation. She did not know she was a sexless machine, and Mr. Hobson's use of the machine as audience encourged hopes in the mature bosom of Mrs. Figgins to which a passing glance in a looking-glass should have given the lie. But Mrs. Figgins did not use a glass. She disliked shocks.

It was not so much a settled convinction as a dream born of gin, an intermitten gleam of hope fostered by her long immunity, her natural optimism, the steady degeneration of Mr. Hobson, and her overweening lust for revenge on Maggie.

She laid no plans, for her hopes were far too faint for that, but she meant, should opportunity occur, to put her ambitions to the test. And the opportunity occurred.

Mr. Hobson, as usual, was sleeping in the parlour after dinner. His sleep was heavy. He no longer played his little games with sleep, approaching sleep gradually, teasing it as if he did not mean to yield to it, savouring it before tasting, yielding at last like a much-wooed girl to the arms of a lover. Such sportive ways had gone, along with the mental gymnastics in complacency with which he used to soothe his soul after dinner. He now fell heavily asleep, but slept destressfully, and awoke too often with shaking limbs and a start which disorganised his digestive apparatus.

Mr. Tudsbury entered Jim Heeler's shop.

"Hullow," said Jim from behind a cheese rampart, "what's up?"

Tudsbury tested a cheese without committing himself. It seemed to give him strength. He sat down by the counter in an odour of cheesiness and leant confidentially across to Mr. Heeler.

"Jim," he said. "I'm against interfering with any man's business, and Sam Minns is a friend of mine, but Hobson's a friend and all, and there's reason in all things. Hobson's spending too much money with Sam."

"He's a bad man to give advice to, Henry is." Mr. Heeler granted the premise.

"And we can't do it in the Moonraker's because of Sam," said Tudsbury.

"Do what?" asked Heeler, making up his mind about a piece of bacon which did not require a microscope to reveal its condition, and marking it "Sixpence, to clear."

"Tackle Hobson," said Tudsbury. "It's got to be done, Jim, and I reckon you and I must do it. There's no one else."

"I'm not anxious for the job. Henry's got that techy lately. I can see him knocking heads off for an ill-advised word. It's a funny thing, Joe, but now he's lost his daughters, there's an unkindly lash about his tongue."

"Aye, he was more considerate once. But there, if a man hasn't a family to get the rough edge of his tongue, he must carry it to his public. Families has their uses. Henry was a mellow man once, but it's sad to think what marriage does sometimes for a parent. He can carry his liquor, but the biggest pot 'll overflow it it's filled up enough."

"Folks that live by being respectable must be respectable." Jim Heeler was oracular but non-committal.

"We'll go across, Jim," Mr. Tudsbury beckoned towards Jim's hat. "Before Henry spills himself and his trade-cart in the police court."

"It's a tough contract," objected Mr. Heeler. "I'm not craving to be principal at a funeral this side of Christmas. I've some old stock to work off, my lad, in the Yule novelties. And sithee, Joe, you've worked up to this. You've brought yourself to point, but it's sprung on me and I'm not ready yet. Henry's my friend as much as yours, but I'd sooner thee took the black eye than me. Henry's had trouble, and it isn't friendly to a man who's had trouble to tell him he's not to forget it."

"If he'd stick to beer for purposes of forgetting," argued Mr. Tudsbury, "I'd have nowt to say. Beer never hurt a man yet, but he's drinking miscellaneous, and in particular he's drinking gin. Gin's nasty."

Mr. Heeler agreed. "I hope you'll break him of it," he said.

"*We'll* break him of it, Jim. Henry has it up against me. Fancies I dressed his daughters fashionably on ten pounds a year! It can't be done, but Henry's grudge doesn't recognise reason nor drapery prices. So you must support me with your common sense. He'll only exercise his wit on me if I'm alone, but you're a grocer. He'll take you seriously.

Mr. Heeler acknowledge the compliment by taking down his billycock and silently signifying his willingness to beard the gin-loving lion in his den. But each gentleman was mightily glad of the other's company.

"Eh," foretold Mr. Tudsbury, "eh, but he will be nowty."

"Aye. Nowty he will be."

"I suppose if I told him it was a mistake to get rid of his daughters, I'd be told I'm angry at losing the clothing contract."

"It wouldn't stop at words." Jim was brief. He looked at the well-meaning Joe out of the corner of his eye.

"But I hold to that opinion, Jim."

The two Samaritans crossed Chapel Street and entered the boot-shop, outwardly smug, self-sufficient tradesmen, inwardly nervous and jumpy as cats. The new assistant, who spent more time and money on his toilet than was recognised as decent in Salford, detained the visitors. Mr. Hobson had come in and managed his dinner. But he was in that condition when sleep is a blessing not only to the sleeper, but the sleeper's relations, employees', friends, enemies, and all that population of his town which cares for peace and quiet. Joe Tudsbury retreated behind Mr. Heeler, which was quite enough to end the cowardice of Mr. Heeler. He waved the smart young man aside and marched up to the parlour door.

But during the brief delay in the shop a surprise, an astounding revelation, had been prepared in the parlour.

Mr. Hobson lay upon the sofa. He slept, but uneasily. He did not snore with the perfect regularity which beautifies snoring into a Hymn to Morpheus. He jerked nasally, he also jerked leggily. He coiled up in one of those queer position frequently achieved by sleeping children. Mrs. Figgins watched his performance whilst she removed everything but the gin-bottle from the table. She went over to put him straight, not in any motherly spirit, but lest he should fall off and waken before she had polished off the bottle. In the act she heard the voice of Joe and the voice of Jim in the colloqy with the shop-server. She was inspired.

The sight which met Mr, Heeler and Mr. Tudsbury as they came in from the shop was of Henry Hobson with his arm round the waist of Mrs. Figgins. They might both have been asleep in that affectionat attitude, or they might both be sunk in that happy oblivion of love, the world forgotten, to which self-absorbed lovers are prone. It did not occur to the Samaritans that one of them slept while the other was very wide awake.

Mrs. Figgins allowed the situation to soak into the minds of the witnesses. Then she very sharply pinched Mr. Hobson's soft body, and simultaneously became visibly aware of the presence of Mr. Heeler. She did not blush, but she contrived a nice confusion.

"Oh!" she said, with the surprise of one suddenly discovered. "Oh, Henry! You'll have to tell your friends about us now."

"What?" gaped Mr. Hobson drowsily, struggling with sleep and the fumes of his morning's excess.

"Tell them we're going to be married, or I shall never hold my head up after what they've seen," and the bashful lady fled from the parlour.

Mr. Heeler noticed that the spruce assistant was gazing at them from the open shop door.

"Get out, you," he said, and closed the door.

"What's the matter?" asked Hobson.

"You can correct me if I'm wrong," said Jim.

"But it appears you're going to marry Mrs. Figgins."

"Art mad?" asked Hobson succinctly.

"No," said Jim. "But I found you with your arm round her waist and a sloppy look on your face, and she says you're marrying her. If you aren't, I've only to tell you your arm was in a foolish place."

"My arm!" he repeated stupidly. "You tell me my arm was round her waist?"

"It was," said Mr. Tudsbury.

"By gum!" said Hobson. "I'm worse than I thought I

was. If my arm can play me a trick like that, there's no knowing that I mayn't have lost control of my tongue as well."

"Do you mean you've spoken to her of marriage?" It is really wonderful how imaginative and vigorous Joe's mind became.

"I mean I don't know, but if she said I had, why, after this, I couldn't swear I hadn't, could I? Found with my arm round Mrs. Figgins's waist! Oh, Jim, and me a churchwarden!"

"She's got no witnesses," said Mr. Tudsbury.

"She's got the shop assistant as to the arm," said Mr Heeler. "Joe, we came on one job and we've found a worse."

"What job brought you?" asked Hobson.

"Nay, we'll pass that now," said Jim. "We'll talk of that another time. But taking this Figgins affair, Henry, I ask you bluntly, have you spoken to her?"

"And I ask you, Jim, is it likely?"

"Not when you're yourself, Henry; but what brought Joe and me along is just the remarkable number of times that you're not yourself."

"Then you think I may have spoken to her?"

There was no explosion, not even the kick of a dead donkey. Mr. Hobson was overpowered by the catastrophe.

"It's a nasty thought, lad, isn't it?" said Jim, with sympathy. "But looking at it all ways up, and allowing for what we saw and what you've just admitted, Henry, I'm bound to give you my opinion that it's possible, and if it's possible you don't need me to tell you you're on toast, with that assistant gaping at you through the door, and all."

"I'll wring his neck," said Mr. Hobson. He brightened at the prospect.

"I wouldn't," said Joe Tudsbury. "I wouldn't make him angry. It might pay to raise his wages."

"You're great at making free with other people's money," said Hobson, with more recovery of spirit.

"Nay, Henry," advised Jim. "He's right. You'll save money by raising that lad half-a-crown a week before Mrs. Figgins gets talking to him."

"What shall I do about her, Jim?" Mr. Hobson relapsed into humility at the name of Figgins.

"Ah, now you're getting beyond my depth. I'll tell you what, though. You've a son-in-law that's a layer."

"Lawyer! I'm to use a lawyer!"

"Well, you can tackle Mrs. Figgins alone if you like, but I don't go out in the rain without an umbrella myself."

"Holy Moses, what a mess I'm in! Women, women, again. Damn it! they cannot be trusted. Daughters or widows, eh, they're anathema."

"Solomon was done by 'em," said Job's comforter Number One.

"You stick to beer, Henry, and you'll be right in future." Job's comforter Number Two was more sanely practical if not more consolatory.

"I'd give summat to know if I'm committed or not."

"There's asking her," suggested Joe.

"And there's giving myself away." Hobson crushed him. "Well, you may be friends of mine, but you're not much use at a pinch. I took a trouble to Sam Minns once and I mind it was just the same. I went to Maggie then, and " - he remembered the result - "I'll never go to her now. If there's a lawyer in the family, I might as well make use of him. I'll send for Albert Prosser."

Resigning His Office

It seemed Albert Prosser's malign fate to buy boots from Maggie against his will. He did not want a pair of boots, but neither did he want to ask Maggie directly for advice about her father's new dilemma. Solicitors should give, not ask, advice.

So he went to Oldfield Road to buy a pair of boots, and introduced the subject of Mrs. Figgins with a casual conversational air.

"Oh, that's what's brought you, is it?" said Maggie. "I was wondering."

Albert gave up subterfuge. "It's so awkward," he said.

"It's not a breach of promise action. There's no action, and we've no clear knowledge if there was a promise. There's a hypthetical action on a possible promise and no certainty about it anywhere."

"And I suppose Father's about the worst frightened man in Lancashire?"

"He's pretty bad."

"He must have been before he called a lawyer into it. Well, it'll do him good. Those boots will last you years," she added, dismissing the subject.

Albert stared. "But what about your father?" he asked.

"Nay. You're the solicitor, Albert, and he's consulted you. I reckon you'll charge him a fee, and I'm not here to do other's people's work for them.

"I thought you might be able to suggest something, Maggie."

"Got nothing to suggest of your own?"

"I've explained my difficulty." He evaded a direct reply.

"All right," she said; "I'll take it on. But you can get the credit, for I'll thank you not to breathe a word to him that I've hand in this. And I wouldn't have neither, if it was any one but Mrs. Figgins. You say there's no certainty. Well, there is."

"You mean he's promised her?" said Albert, startled.

"He may or he mayn't and I don't think he has. He's losing grip of himself, but I'd say he's not so bad yet as to promise marriage to Mrs. Figgins. Leastways, Albert, I hope he's not. He'd be beyond repair, if he'd gone that far, and I'm calculating on having the repairing job to do one day. And, anyhow, he's paying Mrs. Figgins nothing. That's straight, and it's not because I mind Father's being out of pocket. It's because I'll none have her in pocket.

"But how avoid it?"

"How! Easy. There may be uncertainty about Father, but there's none about Mrs. Figgins. It's certain she's a thief, and you can take a search warrant and your wife, and go down to where Ada Figgins lives. You'll lay no hand on Ada.

She's a poor scrap, but she did a big thing once, and I'll give you a week's takings if the room's not half full of things from Father's house. Half full, and Mrs. Figgins there for months? It'll be full and overflowing. Well, Mr. Lawyer, you can see the rest. No prosecution for theft, no action for breach of promise. Frighten her and get your paper signed, and if there's anything good amongst the stuff she's stolen, get it back. Take Alice with you to identify the things. And that's about all as I can think of, except that when you charge Father for your services you might think on it to be moderate, seeing whose brains it is you're going to use in this. Goodnight. Oh, how's Alice?"

"She's very well, thank you. And - "

"Yes," said Maggie, "I'll send you the boots." She had two customers waiting, and no time to waste on Albert's thanks.

It was, in fact, an admirable scheme, and succeeded on the main issue. Mrs. Figgins had really hardly hoped to succeed. She acted more on impulse than from a considered plan, though she had undoubtedly proved her genius for making the most of opportunity. But she had overreached herself and was afraid of her own success. A colourable imitation of a police search of Ada's room cowed her to immediate poltroonery, but it was one thing to intimidate her into signing a well-worded denial of any matrimonial pledge from Hobson and another to tie her tongue. Sober, she was scared and silent, but gin inspired her to eloquent disquisitions on the greatness she should enjoy in a juster world than this one, where poor folk are "put upon."

No doubt the babblings of a Mrs. Figgins in her very disreputable cups were to be ignored by the discreet, but her auditors were indiscreet, and, supported perhaps by a chance remark from the spruce assistant, some rumours of his warden's association with Mrs. Figgins reached Mr. Blundell. As a scandal it was distinctly vague, but, unfortunately, there was no vagueness at all about Hobson's Moonraking. That was rank, and even Mr. Blundell, tolerant to excess, could no longer ignore it, especially when fortified by the subterranean rumours of his discreditable connection with a charwoman.

The upshot was that Mr. Blundell visited the shop. His part of the interview was masterly in its tactful circumlocution. Hobson's part was explosive. He resigned his office, and with it, as he soon discovered, that still valuable share of the churgoers' bootmaking which depended on the vicar's favour.

On the other hand, Maggie still taught in the Sunday-school, and the cellar of Oldfield Road was getting too small for her increasing trade.

"If I said twenty years before you were the biggest man of the three, I made a bad mistake," she said. "For twenty months are nearer it."

Will didn't contradict her either. "We're getting on," he said, with a confident ring in his voice which made Maggie look at him,; ostensibly it was only the ordinary look of any half at the other half of the commonplace union. But Maggie smiled sweetly when she looked at something else.

CHAPTER FIFTEEN

Time To Stand Up

Will Mossop might well be confident. The most wonderful thing in the world was happening to him. His wife was going to have a child, and the marvel and the joy of it were almost more than Will could bear. But he could stand good luck better than before Maggie took him in hand.

Maggie was a little mixed about it. She was glad, but Will was new to fatherhood, while for her the child now leaping in her womb was a second baby to her and she felt a little jealous for her first. Will was her first and she foresaw that she must lose her grip on him. The time was coming, when her education of Will Mossop must bear fruit, when he must stand alone a man in the world of men; and like any other mother she resented the untying of the apron-strings.

She was proud of the man she had made of him, but pride still struggled with her zest for mastery. She must let go, but there was agony for her in the relaxing of control though it was she and she alone who had fitted this man to stand alone.

It was the day after their first annual stock-taking, and Will came in from an errand of whose nature he had not told her. Lately, he had taken to such small habits of independence, and when it came to bowing to the inevitable, Maggie found she had a back which bent, as a Scotsman jokes, "wi deeficulty."

"Where have you been?" she asked.

He took out his cheque-book and showed her a counterfoil. "That's what I've done," he said. "A hundred and twenty pounds to Mrs. Hepworth. That's her capital and twenty per cent. We can do without her now."

"Looks like you can do without me too," she said. "Going and doing a thing like that on your own."

"Maggie!" he said, downcast, "I thought to please you."

"The queer thing is you do," she said. "But I like to have a finger in the pie."

"God know you made the whole pie, Maggie, and I'm sorry I upset you. I mean to give you a little surprise."

"It's all right, lad," she said. "I'm none complaining. You're a fast traveller, but I started you on the road."

"I reckon we'll travel together, lass, you and me and - and him. Maggie", he added shyly. "I'd as lief he weren't born in a cellar, too."

"He won't be," Maggie said. "There's time enough for that."

"Aye, but the business could do with a move, and all. We've a year in this place, and we're growing big for it."

"We'll flit," she said. "But I'm in two minds where. There's a good house near Vickey's in Fitzwarren Street to let."

"Fitzwarren Street! By gum!"

"What's to do? Fitzwarren Street is nothing so grand, but it might do as a stepping-stone to the Crescent, only I favour living at my shop, myself, for the present and I haven't found a shop to suit my taste. We'll be on the main road when we make a move."

"Aye," said Will, filling a pipe, whilst Maggie watched him quizzically. Smoking was a new habit with Will, but she liked to see him with a little vice. It completed her handiwork.

"How's Father lately? Have you heard? " she asked.

"It's a rum thing, lass, but I was thinking of him myself at that moment. It's wonderful the way we think together."

"I was thinking of his shop 'ud do for us," she said.

"Nay, then, you thought ahead of me that time, Maggie. Do for us? Hobson's? We're none that size just yet."

"We're a bigger size than he is now if all we hear is true. What was it you were thinking of him?"

"Just thinking back a bit on this full year that's past since you and me walked out of Hobson's shop."

246 Hobson's Choice

THE MANCHESTER AND SALFORD BANK MOSLEY STREET

"We'll happen walk in it again some day," she said. "I'm thinking forward myself."

"Aye," he agreed, looking at the needlework on Maggie's lap. "By gum, lass, it 'ud be great to have him born at Hobson's."

"It's in my mind," she said; "but the first move's got to come from Father."

"And that's a bit unlikely in the way things are," said Will.

"You never know," she said. "There's no great hurry for our flitting yet."

But the flitting was to come.

The Green Rabbit *or* Tubby The Housemaid

Hobson was desperately frightened by the affair of Mrs. Figgins. He gave Albert Prosser credit for accomplishing his rescue, and even acknowledged that lawyers, properly employed (that is to say, for him and not against him), had their uses; but he had lost his position at the church and its correlated advantages. He had to blame something. He did not blame himself, and, naturally, he did not blame the Moonraker's. He blamed women.

"Eh!" he said ruminatively. "I might have known better after my experience with daughters. I made a mistake and I acknowledge it. I was let down by a woman once and I'd no more sense than to ask for trouble again. I fancied I could make a machine of a woman and I were wrong. A machine's serviceable to man, and a woman's a thorn in the flesh of man. A machine's reliable, and the only reliable thing about a woman is that she's unreliable. I say nowt about my Mary. She's in her grave, but I put my head in a noose when I got daughters, and I did it again when I engaged Mrs. Figgins. But I've stopped doing it. I've been a fool twice, but I'm none a fool all the time."

He entered the shop and raised the trap.

"Tubby, he said, "I want you. I'm going to save you money. You can bring your clothes with you in the morning and put them upstairs here. If you can't make a bed you can learn, and likewise with the cooking of bacon. I appoint you to do for me in the place of my daughters who've deserted me, and Mrs. Figgins who betrayed me."

And with his domestic affairs at last settled solidly on the bed-rock of masculinity, Mr. Hobson strolled out to the Moonraker's. Mr. Heeler and Mr. Tudsbury attempted no further protest. They were too awed by the dire result of their first to have a stomach for more. Now and then one or other of the Moonraker's company would open his mouth to address Hobson when his orders followed each other with exceptional rapidity, but remembrance of the unhappy experience of Heeler and Tudsbury, those instruments of doom, froze the friendly protest on their lips, and Hobson drank unchecked of man.

But not of God. God gave Henry Hobson a magnificent constitution, but He appoints a breaking-point and Hobson reached it one morning shortly after Maggie's talk with Will.

This is not a subject on which one wishes to enlarge; but the fact is, that when Mr. Hobson awoke on that morning, he thought a green rabbit was running about his bedroom.

If he was frightened by Mrs. Figgins he was appalled now. Mrs. Figgins had followed Nature's law, and, being a woman, made a nuisance of herself, but Hobson was aware that green rabbits are unnatural. They are unhealthy, and Hobson liked health. He liked to be healthily lazy in bed after Tubby had brought up his shaving-water. He only broke the spell of glorious sloth when the water was cooling to the point beyond which shaving is uncomfortable.

But today he had no period of inert bliss. He saw the rabbit and he pulled himself together. He did not pursue the rabbit with a toothbrush. He had courage to forget the rabbit. He told himself the rabbit was not there. He made an effort and proved himself of hero's mould. He cast the bed-clothes from him and he rose, though every limb was trembling like a jelly. Never did Hobson rise to greater heights, but black depression had him by the throat. It was the end of the tether, and he realised it, yet, realising, struggled on. Nobody should ever know. Hobson would "carry on," doggedly, obstinately, to the bitter end, ignoring symptoms, scorning all augury, living his life as he had lived it till the crack of doom.

It was preposterous, but it was magnificent. Hobson defied his fate. He nailed his colours to the mast. He was an Englishman, and an Englishman never knows when he is beaten.

His hand trembled, but he took his razor up. He opened it, and then his great unhappiness surrounded him, pressed in upon him till it mastered him and seemed a thing unfightable and not worth fighting. Life was hateful to him. All, all, was gone, even the Moonraker's and the god of wine deserted him. He was an old man and he was not happy....with the razor in his hand and the recollection of the green rabbit in his mind. He raised the razor.

With a shuddering impulse which shook the floor he threw it from him, as far from him as he could, which happened to be through the window into the yard below, and staggered panting to the bed.

Tubby Wadlow, preparing breakfast in the parlour, heard the crash of glass and the heavy fall of Hobson to bis bed. He dashed upstairs.

"Tubby," said Hobson from the bed, "you haven't the sense of a louse."

"I came to see what's the matter," apologised Tubby.

"You can't see what's the matter. No one can see what's the matter but a doctor, and if Dr. Macfarlane's not here in five minutes you've a good chance of getting yourself hanged for murder."

Tubby went down the stairs with remarkable pace. "And," called his master, "go to Mr. Heeler and tell him I'm very ill."

Hobson felt slightly better. "Eh!" he remarked; "I'm in a bad way, but I'll cheat the undertaker yet. I come of a long-lived race, and Hobsons don't die before their time. But I'll wind that doctor up if he don't cure me sharp. I'll none pay doctor's bills for long, and I'll none let him think he's got a softie neither. I'm none fit for it, but I'm going down-stairs. Doctors shan't catch me looking helpless in my bed."

He began to dress and presently heard Tubby return. "Tubby," he called. "I'm gettin up. Is breakfast ready?"

"I didn't think you'd want none," Tuby replied.

"I don't pay you to think," remarked Mr. Hobson.

"I'm coming down to breakfast, so see it's ready. I'll see Mr. Heeler and the doctor down there."

Tubby resumed his preparations. They were not distinguished for competence, nor was the parlour fireplace intended for the cooking of bacon; but it was nearer the parlour table than the kitchen range, and Tubby was allowed to run the house on easy terms. The room was very dirty, but Tubby was without prejudices, and, for Hobson, it was worse than in the days of Mrs. Figgins by a quite imperceptible degree. According to his lights Tubby did his best, but it was not a very willing best. He "obliged the master," hating it. Jim Heeler came in with deep anxiety written on his face.

"I'll go straight up to him, Tubby," he said.

"Don't do that, Mr. Heeler: he's getting up."

"Getting up? I thought it was something serious."

"If you ask me, it is."

"Which way?" asked Mr. Heeler.

"Every way you look at it. Mr. Hobson's not his own old self and the shop's not its own old self, and look at me." Tubby in the character of a cook-housemaid was something to look at. His honest old face attempted tragedy and achieved the drollest look imaginable. He had a toasting-fork in his hand and an abandoned apron of Alice's round his waist.

"Now I ask you, Mr. Heeler, man to man, is this work for a foreman shoe-hand?"

"By all accounts there's not much else for you to do, Tubby."

"There's better things than being a housemaid - if it's only making clogs."

"I'm told there's not much margin on clogs."

"Well, summat's better than nowt, Mr. Heeler, and

there's nothing else wanted here. Hobson's is in a bad way and I'm telling no secret when I say it. It's a fact that's known. And who's to blame, eh? Tell me that?"

"I don't think you ought to discuss that with me, Tubby," said Mr. Heeler, but Tubby was not to be snubbed.

"Don't you?" he said. "I'm an old servant of the master's and I'm sticking to him now when everybody's calling me a doting fool because I don't look after Tubby Wadlow first; and if that don't give me the right to say what I please, I don't know right from wrong. I'll tell you what it is. Temper's ruining this shop: temper and obstinacy."

"They say in Chapel Street that it's Willie Mossop."

"Willie's a good lad, though I say it that trained him. Offered me a job t'other day, did Willie; and I'd have taken it an' all if I could have brought myself to leave Mr. Hobson. That tells you if I've a right to speak my mind. Letting my interests pass, I am, and cooking bacon for Mr. Hobson when I might be working at my trade for Willie Mossop. But listen here, Mr. Heeler, and I'm telling you no lie. Willie did us a thick'un. He hit us hard and I'm not denying it, but we'd have got over that all right. With care, you understand, and tact. Tact. That's what the gaffer lacks. Miss Maggie, now: well, she's a marvel, aye, a fair knock-out. Not slavish, mind you. No. Stood up to the customers all the time, but she'd a way with her that sold the goods and made them come again for more. Look at us now. Male assistant in the shop."

Mr. Heeler nodded understandingly. "Costs more than women," he said.

"Cost!" retorted Tubby with deep disgust. "They're dear at any price. Look here, Mr. Heeler, take yourself. When you go to buy a pair of boots, do you like to be tried on by a man or a nice soft young woman?"

"Well - " said he, smirking a little.

"There you are," said Tubby. "Enough said. Why, it stands to reason. It's human nature."

"But there are two sides to that, Tubby," said Mr. Heeler. "Look at the other."

"Ladies?" said Tubby. "Ladies that are ladies wants

trying on by their own sex, and them that aren't buy clogs. It's the good class trade that pays and Hobson's have lost it."

As Tubby stated his theory of the human boot-shop Mr. Hobson came into the parlour. No one but Mr. Hobson would have attempted to come downstairs alone. Lots of people in Salford would have got up, like him, to face the doctor standing, but to descent the stairs alone was an act of pig-headed obstinacy, for which Hobson was to pay. His head swam and his legs trembled, but he achieved the impossible, and got down the stairs without accident, but with his confidence thermometer at zero. He was collarless, not that anything besides his exprerssion of supreme self-pity was needed to demonstrate his invalidism, but because his shaking fingers had been unequal to buttoning the "dicky" which by the way, was quite decorous wear for week-day use. And he was shaken to the marrow. Physical weakness humiliated him. It was more than disturbing, it ravaged the soul of Mr. Hobson as nothing, not even his daughters' revolt, had done before. Even the losing of a churchwardenship is a little thing compared with having one's inside turned to water by the familiar sight of one's own staircase. Orestes in his agony knew no such affliction as the smell of cooking bacon which now tortured the suffering body of Mr. Hobson.

Jim Heeler met him at the door with friendly sympathy, and took his arm.

"Oh, Jim! Oh, Jim! Oh, Jim!" said the sufferer, with acute melancholy.

Tubby fluttered round the fire and put the smoking bacon on the table. Mr. Hobson choked alarmingly and made vague movements with his hand.

"Air," commanded Jim, and Tubby opened the window.

Mr. Hobson took the bacon dish and threw it through the window, where, presumably, it kept his razor company.

"Bacon!" he said. "Bacon, and I'm like this."

He sank upon the sofa. "Close the window, you blithering ass. Do you want me to catch my death of cold?"

Tubby closed the window, making a mute appeal to Mr. Heeler.

"Where's the doctor?"

"Coming, sir," said Tubby.

"Coming? You mean to say he isn't here? A man like me sends for a doctor and he takes his time like this! I might be dead for all he cares; aye, and for all anybody cares either."

"Nay, Henry, come lad, I'm here," said Mr. Heeler. "And I care. But it's awkward to be ill in a place with no women about."

"It'll be awkward, then," said Hobson.

"Shall I go for Miss Maggie - Mrs. Mossop, I mean?" suggested Tubby.

"I think your daughters should be here," Jim backed him up.

"They should," said the patient; "only they're not. They're married, and I'm deserted by them all, and I'll die deserted; then perhaps they'll be sorry for the way they've treated me. You can go for Maggie, and you can go for the devil. It doesn't matter who you go for, I'm a dying man."

It might or might not have been meant as a command to go for Maggie. Tubby chose to consider it one, and went. He was not called back.

"Well, this is very sudden," said Jim. "You've never been ill in your life. What are your symptoms, Henry?"

"I'm all one symptom, head to foot. But we'll know soon how near the end is when that docotor comes." He turned a panic-stricken eye on Mr. Heeler. "I'm frightened of myself, Jim, I haven't washed this morning. Couldn't face the water. The only use I saw for water was to drown myself. The same with shaving, only worse. I've thrown my razor through the window. Had to, or I'd have cut my throat. I'll never trust myself again. I'm going to grow a beard - if I live."

"You'll live, Henry. Salford can't lose you, lad; but I fancy a doctor could improve you. What do you reckon is the cause?"

"Moonraker's," said Hobson succinctly.

"You don't think - - " said Jim, concealing his agreement.

"I don't think; I know," stated Hobson. "I've seen it happen to others, but I never thought that it would come to me."

"Nor me neither," lied Jim. "It's a hard thing if a man can't take a drop of ale without it's getting back at him like this. Why, it might be my turn next!"

But Hobson had no sympathy to waste on the huypothetical case of Mr. Heeler. He groaned heavily.

"It's not the deserving who are singled out for suffering in this world," he remarked. And then the spruce assistant opened the shop door and showed in Doctor Macfarlane.

A Tussle With The Doctor

Scotland is on the whole a healthy country, yet the University of Edinburgh turns out more doctors than any other University in the United Kingdom. That accounts for the extraordinary number of Scotch doctors in Lancashire. They come because they are not needed in the land of their birth and the fare to Lancashire is not excessive; and they remain because forceful bullying goes further with a Lancashire patient than tact and a bedside manner. Also, they do not take return tickets to Scotland, which in itself is reason enough for remaining.

Robert Macfarlane had remained a long time in Salford. He knew ther breed and how to deal with it.

"Good morning, gentlemen," he said, and was passing through the room. "My patient will be upstairs, I belive."

"My lad," said Mr. Hobson, "there's a man in this town by the name of Brown. A fellow came up to him one day in the street and said 'You're Mr. Robinson, I believe?' 'If you believe that,' says Brown, 'you'll believe owt.'"

"If I'm to apply that story to present circumstances, sir, I must conclude my patient's up, and I've great objection to being called out at this hour to a patient that's well enough to be up." He addressed Jim: "Are you Mr. Hobson?"

"Certainly not," said Jim: "I'm not ill."

"Hum," said the doctor. "Not much to choose between

the pair of you. You've both got your fate written in your faces."

"Do you mean that I - - ?"

"I mean he has and you will."

And having finished with Mr. Heeler the doctor turned to Hobson.

"About time you took a bit of notice of me." said Hobson.

"I'm noticing you, sir," said he, sitting by him and taking his wrist.

"I've never been in a bad way before this morning. Never wanted a doctor in my life."

"You've needed, ma mannie, but ye've not sent."

They have the habit of the Eleventh Hour with doctors in Salford, and Macfarlane resented it. It meant hard work and light bills.

"But this morning - - -" proceeded Mr. Hobson.

"I ken - well."

"What! You know what's up with me?"

"Any fool would ken but one fool, and that's yourself.

"You're damned polite."

"If ye want flattery, I daresay ye can get it fra your friend. I'm giving ye ma medical opinion. Which do you prefer?"

"I want your opinion on my complaint, not on my character," said Hobson.

"Your complaint and your character are the same. And - - " he glanced at Jim - "I'll tell ye something for your good. A man is known by the company he keeps, and I mislike yours." Jim rose in wrath.

"Am I to stand this, Henry?" he asked.

"Sir," said Macfarlame, "if I am to interview a patient in the prescence of a third party, the least that third party can do is to keep his mouth shut."

"After that, there's only one thing for it, Henry. He shifts on or I do." Mr. Heeler delivered his ultimatum with confidence, but he was to receive the shock of his life.

"You'd better go, Jim," said Hobson.

Charitably, Jim put it down to Hobsons's sickness. He controlled himself. "There are other doctors, Henry," was all he said.

"I'll keep this one," said Hobson, and explained. "I've got to teach him a lesson. Scotchmen can't come over Salford lads this road. I can bully as well as a foreigner."

"Eh, Henry, you frightened me, but if that's it, I'll go. Not but what I'd like to stay and watch you take him down."

"Leave him to me," said Hobson. "I'll make a job of it." And Mr. Heeler went.

"That's better," said the doctor. "Now we can get to business. Will you unbutton your shirt?"

"No hanky-panky now," said Hobson, looking apprehensively at the stethoscope and baring his chest to it as if expecting to be stabbed. The doctor went on with his examination without comment. He was soon satisfied.

"Aye," he said, rising. "It just confirms ma first opinion. Ye'll have had a breakdown this a.m.?"

"You might say so." Hobson did not mention the green rabit in so many words, but the doctor understood him very well.

"Melancholic? Depressed? Imaginative?"

"Question was whether the razor would beat me or I'd beat razor. I won - that time. Razor's in the yard. But I'll never dare to try shaving myself again."

"And do ye seriously require me to tell ye the cause, Mr. Hobson?"

"I'm paying the brass to tell me."

"Chronic Alcoholism, if ye ken what that means. A serious case."

"I know it's serious. What do you think you're here for. It isn't to tell me something I know already. It's to cure me."

"Very well, I will write you a prescription." He sat at the table, produced paper and pencil, and began to write.

"Stop that," said Mr. Hobson angrily.

"I beg your pardon?" Macfarlane was icily polite.

"I won't take it. None of your druggist's muck for me. I'm particular about what I put into my stomach."

By this time they had each other's measure very well, and, as a matter of fact, were thoroughly enjoying themselves: Mr. Hobson was demonstrating his Lancashire independence to the foreigner from Scotland; and the equally obstinate doctor was determined to teach Mr. Hobson a lesson for defying his professional authority. Each saw the other's point of view and warmed to battle.

"Mr. Hobson," said the doctor, "if you don't mend your manners, I'll certify you for a lunatic asylum. Are ye aware that ye've drunken yourself within six months of the grave? Ye'd a warning this morning that any sane man would listen to, and ye will listen to it, ma mannie."

"By taking your prescription.?" sneered Hobson.

"Precisely. Ye will tak' this mixture, Mr. Hobson, and ye will practice total abstinence for the future."

For the moment he was beyond anger. "You ask me to give up my reasonable refreshment!".

"I forbid alcohol absolutely," came firmly. Macfarlane thought he was winning, but decived himself. Hobson was staggered by the sheer impracticability of his demand, but he came up strongly.

"Much use your forbidding is. I've had my liquor for as long as I remember and I'll have it to the end. If I'm to be beaten by beer, I'll die fighting; and I'm not practising unnatural teetotalism for the sake of lengthening out my unalcoholic days. Life's got to be worth living before I'll live it."

The doctor took his hat. He hadn't finished with Hobson, but he thought the hint would frighten him.

"If that's the way you talk my services are of no use to you."

Hobson was not frightened. "They're not," he said; "I'll pay you on the nail for this."

"I congratulate ye on the impulse," said the doctor.

"Nay," said Hobson genially, sorting small change from his pocket, "no need to take it sourly, lad. It's a fair deal and I've had value. Thou's been a tonic to me. When I got up I never thought to see Moonraker's again, but I'm ready for my early morning draught this minute."

Macfarlane put his hat down. He liked a tussle, and a case of such egregious obstinacy was worth wasting time on. This was a challange and he took it up.

"Man, will ye no be warned?" he said, relapsing in his earnestness into a broader Scots. "Ye pig-headed animal, alcohol is poison to ye, deadly virulent wi a system in the awfu' state ye're in."

"You're getting warm about it. Will you take your fee?"

Macfarlane proved his worth. He waved the bawbees from him.

"Aye, when I've earnt it," he said. "Put it back in your pocket, Mr. Hobson. I haena' finished with ye yet."

"I thought you had."

"Do ye ken that ye're defying me? Me, Robert Macfarlane of Edinbro' University? Ye'll die fighting, will ye? Aye, fighting spectres and incorporeal ghastliness. It's a gay high-sounding sentiment, ma mannie, but ye'll just no do it, do ye hear? Ye'll no slip fra me the noo. I've got ma grip on ye and I'll no leave go. Ye'll die sober and ye'll the longest time ye can before ye die a natural death. Have ye no a wife, Mr. Hobson?"

Hobson, rather impressed by his sincerity, pointed solemnly at the ceiling. Macfarlane misinterpreted.

"In bed?" he asked.

Hobson shook his head. "Higher than that."

"It's a pity. A man like ye should keep a gude wife handy. Have ye no female relative that can manage ye?"

"Manage!" quoth Mr. Hobson angrily.

"Aye," and the doctor was noticeably calm, "Keep her thumb firm on ye."

Hobson was grim. "I've got three daughters, Dr. Macfarlane, and they tried to keep their thumbs on me. They're married now - and queerly married, too."

"You drove them to it, then."

"They all grew uppish. Maggie worst of all."

He caught at the name. "Maggie? then I'll tell ye what ye'll do, Mr. Hobson. Ye will get Maggie back. At any price, at all costs to your pride; as your medical man I order ye to get Maggie back. I don't know Maggie, but I prescribe her in the dark, and - damn ye, sir, are ye going to defy me again?"

Hobson was, but the doctor's vehemence was telling. Besides, the thought of Maggie had been present at the back of his mind since his attack, though he did not see how he could ask her to come. If Macfarlane could do the asking for him - but no.

I've escaped from the thraldom of women once," he said; "and - ".

"And a pretty mess you've made of your liberty. Now this Maggie ye mention. If ye'll tell me where she's to be found, I'll just step round and have a crack with her maself, for I've gone beyond the sparing of a bit of trouble over ye."

"You'll waste your time. She'll not come back," said Hobson with a fine concealment of the hopes which leapt within him.

"Oh, now that's a possibility," said the doctor. "If she's the sensible body I take her for, I concur with your opinion she'll no come back to the likes of ye; but women are a soft-hearted race, and she'll maybe take pity on ye after all."

"I want no pity," he growled.

"If she's the lass I think she is, ye'll get no pity. Ye'll get discipline, and Dear kens ye need it sore. Ye've asked me for a cure and Maggie's the name of the cure ye need. Maggie, sir, do you hear? Maggie!"

CHAPTER SIXTEEN

Maggie's The Medicine Needed

Maggie spared Dr. Macfarlane the trouble of seeking her at Oldfield Road. It was early when Tubby burst into her cellar with a white face, and the shops of the neighbourhood had not yet taken their shutters down, but Maggie was up and at work.

Tubby remember his rebuff and meant to make no mistake this time.

"The master's had a turn and he's desperate bad, he said. "The doctor's with him now."

"I've been expecting it," said Maggie calmly, going for her hat.

"Shall I come with you?" Will asked.

"No," she called from the bedroom. "Time enough for that when I've seen for myself. I'll happen send Tubby for you, and if I do, think on to come quick. Now, Tubby," she said, ready before he had recovered his breath, "you'd best go round for Mrs. Prosser and Mrs. Beenstock. If he needs one he'll need all."

"He didn't mention them." said Tubby.

"But I do," Maggie said. "They've more time on their hands than me, and if he wants nursing it'll be turn and turn about. I've my living to earn and they're fine ladies. So be sharp."

She lost no time herself, and opened the parlour door as the doctor "prescribed" her loudly.

"What about me?" she asked.

The doctor gasped, then took an appraising look at her. "Ye'll be Maggie?" he asked.

"I'm Maggie."

"Ye'll do," he said, satisfied. "You're wanted here."

Hobson considered a protest against the coming of this daughter whom he had - expelled, but decided to leave it alone.

"I'm married," she said quietly.

"I know that, Mrs. - - ?"

"Mossop."

"Your father's drinking himself to death, Mrs. Mossop."

"Look here, Doctor," said the patient, "what's passed between you and me isn't for everybody's ears."

"I judge your daughter's not the sort to want the truth wrapped round with a feather bed for fear it hits her hard."

"Go on," she said; "I'd like to hear it all."

"Just nasty-minded curiosity," grumbled Hobson, but it was only for form's sake. Maggie's presence made him happy.

"I don't agree with you, Mr. Hobson. If Mrs. Mossop is to sacrifice her own home to come to ye, she's every right to ken the reason why."

"Sacrifice!" he shouted. "If you saw her home you'd find another word than that. Two cellars in Oldfield Road."

"I'm waiting, Doctor," Maggie pointed out.

"I've a constitutional objection to seeing patients slip through my fingers when it's avoidable, Mrs. Mossop," he explained; "and I'll do ma best for your father, but ma medicine will na do him any good without your medicine to back me up. He needs a tight hand on him all the time."

Mr. Hobson controlled fluency. He itched to speak, but only shuffled under Maggie's eye.

"I've not the chance I had before I married," she said.

"Ye'll have no chance at all unless ye come and live here. I willna talk about the duty of a daughter, because I've no doubt he's acted badly by ye, but on the broad grounds of humanity it's saving life if ye'll come."

"I might," she said.

"Nay, but will ye?"

Maggie was not committing herself. "You've told me what you think. The rest's my business."

"That's right, Maggie," said Hobson, seeing his opportunity to get back at the doctor. "That's what you get for interfering with folk's private affairs, Dr. Macfarlane. So now you can go with your tail between your legs."

Maggie's eye met the doctor's, and he saw the smile in it. She was not smiling at him, and he saw in it the reply he hoped to get. "On the contrary," he said, "I am going, Mr. Hobson, with the profound conviction that I leave you in excellent hands. One prescription is on the table, Mrs. Mossop. The other two are total abstinence and - you. Good-morning."

Maggie saw him amiably to the door, then she turned and faced her father. The clock had gone full round, and Maggie was not averse from savouring her triumph. She, the ejected, was required as she had known she would be, and it was for her to state the terms on which she would return to Hobson's roof. She was not there to make the terms harsh, but to define them firmly. She noted the marks of weakness in the man, the comfortless disorder of his room, touched the dust-laden mantelpiece and abominated the result upon her finger. Silently she took in everything and silently he watched her do it, shifting uneasily upon his sofa. Then she took up the prescription and opened the door. Tubby was just entering the shop after taking her message to her sisters.

"You're soon back," she said.

"I took the tram," he explained.

"It's not so bad as that," she said. "Still, they'll be here the sooner. Go round to Oldfield Road again and ask my husband to come here, and get this made up at Hallow's on your way back. You needn't take another tram."

There was not need to hurry back to her father. A little suspense would do no harm, and having already gauged the domestic situation, she proceeded to sum up the shop.

The assistant made a slight protest as she opened the sales book. He did not repeat it. The book was soon inspected. There was so little to inspect, but it appeared to give her considerable satisfaction.

"You've not been overworked, my lad," she told him,

and returned to Mr. Hobson who was still pitying himself on the sofa.

He had his speech prepared. "Maggie, he said, "you know I can't be an abstainer. A man of my habits, at my time of life-"

"You can if I come here to make you," she assured him.

"Are you coming?" he asked, trying not to appear eager.

"I don't know yet," she said. "I haven't asked my husband." And she meant it, only Hobson was not awake to the new Will Mossop, the Will of Maggie's making who nowadays was worth the asking.

"You'll ask Will Mossop! Maggie, I'd better thoughts of you. Making an excuse like that to me. If you want to come you'll come so what Will Mossop says, and well you know it."

"I don't want to come, father. I expect no holiday existence here with you to keep in health. But if Will tells me it's my duty I shall come."

"He'll tell you nowt and you needn't pretend to me. He's not the man that wears the breeches at your house."

"My husband's my husband, Father, so whatever else he is. And my home's my home and all, and what you said of it just now to Dr. Macfarlane you'll pay for. It's no gift to a married woman to come back to the house she's shut of."

Maggie was warm, and perhaps warmer than she meant to be because she really was not sure of herself. For once, she was in two minds. The house was a desolation, the business a disaster. She could clean the one and revitalise the other by adding her own to it, but she foresaw a tough struggle before she had her father licked into shape again. He had slipped further downhill than she expected and, honestly, she doubted her strength, or not so much her strength as her time. She had not many months in hand before her own concerns must take the place of all else, and of the two duties - to her father and her child - Maggie had no doubts at all as to which came first. She told the simple truth she said she must ask Will. It was up to Will. Was he big enough, had he grown sufficiently, had he yet the self-confidence to run Hobson's shop single-handed? For that was what it came to. She must devote herself exclusively to her father if she was to pilot him to smooth water before another life demanded her undivided attention. Inevitably, it was "up to" Will Mossop.

Those were her thoughts, but Hobson could not read them, and saw she saw no reason to tell him. But, at her hint of possible refusal, he was alarmed. Practically he pleased with her to come back. He, who had turned her out, and vaunted his hard-won freedom from the shackles of unreasonable women. He wanted to live and he wanted Maggie to help him.

"Look here," he said, "you're talking straight, and I'll talk straight and all. When I'm set. You're coming here. I didn't want you when that doctor said it, but, by gum, I want you now. It's been my daughters' hobby to cross me. Now you'll come and look after me."

"All of us?" inquired Maggie maliciously, hearing Alice's voice in the shop.

"No, not all of you. You're the eldest."

Alice came in. Tubby had overdone it again in the delivery of his message. She was dressed in half-mourning, but a word with the assistant in the shop had mitigated her alarm. Her face showed exasperation more than any other emotion - no one likes to be keyed up to tragedy and to find it is, at most, tragi-farce - and did not lighten when she saw herself forestalled in daughterly duty by Maggie.

"You been here long, Maggie?" was her greeting.

"A while," said Maggie dryly.

"Oh, well," Alice excused herself, "a fashionable solicitor's wife doesn't rise so early as the wife of a working cobbler. You'd be up when Tubby came."

"A couple of hours earlier," said Maggie

Alice shrugged her shoulders prettily. She had not improved, and her perceptions of what was and was not "common" had grown acute. Early rising was "common." She turned to Mr. Hobson.

"You're looking all right, father," she remarked,

"You've quite a colour."

"I'm very ill," he told her crossly.

"He's not so well, Alice. The doctor says one of us must come and live here to look after him."

"I live in the Crescent, myself," said Alice, settling her part.

"I've heard your house was that way on," said Maggie dryly. "It's a nice address, but I'm told the rents are going down on account of the smoke."

Then Vickey swam in. In a pretty tremor, flushed, effusively she crossed to the sofa with the tenderest gesture in the world, and sank effectively to her bended knee before the author of her being.

"Father! You're ill."

He lifted her gently. "Vickey! My baby!"

He gazed at the others. "At last I find a daughter who cares for me."

"Of course I care," said Vickey, but caught a quizzing look in Maggie's eye which brought her sharply to her feet. "Don't the others?"

"The doctors says one of us must come and live here to look after him," said Maggie.

Vickey was perfectly sweet about. "I wish I could, but of course it can't be me. In my circumstances, Maggie," she explained.

"What circumstances?" asked Maggie bluntly.

Vickey came to her, blushing divinely, and whispered in her ear.

"What's the matter?" growled Hobson. "What are you whispering about?"

"We'll settle who's to stay here amongst ourselves," said Maggie. "And you'd look all the better for a wash. You're well enough for that, and just think on to put a collar round your neck against Will comes. I've sent for him."

"Put a collar on for Will Mossop! There's something wrong with your sense of proportion, my lass."

"Father," she said, "I can go home or you can put a collar on for Will. I'll have him treated with respect."

"I expect you'd put a collar on in any case, father," suggested Alice tactfully.

"Of course I should. I'm going to put one on. But, understand me, Maggie, it's not for the sake of Will Mossop. It's because my neck is cold."

The Phenomenal Will Mossop

For just a moment, Maggie toyed with the thought of Hobson comfortably installed (so far as externals went) in Alice's large house in the Crescent, or Vickey's scarcely less roomy house in Fitzwarren Street. It was a temptation, and she knew that, by putting on her full pressure with their husbands, she could manage it. But there would be complications over the shop, and, after all, she preferred her father to be happy. He would not be happy with Alice or Vickey. He liked his groove and the air of Chapel Street.

Maggie was no shirker, but if, symbolically, her return to Hobson's was a triumph, practically it was a trouble. Still, she would shoulder her burden if Will could shoulder his - the shop. She did not question his competence, but his confidence, and that she meant to test. She could get its measure by observing him with her sisters. Therefore, to hold them till he came, she treated the question as still an open one.

"Now then," she said briskly, as Hobson disappeared, "which of us is it to be?"

"It's no use looking at me like that, Maggie," said Vickey, virtuously indignant. "I've told you I'm expecting."

"I don't see that that rules you out," said Maggie, giving nothing away about herself. "It might happen to any of us."

"Maggie!" expostulated Alice, who had nothing to give. Babies, perhaps, were "common."

"What's the matter? Children do happen to married women, and we're all married."

"Well," said Alice, not so much commenting on Maggie's statement of fact as replying to the question of her eye, "I'm not going to break my home up, and that's flat."

Maggie refrained from making the suggestion that her home could very well house Mr. Hobson.

"I see," she said; "one of you has a house full of furniture and the other has a baby coming, so father can drink himself to death for you."

"It is the duty of the eldest," said Alice. "I'd come if there were no one else."

"Duty!" said Vickey. "I'd call it a pleasure to live here after a year of two cellars."

"I've had thirty years of the pleasure of living with father, thanks," said Maggie dryly. "But it's for my husband to say."

At that moment Will Mossop was in the shop. He did not need to imitate Maggie's movements in it, because he had walked up with Tubby and had very thoroughly pumped him. He knew most of what there was to know of the state of Hobson's trade. Nevertheless, he was looking expertly at the stock-in-hand on Hobson's shelves when Maggie came to him.

"You're of one mind with me," she said, approving his occupation. "Do you feel like taking Hobson's on.?"

"You and me can manage it easy," he said.

"Aye" she said, "easy. But I'm asking you to manage this alone. Close Oldfield Road, I mean, and come here with our trade. I'll sit me down and watch you run it."

"Without your help?" he gasped.

"I reckon I've brought you up," she said.

"You've to stand on your own legs some time, and now's as good as any other."

"By gum," said Will.

And "Well?" said Maggie.

"Aye," he replied. "Aye, and I'll do you credit, lass."

Things were going very well for Maggie. Will, it appeared, was ready to take his full share of the burden and she liked his assurance. But she was curious to see how he would stand up to her sisters and, after them, to Hobson. She gave him a hint.

"You can prove it now," she said; "Alice and Vickey are in yonder and you can take a high hand with them. And with father, and all. He's not too ill to stand it, so you don't need to be slow with him."

"I don't mind them," said Will, "but I'll have to see about your father. I'm short of practice in taking a high hand with him. But I'll tell you what, Maggie," he was saying, as they returned together to the parlour where Alice and Vickey were holding an indignation meeting about Maggie's absurd pretensions regarding her louse-spirited, unpresentable oaf of a husband, "we'll cut it short, for I'm busy at my shop to what they are at his. It's a good old has-been is Hobson's."

Which, on the whole, was hardly calculated to charm the waiting sisters.

"What on earth do you mean?" asked Alice, vouchsafing no other greeting. "It's a good business still."

"Is it?" asked Will. "You try to sell it, then, and you'll learn something. Stock and goodwill 'ud fetch about two hundred."

"Don't talk so foolish, Will," said Vickey politely. "And the value of father's shop is no affair of yours either."

"Now I thought maybe it was. If Maggie and me are coming here - "

"You're coming to look after father," stated Vickey.

"Maggie can do that," he said. "I'll look after the business."

"You'll do what's arranged for you," said Alice sharply, watching for his collapse. Surely this astonishing inflation of Will Mossop could not persist? No doubt Maggie had breathed it into him in the moments she had had alone with him in the shop, but the ridiculous balloon only needed pricking to collapse. But he did not collapse.

"On the contrary, I'll do the arranging," he said. "If we come here, we come on my terms."

Alice was bereft of speech, but Vickey rallied. "They'll be fair terms."

"I'll see they're fair to me and Maggie," said the phenomenon called Will Mossop.

"Will Mossop!" Alice almost screamed, her voice beyond control. "Do you know who you're talking to?"

SALFORD FOOT BARRACKS, REGENT ROAD, AND FREE LIBRARY.

"Aye," said Will, sitting very naturally; "my wife's young sisters. Times have changed a bit since you used to order me about this shop, haven't they - Alice?"

"I'm Mrs Albert Prosser now," she said, with dignity.

"So you are," he agreed, "to outsiders. And you'd be surprised the number of people that call me Mr. Mossop now. We do get on in the world, don't we?"

Maggie exulted in him. He was not only standing up to those once terrible sisters of hers and giving better than he got: he was saying the things she would have said herself, and she was more than satisfied. The air balloon of Alice's imagining did not shrivel. It grew. It was impervious to pricks, to scorn, to reminders of its past. It almost bounced, but not quite. Will's was a character of perfect simplicity. He went as far as he was certain of himself, but not an inch further. A man who bounces trades on other people's ignorance, and hopes to be taken for better than he is. Will's knowledge of himself was founded on a rock, and he did not overstep its bounds. But when Mr. Hobson came in (with his collar on) Will remembered that he was expected to take a high hand.

"Good-morning, father," he said. "I'm sorry to hear you're not so well."

"I'm a changed man, Will."

"There used to be room for improvement," quoth Will truthfully.

"What!" roared the burgess, leaping to his feet.

"Sit down, father," said Maggie, and he sat.

"Aye," said Will; "don't let us be too long about this. My time's valuable. I'm busy at my shop."

"Is your shop more important than my life?" asked Hobson, sarcastically.

Will weighed his answer. "That's a bit like asking if a pound of tea weighs heavier than a pound of lead," he said. "I'm worritted about your life because it worrits Maggie, but I'm none worritted that bad I'll see my business suffer for the sake of you."

Alice was outraged. "And we're to stay here and watch Maggie and Will abusing father when he's ill!"

"No need for you to stay," said Will.

"That's a true word, Will Mossop. Neither of them 'ull leave their homes to come to care for me, and a business is more than a home. They're not for me, so they're against me."

"We're not against you, father. We only want to stay to see that Will deals fairly by you." Alice made it worse.

"Oh," said her father, "I'm not capable of looking after myself, aren't I? I've to be protected by you girls lest I'm overreached, and overreached by Will Mossop! I may be ailing, but I've fight enough left in me for a dozen such as him; and if you're thinking that the manhood's gone from me, you can go think it somewhere else than in my house."

Vickey tried tenderness. "But, father, dear father - - "

"Vickey," he said, "you'll not wheedle me this time. You've tried it once too often. I'm not so dear to you if you'd to think twice about coming here to do for me, let alone jibbing at it the way you did. A proper daughter would have jumped, aye, skipped like a calf by the cedars of Lebanon, at the thought of being helpful to her father."

"Did Maggie skip?" put in Alice.

"She's a bit ancient for skipping exercise is Maggie," ruled Hobson, sticking to his faith in the matter of Maggie's age, "but she's coming round to reconcilement with the thought of living here, and that is more than you are doing, Alice, isn't it?" Alice did not reply. "Is it?" he asked.

"Are you, either of you two, willing to come?"

Alice was silent. Vickey threatened volubility, but he cut her short.

"Open the door for them, Will, they've homes to go to."

Boldaciouness

Of course, in the end, it would have anyhow come to that, but, given the chance, Alice and Vickey might have made a better show of it. Mr. Hobson was quite aware of that, but he did not tell Will to open the door for them (and thus, in a sense, make Will the instrument of their outgoing) without a very decided object. He did it not so much to emphasise his displeasure with them as to placate Maggie.

High hopes had come to Hobson. He dreamed again the dream he had that sun-kissed Sunday afternoon as he left the Butting Ram at Besses - the dream of Willie Mossop given back to him in eighteen shilling servitude and Maggie restored to wageless work. It was a sharp reaction from his early morning gloom, but his natural optimism asserted itself strongly as he wove he sanguine web. A little tact, such as he had exercised in letting Will show out the sisters, a little flattery, such as he now prepared to bestow, and the thing was done. Quarters at Chapel Street were more than fair compensation for the loss of anything they were to give up. They had an independent home, but what a home!

He expanded his chest, in the mood for fluency, and his face was bland benignity.

"We're well shut of the pair of them," he said.

"They've got stiff necks with pride and haughtiness because they've got gold rings around their fingers, and the difference atween you two and them's a thing I ought to mark and that I'm going to mark. There's time's for holding back and time's letting loose and being generous, and I know which sort this is. You're coming here to this house, and you can have the front bedroom for your own and the use of this room split along with me. Maggie 'ul keep house, and if she's time to spare, she can lend a hand in the shop. I'm finding Will a job. You can come back to your old bench in the cellar, Will, and I'll pay you the old wage of eighteen shillings a week, and you and me'ull go equal whacks in the cost of the housekeeping. And if that's not handsome, I don't know my knee from my elbow. I'm finding you a house rent-free and paying you half the keep of your wife."

Will looked humorously at Maggie, and took his hat up. "Come home, Maggie," he said. She rose obediently, proud of her tactician, proud to take her orders from him. The benignant Mr.Hobson stared in blank amazement. "It may be new to you," Will condescended to explain, "but I've a business round in Oldfield Road, and I'm neglecting it with wasting my time here."

"Wasting time!" echoed Mr.Hobson. "Maggie, what's the matter with Will? I've made him a proposal."

Will laughed.

"He's a shop of his own to see to, father," Maggie said.

Mr. Hobson was incredulous. Hobson's was Hobson's. "A man who's offered a job at Hobson's doesn't want to worry with a shop of his own in a wretched cellar in Oldfield Road - unless he's a fool."

"I'm not fool," said Will: "not now, so what I used to be. We've been a year in yonder cellar and do you know what we've done? We've paid off Mrs Hepworth what she lent us for our start and made a bit o'brass on top of it. We've

ST. ANN'S SQUARE.

got your high-class trade away from you. That shop's a cellar, and, as you say, it's not much cop, but they come to us down there and they don't come any more to you. Your trade's gone down till all you sell is clogs. You've got no trade and me and Maggie's got it all, and now you're on your bended knee to her to come and live with you, and all you think to offer me is my old job at eighteen shillings a week. Me, that's the owner of a business that is starving yours to death."

"But - but," stammered Hobson, who was still living in the past and the golden glamour of his reborn dreams. "You're Will Mossop. You're my old shoe-hand."

"Aye, I were, but I've a move on me since then. Your daughter married me and set about my education. And now I'll tell you what I'll do, and it'll be the handsome thing, and all, from me to you. I'll close my shop - "

"Oh? That doesn't sound like doing so well."

"I'm doing well, but I'll do better here. It's a good address, for the time being, and I'll transfer to it. And what I'll do that's generous is this. I'll take you into partnership and give you your half share on the condition you're a sleeping partner, and you don't try interference on with me."

Mr. Hobson was nearer sudden death by apoplexy than ever before, and he had had narrow squeaks. But on the strictly homoeopathic principle of curing shock by shock, Will's next words probably saved his life.

"William Mossop, late Hobson, is the name this shop'ull have."

"Wait a bit, Will," said Maggie. "I don't agree to that."

Hobson turned to her with relief. The portent of Will Mossop was beyond him, but Maggie, as he always said, had sense, though she made monstrous use of it.

"Oh, so you have piped up at last," he said. "I began to think you'd both gone mad together."

Maggie's reply was not addressed to him. "It had better not be 'late Hobson,'" she said quietly to Will.

"I'm none dead yet, my lad," said Hobson, "and I'll

show you I'm not, and all. But just a moment first. I want to know if I'm taking this in right. I'm to be given half share in my own business on condition I take no part in running it. Is that what you said?"

"That's it," said Will.

"Well, I've heard of impudence before but - - "

"Oh, that's settled, father. Quite settled. It's only the name we're arguing about, and I think 'Hobson & Mossop' is best," said Maggie to Will.

Will didn't. He differed from Maggie and he meant to have his way. "The best I'll do is this, 'Mossop & Hobson.'"

And he did. Will Mossop met her eye, and it was not he but she who quailed. He had hurled defiance at her sisters, he had bearded Hobson, and now he took his courage in both hands and challenged Maggie herself. He wanted his name first on Hobson's signboard. It was his due and he desired it. He desired it so much that he dared Maggie to oppose him. And she let him have his way, not, indeed, because she must, for she hardly made a fight of it, but to reward him, to encourage his confidence and to let Hobson see for himself that Will was "Gaffer."

"'Mossop & Hobson,'" he said, "or it's Oldfield Road for us, my lass."

"Very well, said Maggie, turning aside very quickly. No one was going to see Maggie Mossop with a tear in her eye, testimony to sheer pride though it was. Hobson's last bewildered protests were lost to both of them. Maggie was ashamed of her weakness, and Will was exulting in his strength. He was looking through into the shop with a proprietary eye.

"I'll make some alterations in this shop, and all," he said. "I will so. Look at that chair! How can you expect high-class customers to come and sit on a chair like that? Why, we'd only a cellar, but they sit on cretonne for their trying-on."

"Cretonne," said Hobson, scornfully. "It's pampering folks."

"Cretonne for a cellar and morocco for this shop," said

Will. "Folk like to be pampered. Pampering pays. There'll be a carpet on that floor, too."

"Carpet! Morocco!" gasped his partner.

"Young man, do you think this shop is in St. Ann's Square, Manchester?"

"No, but it's going to be," said the astonishing Will.

"What does he mean?" Hobson appealed to Heaven.

Will explained. "It's no further from Chapel Street to St. Ann's Square than it is from Oldfield Road to Chapel Street. I've done one jump in a year, and if I wait a bit I'll do the other. But this will do to put me on."

Mr. Hobson could stand no more. It was his parlour, and his parlour was sanctuary, but he fled from it abruptly. He left them victors, and the victory was overwhelming for one of his conquerors. Will Mossop woke up as from a dream. He looked about him dazed.

But Maggie was alert. "A breath of air 'ull do him good," she said. "I'll take him round to Bexley Square, and Albert can draw up a deed of partnership."

"Maggie," said Will, contrite, "I bore on him too hard. I've said such things, and they sounded as if I meant them, too."

"Didn't you?"

"Did I?" he asked himself aloud, and said, wondering, "Yes. And I did. That's just the worst ... from me to him. You told me to be strong, and use the power that's coming to me through you, but he's the old master, and - - "

"And you're the new," she reminded him. She wasn't going to let him slip back into humility.

"Master of Hobson's! It's an outrageous big idea. Did I sound confident, Maggie?"

"You did all right."

"Eh, lass, but I weren't by half so certain as I sounded. Words came from my mouth that made me jump at my own boldaciousness, and when it came to facing you about the name, I tell you I fair trembled in my shoes. I was carried away like, or I'd not have dared to cross you, Maggie."

"Don't spoil it, Will. You're the man I've made you and I'm proud."

"Maggie," said Will, "I wanted his name on the signboard. He'll be born at Hobson's now. And that reminds me. I've got a job to see to," and he took her hand.

"What are you doing?" said Maggie, wrenching her hand free. "You leave my wedding ring alone."

"You've worn a brass one long enough."

"I'll wear that ring for ever, Will."

"I was for getting you a proper one," he said regretfully.

"I'm not preventing you. I'll wear your gold for show, but that brass stops where you put it, Will, and if we get too rich and proud we'll just sit down together quiet and take a long look at it so as we'll not forget the truth about ourselves. I'll go and tell father about that walk now," she added.

Will Mossop, left alone in Hobson's parlour, felt a great wonder rise within him. Here he had come, a stripling lad apprenticed to the trade; there in the cellar underneath learnt his craft, and loved his work, and laboured many years for eighteen shillings a week. There in the shop Maggie commanded him to walk with her upon a Sunday afternoon, and there he had defied her father. From that shop they had gone, and to it they returned. They returned as - This, and he saw the signboard shining like a blaze across the heavens.

"By gum!" said Will Mossop. "By gum!" And again he said "By gum!"

William Henry Mossop

A stout gentleman, with a clear eye, and a healthy glow upon his cheeks, was wheeling a perambulator in Peel Park. The perambulator contained William Henry Mossop who, to his mother's vast satisfaction, had been born precisely three days before his cousin Mary Victoria Beenstock.

William Henry was awake. His eyes were fixed upon and his mind entranced by the gold watch-chain on Mr. Hobson's stomach, but Mr. Hobson had the idea that his grandson's air of rapt attention was due to the words of wisdom which poured from Mr. Hobson's lips. As an audience he considered William Henry preferable to all the

Moonrakers in the world. "You've chosen to be my grandson and you're shaping well. You domineer over your mother, you make the house a Bedlamish torment if you're none done by us as you've a mind to be. You've learned to handle a mother, to put a woman in her right place of service and obedience, at start, and I can tell you from experience, my lad - - "

William Henry blew bubbles. Mr. Hobson blinked. A foul suspicion crossed his mind. His grandson was satirising his wisdom pictorially. He produced a yellow handkerchief and removed the bubbles hastily.

"Ugly habit," he reflected. Mr. Hobson never spat himself.

"Gander!" cried William Henry.

"Gander!" Mr. Hobson snorted. He disliked this contraction of his grandson. William Henry had invented it some four or five weeks ago and Maggie was impressed by his achievement, but Mr. Hobson regarded the word coldly. "Gander," taken literally, was too cynical of himself to be pleasant, especially from a two-year-old.

"Perverse! Aye, William Henry, you're the son of Maggie, but I'm glad to think there's not much of William Mossop in your character. It's hardy Hobson stuff, determined, resolute, intelligent, like me, wondrously intelligent. I've pulled through a world of trouble by my intelligence. I made one mistake, but I retrieved it. I'd let females follow their own noses and trouble came. But I took measures, my lad, and I brought your mother back, I restored the natural condition - woman waiting on man. And though you might say, William, that Maggie reformed me compulsorily, I'll ask you this, my lad. Wasn't it the higher intelligence of myself transmitted to her and trained by me in her that came back to my enlightenment? Aye, lad, all wisdom affecting myself radiates originally from myself, or I'd none touch it.

William Henry cooed concurrence, but the excellent self-content of Mr. Hobson was interrupted by the appearance of Tubby Wadlow.

"Eh, Tubby, owt wrong at shop?" inquired the nominal senior of the business.

"Missis is there," answered Tubby dryly. "And she thinks it's time the young master was back," he added.

"Tha's sent from thy bench with a message like that!" said Mr. Hobson resentfully. "Does she reckon I'm same age as him in the pram and need thee for a nurse?"

Tubby smiled gently. To fetch Mr. Hobson and the heir back was part of his daily round. And always Mr. Hobson resented the interruption of his eloquence. William Henry howled abruptly. He knew that Tubby's coming signified food, and disliked postponement. Mr. Hobson looked at him stoically, Tubby looked with sympathy. He howled again. Without another protest Mr. Hobson turned the pram homewards. The howls ceased magically and there was a beautiful calm.

"Aye," marvelled the fond grandfather, "it's a wonderful instinct in children, is food-time."

"Nature furnishes her own with most of their wisdom," agreed Tubby, relishing the sight of his own paunch.

Mr. Hobson was severe. "I don't agree with you, Tubby Wadlow. That child is Hobson, my family, and by consequence inherits twice double the wisdom of nature."

"Aye." The foreman's eyes grew bright. "I was forgetting thy qualities, master."

Mr. Hobson grunted, half mollified.

Tubby had faith in Mr. Hobson, a blind faith, and he flattered sincerely.

"Aye, it's a great thing now, the boot business of Hobson's, Hobson's still, Mossop being only needful because you hadn't a son."

Mr. Hobson smiled, quite mollified.

"Aye, and this young Hobson, he's one of the lords of earth. Master, it's because I've been foreman to yours that I tremble when I look on his face. Eh, the love I have for him brings near to me the unheard music, the deep song of the old world. Man lifting up his head out of chaos always, for those who do not lift their heads are not counted. They are the chaos. It's a hard saying, but a true one. But to me the stars shine like swords, the swords of justice, and the sun as an everlasting challenge. For life is a breaking. As your grandson breaks through from wizend babyhood into the round flesh of boyhood, and thence to the full firmness of manhood, so the general life breaks, breaks through from the dark caves of its infancy into phase after phase, clearness and lightness, brightness and glory, wonder and majesty increasing as it goes. The trials greater, the evils greater, the fall greater, the darkness of failure greater if we refuse our advance - -"

"If Maggie knew you came out here to spout, my lad, she'd send some one a bit rustier in the tongue," said Mr. Hobson, with feeling. He still disliked rival oratory.

"I cannot look on the child and not be moved," said Tubby simply.

Mr. Hobson took this, as it was, for a compliment to his grandson, and, by implication, to himself, the source of all the child's excellence; and the two old men, paunchy, kindly and well-contented, pushed the pram out of the Peel Park gates and along to Chapel Street.

And there was Will Mossop waiting for them on the doorstep with paternal joy on his face, and there, as they hauled the pram through the shop, was Maggie on the parlour threshold with maternal satisfaction on her face, and in every inch of her body.

THE END